Seesaw

Short Story Collection

By Rosen Trevithick

2nd Edition

Thanks to:

TextMender Editing Services
www.textmender.com

And to:

With Words Editing Services

Contents

Preface

It's New Year's Eve 2011 and I'm sitting in the emergency dentist's waiting room with toothache. So severe is the pain emanating from my upper left premolar that I can barely twitch without gasping in agony. Suddenly, I notice a lady in a yellow dress and my heart leaps — she's reading a Kindle! Immediately, I dive into my bag, where I have a wallet full of business cards. I'm going to sell her a copy of *Straight Out of University*, if it's the last thing I do. Every cloud has an amalgam lining.

As I accost a stranger, hoping to make my fifty-fifth sale, I have no way of knowing that in less than two months' time, I will have sold 11,000 books, and readers will have downloaded a further 17,000 freebies.

One day, my readership comprised mainly friends and family, then suddenly men and women from all over the world, were reading my books — mostly humorous or psychological short stories. It was exciting and terrifying in equal measure.

My first download was my favourite. It was autumn 2010, and I sold a copy of my debut novel, *Footprints*. For many years, severe bipolar disorder has stood between me and employment. Then, suddenly, I earned a pound — one whole pound of my very own — not administered by the DSS, not borrowed from my parents, and not an M&S voucher gained by taking an old shirt to Oxfam.

Naturally, I love writing — novels don't leak from begrudging fingertips. Creative writing is something I've done for as long as I can remember. It's not only an entertaining pastime, but a tool that I use to help me make sense of the world. Life can be a confusing ordeal for even the healthiest mind, and I often find myself turning to words to help me find perspective and comfort. Nothing helps you see the funny side of a mortifying experience, like turning it into a storyline.

Likewise, the nasty people of the world are much easier to tolerate if you use their most ridiculous features to build fictional characters that you later mock to death.

Being able to use an activity that I love to earn the cost of a bar of chocolate was the icing on a particularly tasty cake.

This small success encouraged a cat fantasy which grew steadily, out of control. I wanted one so badly that my author profile reported two, despite the reality of a cat-free existence in a damp, dark flat. I wondered how many business cards I would need to drop on trains 'accidentally', before I sold enough novels to cover the cost of catty living.

To speed up cat acquisition, I decided to start writing short stories to attract new readers. I began with one which became my personal favourite, *On the Rocks,* and celebrated with friends when the download count hit 100.

As time went on, my series of short stories quickly took on a life of its own, with hundreds, sometimes thousands of copies, downloaded every day. After dozens of reviewers referred to my shorts as "captivating", "moving", "thought-provoking" and "hilarious", it didn't take long to realise that they deserved a volume of their own.

This collection has no deliberate theme. However, the contents have naturally clustered around two prevailing topics: romance gone humorously wrong, and sombre psychological experiences. Being a bipolar, ginger sex-goddess, I have absolutely no idea how this came about!

You will find that the stories in this anthology are very much grounded in the here and now. You won't find a fantasy, historical or geographical adventure, but you will find humour, mystery, sarcasm and provocation. I wrote these stories to explore and understand the world that we live in.

Perhaps the most well-known story in the

collection is *Lipstick and Knickers*. It led Amazon's fictional comedy chart for almost three weeks. Because it was based on a play performed by my theatre group, The Coffee House Players, writing it evoked many happy memories.

However, I had the most fun writing the farcical *London, the Doggy and Me*. The tale was inspired by something that happened to a friend, an incident which made me chuckle so often that eventually I had to write an adaptation.

On the Rocks and *The Other Daughter,* on the other hand, were at times emotionally draining to write, but I am glad to have tried my hand at something less slapstick, and the finished stories are among my personal favourites.

I was in two minds about whether to include *The Selfish Act* because I wrote it to reinforce a perspective on a controversial news topic, rather than to entertain. However, it generated such strong, positive feedback that, in the end, I knew it had to be part of this volume.

I toyed with the idea of naming this anthology, *The Cat Fund* and channelling the royalties into funding for my eagerly awaited feline friend. But a more pertinent title emerged. Earning a little money through writing has given me the confidence to kick my debilitating illness in the face and put in motion the very first wheels that may eventually allow me to attempt, at least part time, self-sufficiency.

It's extremely difficult to work a conventional job when battling an unpredictable, chronic illness. My mood problems inhibit getting to sleep, medication hinders waking up, unpredictability compromises reliability, and typical day-to-day work stressors can trigger life-threatening mood episodes. It feels like being trapped in a giant self-defeating loop.

I've watched the people around me gain jobs, earn promotions, and buy their own homes, all the while feeling that my own potential has been locked away in a place that I badly want to access, but can't.

Volunteering has been beneficial and I am lucky to have found an organisation that is happy to fit in around my health needs. However, I still feel frustratingly limited by my illness, which often seizes entire days for its own selfish indulgence, preventing me from completing my shifts.

At the time of my diagnosis, over a decade ago, my cognitive skills were severely impaired. I had to take a much-unwanted break from university. For two years, I found it almost impossible to read, my memory was poor, and although I kept writing, little of it made sense. It was a huge relief when basic skills started to return. I cannot tell you how overjoyed I was when I found that I could, once again, write fiction.

It is incredibly satisfying to have found an ability that has prevailed, despite the constant obstacles thrown into my path.

Perhaps one day, I will be able to buy my dream cottage with a bay window that allows me to write overlooking the sea. I will have at least one cat. However, for now, I'm just happy to be contributing to my own rent.

Thus, this anthology is called *Seesaw* because, like my life, the contents alternate between extremes of the serious and the downright silly.

Acknowledgements

I could thank the people who've helped me to put this book together. However, it would be more fitting to thank the people who have provided the long-term support that has allowed me to reach a quality of life where writing a book is possible.

Without trying to sound like a melodramatic Oscar winner, thanks to: Mum, Dad, David, Suzi, Becca, Avi, Dan, Helen, Katy K, Sam, Kate H, Alice, Nadene, Indrani, Therese, Mathias, Kathy, the Holloways, Dom, Fred, Becky B, Dr Gancz, Dr Hayes, The Coffee House Players, Workways Exeter and multiple Citizens Advice Bureaux.

Thanks also to Olivia Wood and Peter Van Der Merwe for contributions that exceeded proofreading, and indeed, my expectations.

Finally, a big thank you to my research team — Facebook friends who have answered ludicrous question upon ludicrous question, for months.

The Other Daughter

"You promised no more!" cried Bethany Jones, furiously flinging the newspaper at her mother. Rebecca was stunned by her youngest daughter's rage; she was usually such a sweet child.

"Calm down!" she appealed.

"You promised!"

With the offending newspaper out of the way, Bethany began hurling the Beatrix Potter tablemats at her mother. One of them knocked over the honey. The next thing she knew, Bethany was next to the fridge, reaching for a photo frame — one of *the* photo frames.

"No!" cried Rebecca.

The kitchen door opened and immediately Bethany stopped in her tracks. Daniel Jones was dressed in baggy striped pyjamas and his tatty black hair resembled a bird's nest. Yet, despite his unkempt appearance, his fatherly presence tempered his hysterical daughter. She placed the photo frame gently down on the table, as if that had been her intention all along.

"What is going on?" demanded Daniel, though the distressed newspaper said it all.

"She promised she would stop," croaked Bethany. Then, she ran out of the room and pounded up the stairs.

Rebecca shrugged, but she couldn't make eye contact with her husband. She started wiping honey off the sugar bowl. Honesty was one of her strongest qualities, but there were more powerful forces at work.

"You did promise you would stop," he said.

Rebecca slumped into her breakfast chair feeling, as she had done for eight years, small and helpless.

Her physical appearance had changed to match her internal misery. She had never been overweight, but the stress of the last decade had robbed her body of anything non-essential. Her once womanly figure now had the shape of a scrawny pre-teen. She often tried to dye her hair back to its original rich brown but there were long periods during which the grey roots were allowed to prosper — the lead up to Christmas was always one of them.

The loss had taken its toll on Daniel too. His face was wrinkled before its time and his shoulders were unusually hunched for a man of his age. If it weren't for his perfect head of jet-black hair, he could easily have been mistaken for a man in his fifties. He had become diminished too.

The pair bore very little resemblance to the bouncy, young couple who had married fifteen years earlier. Daniel had been the lead guitarist in a locally popular band and Rebecca was an art teacher who sold a few paintings on the side to allow Daniel to stay in self-employment. The transformation to the hollow people they had become was tragic, but then terrible things *do* terrible things to people, and what they went through would rot any parent.

Eight years ago, their three-year-old daughter had been snatched from a department store.

At first, they thought Millie had just wandered off, but when the minutes changed to hours and the hours changed to days, they eventually had to face the fact that abduction was the only likely explanation. It wasn't something that any parent is ever equipped to deal with.

Rebecca remembered the day vividly. It had been drizzling outside and their clothes were damp. Judy Garland's 'Have Yourself a Merry Little Christmas' was playing over the speaker system as she browsed perfume. That dreadful day was lodged in Rebecca's memory like a painful splinter.

Since then, the house they lived in had become like a show home. Items were purchased and the house was kept tidy, all to provide a healthy environment for their other daughter. However, there was no passion behind any of the new acquisitions. The only items that were treasured were the ones they'd had for eight or more years — the things Millie had touched, the things Millie had looked at, the things that depicted Millie. Photographs and her crocodile dinner plate were revered. They were placed on walls and mantle pieces and nobody was allowed to touch them except Rebecca. She found comfort in dusting them — making it appear as though Millie had never left.

The sparse scattering of photographs of Bethany showed her growing and changing whilst Millie remained untouched by time.

There were very few Christmas decorations; there hadn't been for years. A few odd pieces of tinsel hugged the banisters and Bethany had hung paper decorations that she made at school, to the light fittings and aged houseplants.

Bethany was angry because her mother was on the front page of today's newspaper under the headline, 'Another Christmas Without My Angel.'

Rebecca knew that she'd promised to step away from the media limelight. However, it never felt right to her. If she left any stone unturned, she would be letting Millie down. She owed it to the whole family to bring Millie safely home.

The press loved Millie Jones. Her enormous blue eyes, golden ringlets and sunny disposition made her highly photogenic. The Jones family were media friendly too — white, middle-class folk whose lives had been brutally torn to tatters by a cruel tragedy. They were articulate enough to give a good interview, and Rebecca was desperate enough to persistently accept media invitations. The once magical nursery school photo had been used so frequently in the press that Millie's glowing face had begun to chill the public — a reminder of thc fallibility of our justice system.

"I was thinking," began Daniel, "perhaps we should go away somewhere this Christmas."

"No."

"Let me continue ..."

"No."

"Hon, we've talked about this — we have to communicate with each other."

"We have to be here in case she comes home."

Daniel sighed and Rebecca saw the look of pity she'd grown accustomed to. She did not understand why *he* pitied her, when she was the one who still had hope — the strong one.

"We've talked about holidays before," Daniel pointed out.

"Not on the anniversary of when she was taken."

Daniel frowned again. "We can go away *after* the twenty-third."

"No."

She saw her husband tug a curl on his head. He's literally tearing his hair out, she thought. It wasn't that she didn't recognise her duty to her husband and younger daughter; it was just that she knew her family responsibilities extended further than the people she could reach out and touch. Millie was out there somewhere, she just didn't know where yet.

Daniel held her hand. "Rebecca, you do know that Millie isn't coming home for Christmas?"

Rebecca grabbed her hand back and rose from her chair. "Natascha Kampusch!" she shrieked.

Daniel closed his eyes and shook his head. "No Rebecca, not Kampusch again. We agreed."

"She came home after eight years."

"I cannot have this conversation again, please!"

Rebecca started pacing angrily around the room, clearing away things that did not need to be moved. "Why am I the only one who wants Millie home?" she demanded.

Daniel got up and embraced his wife with both arms, stopping her frenzied scurrying. He took her hand and held it firmly so that she couldn't shake him off.

"You're not the only one who wants her home," he told her. She saw great sorrow in his eyes and wondered why he tried so hard to hide it.

* * *

The rest of the day continued with an eerie level of raw tranquillity. It was a familiar atmosphere, particularly on days when Millie had been mentioned.

Bethany walked herself to school. Daniel made an excuse to spend the day in the garden. Rebecca sought refuge in Millie's room. She read *Dear Zoo* to herself, imagining Millie on her lap as they lifted the flaps. "He was too fierce!" she heard Millie say. She felt a shiver as she remembered the rich sound of her daughter's voice. It had been deep for a child, but with a built-in giggle. She was a perpetually happy soul. Rebecca remembered Millie's laugh when she had played peek-a-boo behind the curtains.

Rebecca had agreed to avoid mentioning their lost daughter too often, to give Bethany the best shot at an ordinary childhood. This meant that the occasions when discussions about Millie *did* happen, it was agonising for everybody.

Bethany often appeared insensitive about matters of Millie. Rebecca tried to remind herself that Bethany had been an infant when her older sister was kidnapped. Her grief had been handed to her, bit by bit, as she grew up. Bethany sometimes talked about what it would be like to have another child to grow up with, but she had no memories of the big sister that she was supposed to love and yearn for.

Their younger daughter was prone to occasional outbursts about her parents, and why they couldn't be more like other people's. Her friends had mothers who weren't sad all the time and who didn't appear on the covers of newspapers and magazines. Her friends had parents who had jobs and went to work rather than living on the royalties from a book that didn't even have a happy ending. Bethany complained that she didn't like the way that people looked at her sometimes. She screamed that her name was Bethany Jones, not 'Millie Jones's sister'.

Bethany said that people behaved oddly around her when they knew she was Millie's sister and Rebecca knew that that was true. It was something her family were all too used to.

Most people pitied Bethany and were overly nice to her, yet some children inexplicably bullied her. Only yesterday, a bigger girl had asked Bethany about her sister and then torn a chunk of hair from her head. Rebecca hated the patronising way people treated her family, but at least their behaviour made sense. Why would somebody bully a girl just because her sister was missing?

It worried Rebecca, but being picked on by an older child was nothing compared to being snatched by a kidnapper. At least she knew about any abuse Bethany suffered.

Rebecca recognised that she had to tread carefully around Bethany, but she didn't like being silenced in her own house. Millie was part of the family and she should be treated as such. Many of the rules she'd agreed to in order to protect Bethany felt unnatural. She felt as though she was being disloyal to Millie.

She enjoyed her alone time in Millie's room. She rubbed baby powder into her arms to evoke happy memories. She relaxed as the sweet scent filled her nostrils. She remembered the sound of Millie sleeping — little snuffles breaking the silence.

Eventually, the peace was disturbed and Rebecca felt an uncomfortable jolt back to reality. Bethany was home from school. Begrudgingly, Rebecca came downstairs as her younger child stumbled inside, bringing with her the scents of the outside world —

rain, petrol and earth.

"What did you do at school today, sweetie?" asked Rebecca, forcing herself to speak.

"Numbers and stuff," replied Bethany, nervously.

"What do you mean? Did you do maths?"

"No, just numbers. Can I go up to my room?"

Rebecca sighed as she watched Bethany slip away. She felt sorrow that her youngest daughter didn't want to spend time with her, but was distressed further by the fact that she couldn't bring herself to object. She comforted herself by imagining what Millie might have done today. Perhaps she would read the Christmas story. When Natascha Kampusch was kidnapped, her captor had given her books.

Through concern that her husband might judge her if he heard she was in Millie's room again, Rebecca decided to stay downstairs and put the television on. Perhaps Sky would run an anniversary feature on the hunt for Millie. It was important that Millie Jones remained a household name. When Natascha escaped from her captors, she asked passers-by to call the police and many ignored her, until she said to one elderly neighbour, "I am Natascha Kampusch," and then the neighbour knew what had to be done.

The news today was dominated by sport. Initially, the reporter speculated about a football transfer. Rebecca felt that a missing toddler was more important than an overpaid sports star, and felt her temper growling. When the world carried on without her like this, she felt as though her feet were trapped in mud whilst a rising tide flooded in.

Then she remembered that Millie was no longer a missing toddler, no longer her tiny blonde girl with curls and a pink gingham dress, but an eleven year old whose hair might no longer be fair or even curly. She certainly would no longer be wearing that beautiful dress with a white bow at the back, or her yellow rain coat. Rebecca felt comfort in remembering Millie's bright blue eyes — one feature that she felt sure time could not change. The scar on her nose would be unchanged too. Rebecca had been horrified when a two-year-old Millie had fallen on a step and cut her face, but now thinking about that little scar made her feel warm and closer to Millie.

The next news story concerned an injunction to prevent a prostitute selling her story to the papers. Apparently, she'd slept with some sort of celebrity. Rebecca felt depressed to live in a world where celebrities were deemed more important than a missing child.

Then, a story began that was every bit as important as a missing child — *another* missing child. Rebecca straightened her spine and raised the volume. What was it about Christmas that made it such a popular time for domestic tragedy? The missing girl was eleven — the same age as Millie was now. A thought suddenly leapt into Rebecca's mind: perhaps the same kidnapper had taken them both. Perhaps he would take this Jemma Bellamy to wherever he kept Millie. Perhaps he would accidentally lead the police straight to her. Hurriedly, she leaned forward to find out as much as she could about the new victim.

It was difficult to concentrate. She wanted to tell Daniel about this new development right away, but she knew she had to get as much information as she could, first. He usually responded to her theories with scepticism and a look of pity, but he wouldn't this time — this time she really had something.

The news reporter described Jemma Bellamy, but there was no photograph yet. The story was just breaking.

Rebecca was just turning up the volume further when the doorbell rang. Her stomach lurched, as it had done every time the doorbell had rung in eight years. As she approached the front door, she saw a familiar sight refracted through the frosted glass. Her heart started pounding in her chest.

She tried to shout "Daniel!", but actually managed nothing more than a faint croak. She yanked open the door forgetting the chain — a measure to protect her other daughter from completing the kidnapper's set. Frustrated, she closed the door again, removed the chain and then, more carefully, opened the door.

Although Rebecca Jones was on first name terms with the visitors, PC Anne Chambers and PC Mark Moore, she did nothing but gawp. This was not a planned visit.

"Can we come in?" asked PC Chambers.

By now, Daniel was with Rebecca at the door. Hers was not the only life dominated by the doorbell.

The eager parents lead the police officers into the living room, without saying a word. They both sat in petrified silence, waiting for the police to break news.

Anne Chambers took off her hat, revealing a head of chin-length yellow hair. Mark Moore, whom Rebecca knew to be heavily balding, kept his on, as he often did.

Rebecca could take the silence no longer.

"Is this about Jemma Bellamy?" she hurried out.

The police officers exchanged confused looks.

"Who's Jemma Bellamy?" asked her husband.

"She's another missing eleven year old," explained Rebecca, then she turned to the police, "isn't she?"

Chambers looked confused. "We're here about Millie."

Daniel took Rebecca's hand and they sat on the sofa, mirroring each other's clenched fists, round shoulders and parted lips. Neither of them was able to speak.

"We think we've found her," announced Chambers.

Rebecca sprang up, her hands rushing to her mouth. She inhaled deeply and then paused, freezing, with her lungs full to the brim. Had this moment really come at last?

"You mean, you've found her body?" asked Daniel, nervously.

"No, we've found her alive."

Daniel sat in stunned silence, as if afraid of waking up from an incredibly wonderful dream.

For Rebecca, it was the most familiar experience in the world. Every day she had played out this moment in her mind. She had always known that it would come. The greatest weight off her chest was not that her daughter was alive — of that, she'd always been sure — but that she didn't have to wait another day to be with her. She would get to see Millie grow up after all.

"Where is she?" asked Rebecca.

"How is she?" begged Daniel.

"I believe she's well."

"Where has she been?" he asked.

"We think she was kidnapped. Millie — or I should say, a girl fitting Millie's description — presented at Paddington Green Police Station, and reported that she'd escaped a kidnapper," explained Chambers.

Rebecca listened intently, but she didn't need to. Her heart already knew the general plot, Chambers was merely filling in the details.

He continued, "We'll need samples from you both for a DNA test, but initial checks support the girl's story."

"Has she got a scar on her nose?" asked Daniel.

"I believe so."

Rebecca jumped in. "You believe so? Haven't you seen her? Can we see her? Is she in your car?" She sprang from her seat and to the window.

"It's not that simple," explained Chambers. "Millie has been through a serious ordeal."

"But you said she was well!" said Rebecca, becoming frantic.

"We are seeking specialist advice on how to proceed. She needs a psychological assessment before social services can decide the best way to proceed."

"What?" demanded Daniel. "What's it got to do with social services?"

"She's our daughter!" shrieked Rebecca. "I want to see her today! Please tell us we can see our daughter today!"

"It's unlikely that you'll be able to see Millie until after Christmas."

It was more than Rebecca could take. She rushed to the nearest photograph — a snap of Millie, aged two, on her toy bike — and thrust it at Chambers. "Look! *Our* daughter!"

She rushed to the fireplace and grabbed three more, including her favourite — Millie holding Bethany the day after she was born. Rebecca threw the photographs into Moore's hands. "Part of *our* family!"

Then, replicating the tantrum she'd seen at breakfast, Rebecca began grabbing anything she could get her hands on, and flinging it in the direction of the police officers. Rationality had left her.

* * *

The one thing Rebecca had not expected to feel during the twenty-four hours following such terrific news was loneliness, yet she felt terribly isolated. She had not been allowed to see Millie and whilst Daniel acknowledged what the officers had said, his manner was detached and standoffish. Rebecca had agreed not to tell Bethany the news until the police had made progress. She knew that it was Daniel who needed substantiation. He didn't dare let himself believe.

Finally, they received a phone call; the DNA test confirmed that the girl found at Paddington Green was indeed their daughter.

Daniel sprang from the bottom of the stairs and rushed out to his shed. He threw old paint tubs, broken flowerpots and cobwebbed bricks out onto the lawn, until finally he found something Rebecca hadn't seen for eight years: Millie's gardening set.

As he took the box of plastic trowels, forks and a toy watering can from under the workbench, Rebecca saw his lower eyelids tremble under the weight of tears.

Rebecca ran into the house. "Bethany!" she cried. "Bethany, come downstairs!"

Daniel placed his arms around his wife, and gave her ear a gentle kiss.

Bethany could clearly tell that something weird was happening. It was not usual for her mum and dad to ask her to sit at the kitchen table in the middle of the afternoon. She frowned and folded her arms.

"What is it? I want to go and play with my DS."

"Bethany, we've got some very wonderful news," smiled Rebecca.

"Is it about Father Christmas?" Bethany asked with excitement. She looked from one parent to the other, waiting for one of them to give something away.

"Better!" grinned Rebecca.

Daniel held Rebecca's arm, to calm her.

"Better than Father Christmas? What could be better than Father Christmas?"

"Your sister is coming home!" shouted Rebecca, with glee.

Bethany didn't respond, she just looked confused.

"I said, your sister is coming home!" repeated Rebecca, with equal delight.

"But I thought my sister was murdered," she said. Even given the recent developments, the statement chilled Rebecca to the core.

"No, she was just taken away from us by a very bad man," Rebecca explained.

Daniel intervened. "Don't worry, you won't have to suddenly adapt. We're going to get to know her again very slowly."

"Get to know her? Daniel, don't talk nonsense!

She's our little girl!"

Bethany was not smiling. She was not smiling in the slightest.

* * *

"Anne said not to get carried away," Daniel reminded Rebecca, as she brought the new curtains in from the car and stacked them next to the boxed Christmas tree.

"And that's another thing I won't miss," laughed Rebecca, "having the police around for tea."

"It sounds as though we'll be seeing a lot of the authorities over the coming weeks."

"Don't be such a pessimist," scolded Rebecca, with an airy breeze in her voice.

"I'm just being realistic."

"Yeah, like when you said she was dead."

"I never said she was dead."

"As good as."

"What I said was, that we had to get on with our lives as though she *might* not come back."

"I told you she was still alive," Rebecca continued, ignoring him. "A mother can feel these things."

"Honey, there was no situation in the world in which I would rather see you proved right. But since it happened, I've taken whatever action I've needed to take in order to keep this family together."

"Yeah, I know," she said, dismissively.

"I'm serious Rebecca. Even if I could have foreseen this, I would spend the years focusing on you and Bethany. It was the only way I could get through each day."

"It's not how I coped."

"Rebecca, every day you expected her home, and every day you were let down."

"Not *every* day," smiled Rebecca.

"No," he conceded, taking her hands and smiling into her eyes, "not every day."

"I'm thinking of writing to Mr and Mrs Bellamy."

"Who?"

"The parents of that missing girl in the news. I was thinking of telling them never to give up hope."

"There's no point."

"Wha-? How can you say that after what's happened to us?"

"Haven't you seen the news? Carl and Sarah Bellamy are dead."

"What?"

"Well, let's not go into that now."

"No, please, I'm interested."

"It said on the news that there was a fire."

"How did I miss that?"

Daniel looked at the piles of books, curtains and Christmas decorations but decided not to comment.

"Their house was burnt to the ground."

"What, after Jemma went missing?"

"According to the news, the couple were dead before the fire started. Nobody knows what happened to their kid. That's why the story is so high profile."

"Shit. I never thought I'd say this, but maybe we're the lucky ones."

"Nobody wins when there's a missing child," replied Daniel, grimly.

Suddenly, they were interrupted by a loud cry from the top of the stairs. "What the fuck...?" yelled Bethany at the top of her lungs.

"Where did you learn words like that?" asked Rebecca, instinctively.

"Whatever is the matter?" asked Daniel, beginning to climb the stairs to meet his daughter.

"Calm down," hushed Rebecca.

"Why should I?" yelled Bethany.

"This is a happy time. Your sister's going to come home," Rebecca told her.

"I don't have a sister!"

Rebecca looked as though she'd been punched in

the stomach. Daniel reached the landing and invited Bethany to share a stair. She refused to sit down.

"What is that?" demanded Bethany, pointing at the pile of things.

"A Christmas tree," said her mother.

"We've never had a Christmas tree before."

"Well, we've never had everybody home for Christmas before."

"I don't have a sister and I don't want a sister."

Rebecca felt cheated. This was supposed to be a perfect time. She wanted Bethany to feel what a joyful occasion this was.

She went into the living room, imagining it alive with the four of them. She retrieved the photo of Millie holding Bethany, hoping that this would help get through to her. She was about to go back into the hallway when she heard Daniel talking. She paused to listen.

"I don't want a sister, Daddy."

"Why don't you want a sister, honey? Sisters are lovely."

"You don't like *your* sister."

"Yes I do."

"You said Auntie Pam has a laugh like a pig."

Rebecca heard her husband chuckle.

"Well, she does, but that's what having a sister is all about."

"Having a sister is about laughing like a pig?"

"No. You make fun of each other, and you fight, but then you love each other anyway."

"Like you and Mummy?"

Rebecca decided it was time to return to them. She went back into the hall to where Daniel and Bethany were sharing a step. She sat down beneath them.

"Look at this photo," she offered.

Bethany rolled her eyes. "I've seen it before."

"Look closely."

Bethany pretended not to be interested but curiosity got the better of her. She took the photo, but could see nothing worthy of close inspection. "What?"

"What's that on the floor next to Millie?" asked Rebecca.

"It's my Peter Rabbit."

"And what do you notice about Peter Rabbit?"

"Nothing special."

"He's already missing an eye," Rebecca pointed out.

"How did I lose his eye when I was only one day old?"

"*You* didn't lose his eye."

Daniel saw where Rebecca was going with this. He smiled at her with admiration in his eyes. At these rare moments, she caught glimpses of why he'd stood by her for eight years of turmoil.

"Millie lost my Peter Rabbit's eye?" asked Bethany, looking affronted.

"He wasn't your Peter Rabbit when his eye went missing," explained Rebecca. "He was Millie's Peter Rabbit."

"I stole Peter Rabbit?"

"No, she gave it to you."

She saw a brief flicker of emotion on her younger daughter's face, and hoped it meant that finally, she could have the family she'd dreamt of for eight years, the family she'd once had, for a few precious months.

"Do you think you can spare some time to meet the person who gave you Peter Rabbit?" asked Daniel.

Bethany nodded. "But I won't have to give him back, will I?"

* * *

The birds were squawking — not singing, but sitting on the roof screeching as loudly as they could. Rebecca Jones hadn't slept a wink, but the gulls were scarcely to blame. How could any mother sleep the night before being reunited with a daughter she'd been separated from for almost eight years?

At first, when told she would only see Millie for an hour, Rebecca had been angry, but now the thought of even one moment with her daughter brought her nothing but delight.

She had only turned her back for a second during that ill-fated day in Debenhams. Now, finally, her punishment had ended.

Would they share words? Or, would their hugs and tears speak for them? Had Millie thought about her family every day, in the way that their lives had been marked by the memories of her?

She pulled the new photo of Millie from her top drawer, for the tenth time that night. She looked at the big girl staring back. Eight years had brought ample changes, but she still had gentle blue eyes and Rebecca found comfort in the fact that she had kept her waves of blonde hair. Rebecca knew she had missed out on a lot, but felt strangely reassured that Millie's hair changing was not one of them.

When Millie was taken, she'd been wearing a yellow coat. For some reason Rebecca had always imagined that she'd turn up wearing yellow. Yet, in the picture, Millie was wearing denim dungarees.

In the photo, Millie looked healthy — perhaps healthier than Rebecca did. She had radiant skin and a faint covering of puppy fat. For the first time, Rebecca felt something other than hatred for her daughter's kidnapper — she felt gratitude. He had kept her daughter safe. She prayed that the same could be said for Millie's psychological well-being.

She had spoken to a woman called Catherine Gaw from social services. Catherine told her that Millie reported that her years in captivity were free from physical abuse, and that although they were quietly optimistic, they couldn't be sure of anything yet. Apparently, their physical examinations had been confounded by Millie's refusal to allow anybody to touch her. This in itself was alarming.

Rebecca couldn't bear to think that Millie had suffered any physical abuse. In the many years that she imagined Millie as a prisoner, she hadn't dared use the "P" word. She had convinced herself that Millie's kidnapper was somebody lonely and otherwise harmless, making a misguided grasp for company.

However, she mustn't dwell on the past on a day like today. It was a time to look forward.

As she imagined Millie's face when she saw her, Rebecca pattered her feet against the bed with anticipation. She could not wait to share her excitement any longer, she flicked Daniel on the face with a finger, and then promptly backed away to make it look as though his stirring was spontaneous.

"What is it?" asked Daniel, with a frustrating level of non-understanding.

"We've got to meet Millie!"

"What time is it?"

"Six forty-five."

Daniel groaned and turned away, burying his head under a pillow. Rebecca couldn't understand why he didn't want to be awake, savouring every moment of this extraordinary morning. She concluded that he just wanted to be at his absolute best for the reunion.

Nobody had expected things to happen this fast. It had first been thought that weeks might pass before Millie could see her parents, but the insistence of both sides had hurried things along. Social services had agreed to a preliminary meeting somewhere neutral, and the family room at the local police station was to be the unlikely setting for this emotional rendezvous.

It was decided that it would be best if Bethany stayed at home with Auntie Pam while her mother and father were reunited with Millie. The occasion was going to be emotional for everybody so social services felt that it would be best to keep things as basic as possible. When they had told Bethany of their plans, she had become very quiet but agreed.

Rebecca wanted more than anything to bring Millie home, but she knew that she would have to wait.

To pass the time, she crept out of bed to have another look at Millie's room. For eight years, they'd kept it the same — not moving as much as a sweet wrapper. In the last three days, Rebecca had slapped on a lick of paint, changed the bedding and put some new books on the shelf. She had to keep reminding herself that she wouldn't be getting her toddler back, but a girl who was only two years off becoming a teenager. She would soon have to talk to her about boys and periods.

The doorbell rang. Rebecca wondered how long she'd spent in Millie's room, just taking in the freshness of the paint.

There was no longer a need to fear the doorbell. Rebecca skipped down to the door, stopping to wipe some dust off the banisters as she leisurely descended the stairs.

That was odd — policeman shapes before breakfast?

Still, what was there to fear now? Rebecca threw open the door, unbothered by the fact that she was in her dressing gown and slippers.

"May we come in?" asked PC Chambers. Rebecca noted that both officers looked more tired than usual. She wondered if they had been working a night shift.

"I didn't do it officer," she quipped.

Rebecca showed the officers into the living room, which was now beautifully dressed for Christmas with an eight foot tree and six separate strings of fairy lights. She noticed something unusual about Moore — he'd taken his hat off.

"Is Mr Jones at home?" asked Chambers.

"Oh, very formal today, aren't we?" she laughed. "Daniel!" she warbled. "He was still asleep last time I checked. I might have to go and wake him. He can sleep through seagulls — it's amazing!"

"I'm awake," yawned Daniel, appearing barefoot in the hallway. "What's going on? There isn't a problem with today's meeting is there?"

The two officers shared an awkward glance. This momentary look cut into Rebecca's core. She shuddered. She was too afraid ask. She stared, eyes wide, feeling her body begin to tremble.

"I'm afraid there's been a development," began Chambers. She seemed to be choking up in a way that Rebecca had never seen in the many years that she'd been dealing with their heartbreaking case.

"You're afraid that there's been a development, or there *has* been a development?" demanded Daniel, with a quiver in his voice.

Time slowed down. Rebecca's surroundings suddenly appeared overexposed and faces faded in and out of focus. She felt light-headed.

Chambers couldn't get the words out, so Moore had to step in. "It appears that the girl we have in our care is not your daughter."

"What?" demanded Daniel.

Rebecca felt herself slipping away from the world. Her husband's words sounded echoic and distant.

"But you said she remembers us? You said she has the scar!" Daniel shouted.

Rebecca could taste something sweet on her tongue and her ears started to buzz. She could feel prickles of sweat all over her face, particularly behind her eyes.

"She does have a scar. She told us that she was Millie Jones. She knew a great deal of detail about your family," explained Moore.

"But you said there was a DNA test!" Daniel reminded them.

"There was."

"The results were positive!" he remembered, vividly.

"That's true. We did obtain a positive DNA result using a hair sample, but a few things didn't add up."

"But DNA testing is ninety-nine percent reliable!" Daniel responded.

"We had reason to believe that the first sample had been contaminated."

"Why?"

"Because the sample DNA was identical to the DNA of your younger daughter, Bethany."

"What? That doesn't make any sense!" Daniel exclaimed.

"It's likely that she swapped her own hair sample for some of Bethany's."

"But that's impossible."

"We usually use a buccal swab for genetic testing, but she couldn't stand anybody touching her. The psychologists felt it would be less traumatic if we used a sample of hair."

Something broke through Rebecca's trance. She remembered something Bethany had told her: an older girl had pulled out a chunk of her hair. At the time, it had seemed like random bullying.

"I don't understand," Daniel said. "Didn't you double check?" he asked Moore. Then he turned to Chambers, the officer he had known and trusted for many years. "How could you let this happen, Anne?"

"We honestly thought the DNA test was just a formality," explained Moore.

"But you said she knew details about our family!" Daniel pointed out.

"From the papers, from your book ..."

"Who in their right mind, would pretend to be our daughter?" yelled Daniel.

"Well, we can't say yet ..." began Moore.

Finally, Chambers cut in, "Jemma Bellamy."

"What? The missing girl off the telly?" asked Daniel.

"It seems she was unhappy in her own home, and

she read about you in the paper ..."

"But she has the scar ..."

"Self-inflicted. She'd been planning this for years."

"Well, didn't you recognise her? Her disappearance has been all over the news."

"Yes, but the appeal didn't have a clear photograph of her," explained Chambers.

"It's likely that they were deliberately destroyed in the fire," added Moore.

"And the photofit was very misleading. The artist got her face-shape all wrong and she had dark hair, completely different eyebrows ..." Chambers told them.

"She dyed her hair to trick us?"

"She was desperate. It's likely that her family abused her."

"Even so, she's not our daughter. Surely what she's done to us is illegal?"

"Perhaps."

"Perhaps? Aren't you going to arrest her?"

"Jemma Bellamy has been charged with the murder of her parents."

Rebecca was amazed to find that she still had the capacity to be shocked.

Daniel looked stunned for a moment and then began to shout. "We thought the girl you'd found was our lovely, sweet daughter, and now you're telling us she's a cold-hearted killer!"

"I really am sorry," said Chambers.

"I really am sorry," parroted Moore.

Some more time passed, some more questions were asked, but no amount of answers would ever make sense of the pain they'd suffered. Nobody would ever understand why one family had been hurt so much.

Eventually, Daniel led the officers into the hallway.

Rebecca felt as though that dreadful day eight

years ago was replaying. Her daughter had been there one moment, and the next, torn away from her. She had been ripped out of her life today as certainly as she had been torn away when she was first kidnapped.

She grabbed a branch of pine between her bony arms, ignoring the scratches from the artificial needles, and hurled the Christmas tree onto the floor. There was a loud splintering sound as branches bowed and baubles shattered. Smashed, shards of sharp plastic tore at her arms and the weight of the tree dug into her thigh.

Rebecca fell back on the floor, buried beneath broken decorations. She began frantically tearing at the branches of the Christmas tree, robbing them of their needles with her bare hands.

Daniel ran back into the room and began freeing her. At first, he removed parts of the tree carefully but then, after removing decorations, he flung them across the room.

Once he'd dug Rebecca out, he began ripping fairy lights and tinsel from the walls, smashing the tiny glass bulbs between his fingers.

They both continued, destroying every sign of Christmas, until eventually Rebecca ran out of energy and broke down in a tearful mess on the floor. At once, Daniel stopped vandalising their home and put an arm around his wife.

"I can't believe she pretended to be our daughter," she said.

Daniel held her close.

"She chose us Daniel," said Rebecca. "She chose *us*!"

Her husband looked puzzled.

"If she wants to be with us, we should meet her," she continued.

"Rebecca! She's been charged with murder."

"But I've already prepared myself to meet her! I've got her photograph!"

"I know." Daniel pulled his wife toward him and began stroking her tired hair.

"I need a daughter!" she cried.

He stopped stroking her hair, "Rebecca, you already *have* a daughter."

* * *

Daniel hadn't left their bed for three days. He said he had the flu but Rebecca knew otherwise. The brief, ill-fated spike of hope had crushed him. It seemed to Rebecca as though he had given up. She'd never seen him that way, not even during the months following Millie's abduction.

"Why doesn't Daddy come downstairs?" asked Bethany.

"Because he's very tired," Rebecca explained, truthfully.

"But he has to come down!" cried Bethany. "He has to go and get my sister from the police station!"

Rebecca realised that this was something she was going to have to do alone.

"Let's go and sit at the kitchen table," she told Bethany.

"No! Tell me now!" demanded Bethany.

Rebecca could have no more told her younger daughter the truth seated at the kitchen table, than in any other part of the house. She stood in the hallway trying to find the words, but instead, large tears dropped from her eyes.

She was surprised to see that Bethany had begun to cry too. "My sister isn't coming home, is she?"

Rebecca shook her head.

"But I bought her a Benjamin Bunny!" sobbed Bethany.

Rebecca didn't know what to do. Daniel was her rock. He usually dealt with difficult situations. All she could do was pick Bethany up and hug her.

She dropped down onto the bottom step of the

stairs, with Bethany on her lap, and let her tears drop into the little girl's hair.

If Daniel were falling apart, what would happen to Bethany? What would happen to her? She couldn't bear the thought of losing either of them.

However, as much as Jemma Bellamy's actions had hurt her family, the scenario felt familiar. Daniel had been right. Rebecca had waited for Millie to run through the door every moment of every day. On a weekly basis she had convinced herself that she'd found new evidence that Millie was about to come home. Every week, her heart had been broken again.

Observing what the ordeal had done to Daniel, she began to understand why he lived his life as though Millie had gone forever. It wasn't that he didn't want her back as badly as she did, he just couldn't cope with endless speculation. This disappointment had left him drained of all energy and fight.

Could any of them carry on like this, with the constant rollercoaster of expectation?

Rebecca knew that she needed to help Daniel through the crisis, the way he'd guided her through the last eight years. However, she could not see a way to relieve his pain. The only thing she could think of to do was to keep going. Being busy didn't ease her inner turmoil, but it didn't make it any worse either. Daniel was right, she already had a daughter and somebody had to look after her.

She took her husband meals and sometimes sat on the bed for hours, waiting for him to talk, but he rarely did.

She wondered what she could do to make things better. She spent hours thinking. She looked on the internet and in magazines, but found her predicament largely neglected in problem pages — naturally. She even spoke to Auntie Pam.

However, deep down, Rebecca knew what she had to do to help her husband return to a mentality that would allow him to move forward. The answer was there, she just hoped that she could find an alternative. The solution was going to be the hardest thing she would ever have to do. She had to begin moving on.

Rebecca spent long hours in Millie's room, noting that the new decoration had brought about a slight change in her outlook. When she changed the bedding, she'd let a part of her toddler go, and yet she was all right. In fact, it felt liberating. However, was she ready to say goodbye to any of the other things she clung to?

The thought of boxing up Millie's books hurt her deep inside, but if she continued behaving as though Millie's return was imminent, she would destroy her husband. She needed to show him a way forward that he could handle.

"Can I come in?" asked a little voice. It took Rebecca by surprise; Bethany had never asked if she could join her mother in her sister's room. Rebecca had found her in there once, playing with some bricks, and had scolded her so severely that she'd been scared to return.

Rebecca hesitated, but then, "Yes, come in."

Bethany crept in quietly, as if afraid that her footsteps might break something. She sat down next to her mother. "Do you think Millie would have liked Benjamin Bunny?" she asked.

"Millie loved Benjamin Bunny," Rebecca smiled. She delighted in being able to share this with Bethany. "The book about him is over there on the shelf."

Bethany didn't move. "Can I look at it?" she asked, softly.

Rebecca took a deep breath, and then with great strength, told her daughter, "You can *have* it."

The little girl beamed. "Really?" she asked.

"Really," repeated Rebecca.

She was struck by how enormous such a little gesture had seemed only moments before. As she watched Bethany carefully turn the pages, grinning as she revealed a new page, she realised that giving Bethany one of Millie's books was not only one of the easiest things in the world, but possibly one of the most enjoyable things she had done in a long time.

Was she ready to take another step for her husband, for her marriage?

Rebecca shared *The Tale of Benjamin Bunny* with Bethany for the first time. Then, she gave her daughter a little kiss on the head, and left her alone in Millie's room.

She planned to make a gesture. It wasn't going to be drastic, but it was the largest step she could manage.

She went into their bedroom and perched on the edge of their bed. She knew Daniel was awake, but he didn't speak.

"I've been thinking ..." she said. He didn't move. "I've been thinking that perhaps, we could go away for the rest of Christmas?"

He stirred. "You don't mean that."

"I do. Let's go away. Let's go away for the whole sodding festive season!"

He turned to face her. "Are you serious?"

"Yes."

For the first time in days, he looked at his wife's face. "I'd like that," he said. He took her hands and pulled her arms around him.

Rebecca imagined moving forwards to a new year without the ghost of Millie. It hurt, but it felt right.

* * *

It was a mild day for late December, but there was no escaping the fact that their trip to Lake Windermere coincided with the depths of winter. Daniel remarked that you needed a certain amount of frostbite to feel seasonal.

Rebecca stopped for breath, and took in the refreshing new surroundings. Something had changed. For the first time in years, she wanted to capture the moment. She asked Daniel for his camera.

Bethany seemed to be enjoying herself too. She looked the part in her green, knitted hat and mittens, with her auburn hair blowing in the chilly wind. The cold put a glow in her porcelain cheeks.

"I've decided I like Christmas Day walks," she offered, illuminating her face with a rosy smile. Rebecca noticed that a recent tooth loss had brought a subtle lisp to her daughter's silvery voice.

"Well, we'll have to take you for walks more often," laughed Daniel.

"Only on Christmas Day. I only like walks on Christmas Day!" The clear blue sky added to the sparkle in her hazel eyes and she chuckled as she teased her father.

A lady in a green waterproof smiled as she passed.

"Hey wait!" interrupted Rebecca.

The lady stopped.

"Would you take a photo of me and my family please?"

The lady nodded. "Of course."

Rebecca grabbed her husband and daughter, and they huddled together, waiting for the camera to document their first family holiday.

There's Something Wrong With the Man Next Door

There's something wrong with the man next door. I can't put quite put my finger on what it is. He's gruff, yet timid and standoffish, in extraordinary measures.

Take yesterday for example — I went to collect the mail in my plunge-line dressing gown. Then, just as I was leaning over the fence, for maximum boobalicious effect, he looked away and scurried back into the house without so much as a wave. These tits have been working for me for fifty years!

My granddaughter thinks I should invite him around for tea and jammy dodgers, but I tried that, or at least, a variation on the idea — I invited him for a three-course candlelit dinner. He said he doesn't really eat and then promptly leaped behind a camellia.

Sometimes, during the late summer evenings, I can feel his eyes watching me in my garden, as I water my flowers. Once I pricked a finger on a tea rose and cried out. He glided up to the fence, but then retreated without saying a word.

My daughter thinks I'm too old to lust over surly neighbours or, indeed, lust at all. I think she'd like me to take up knitting and join the Women's Institute, but that's not my style and it never will be. I want that man in my bed, and I want him there now.

This morning, as I hung my sexiest knickers on the washing line, I put "Love is in the Air" on the radio and danced a sexy Zumba number. I made it look impromptu but, of course, I'd practiced it many times in the spare room. And what did my neighbour do about my captivating display of femininity? He ran away and hid inside his tool shed.

I just can't work out what's the matter with him. I'm bringing out all of my best moves, and yet he's still not asked me out, or even *in*. There's something deeply sinister going on and I plan to get to the bottom of it.

Surely the age difference can't be putting him off? He's no spring chicken himself. He's good-looking, with high cheekbones and porcelain skin. He has interesting eyes — they appear a different colour every time I strain to look at them. However, his thinning grey hair tells me that he's at least sixty-five. Mind you, his physical strength could be indicative of a younger man. I've seen him lifting patio slabs as if they were squares of foam. He's speedy too. Once I saw him in the garden, and by the time I got outside, he was half way down the street.

I've decided to have it out with him. Why doesn't he fancy me, or at the very least, say "Hello". Today is the day that I will solve the mystery that has been puzzling me ever since he first swooped into my life.

After liberally applying perfume, I unfasten the top three buttons of my blouse. Then, I walk the thirty yards to my front gate, open it, walk through, close it again, walk two steps to his gate, open it, walk through, close it again and walk the thirty yards to his front door, all the while wondering if leaping over the fence would have made me look more vital.

I ring the doorbell. I see a curtain move and catch a glimpse of him peering out at me. His pale face looks ghostly and hostile. Now that he knows I've seen him, he has to come to the door. It would be rude, even for him, to leave me standing on the front step, attracting bees.

Slowly, the door creeps open. He stands in the opening, looking unreasonably troubled.

"Can I come in?" I ask.

"No," he says. His voice is deeper than I imagined and there's something profoundly sexy about his rudeness — overwhelmingly so. I fan myself with my hand.

"Please, we need to talk."

"I don't know you," he mutters.

"Well, why not?" I blurt.

To my surprise and delight, he opens the door! I'm intrigued when it reveals a dark hallway with mahogany panelling. It is very different from my own breezy, floral décor, but I suppose I could get used to it.

"Could I have a cup of tea?" I ask, hoping to see more of the house.

"Don't have any."

"Not to worry, coffee will do."

"Don't have any."

"What sort of person doesn't have any tea or coffee?" I ask, then regret it. I should be friendly even in the face of rudeness. It is no use us both being bad-mannered. I know from years of reading *Take a Break* magazine that opposites attract. With that in mind, I try to look as friendly as possible, starting with an enormous smile.

"What are you doing?" he asks.

"Extending the hand of friendship," I sing, extending my hand, which he shrinks away from.

"All right, fine," he begins. "You want to know why I don't want to get to know you? You really want to know?"

I nod, enthusiastically. It's the answer I've been waiting for.

However, instead of speaking, he takes his fingers to his lips and holds them apart, revealing his teeth.

"What?" I ask.

"My theeth!" he explains, still stretching his lips.

"What about them?"

He points at two particularly long choppers at the front.

"What? They're not that bad. If they're really destroying your confidence, you could always get them filed."

"I don't want to get them filed!"

"Well then, what's the problem?"

"I'm a vampire, aren't I?"

It wasn't what I was expecting. I'm silent for a

moment, trying to check that I've heard correctly. I rotate a finger in one of my ear holes. Then, I fall about laughing. Hooray! The sexy neighbour isn't just beauty and brawn — he also has a sense of humour.

"I'm glad you think it's funny."

"Are you a goth? Is that why your house is decorated all funny?" I ask, looking around the hall. "Aren't you a little old for that? I mean, I like it — I love anything a bit kinky, me — but ..."

"I really am a vampire."

"All right, turn into a bat."

"If you're not going to take me seriously, you can sod off."

I take a moment to reflect. He's pale, he's unusually strong and he's shockingly antisocial. He doesn't eat and there are no tea making facilities in the house. He's either a vampire or a nut job. Neither is ideal. I feel empty, as months of fantasies turn to dust.

"Do you want to know why I keep my distance from you?" he asks.

For a moment, I just stare, open-mouthed. Then, I nod. It *is* the reason I'm here, even though suddenly I'm much less interested in the answer.

"It's because I want to drink your blood."

What? I back away, toward the door. I'm beginning to wonder if he's criminally insane. I want to go home. I *need* to go home, or at least anywhere that's not here.

"But don't worry, I'm a vegetarian," he adds.

"I'm going to leave now."

"Wait! I love you."

"What? You don't know me."

"It's a monster urge thing. My vampire senses told me that I loved you, the first time I set eyes on you."

Without turning my back to him, my hands pursue the doorknob.

"I'm not actually going to drink you," he

explained.

"Get away from me!"

"We could make this work! I could protect you!"

"Don't come any closer."

"Aren't you going to tell me that you trust me?"

"Why would I?"

"I've seen the way you try to catch my attention. I know you want me."

"You're mistaken."

"I'm not."

"Well, I've had a change of heart."

"*We could make it work!*"

"Why on earth would any woman want to be with a man after he's proclaimed that he wants to drink her blood?"

"But I've seen the way you look at me."

"*Looked* at you!"

"This doesn't change anything."

"It changes everything!"

"We could have such adventures!"

"At our time of life? I was looking for companionship, perhaps a little sex ... But that's when I thought you were normal! I don't want to date a vampire."

"You're in your sixties; men don't grow on trees."

"They don't hang from trees either."

"Why are you so hung up on the bat thing?"

Finally, I manage to find the door handle. I let the bright world outside flood in. He retreats into the shadows. Then, I run. I run as fast as I can, out into the garden. I leap over the fence, snagging my petticoat. A splinter breaks the skin on my finger. I see him watch me through the window, thirsting for my blood.

For a moment, I mentally punish myself for getting a man so wrong. You think a little doom and gloom is a sexy facade, and then you realise that it's actually indicative of living in a coffin. However, I soon realise that there was no way I could have guessed that he is a vampire.

At least he is vegetarian, which means that I can wait until after I've found a plaster before putting my house on the market.

London, the Doggy and Me

If the dog hadn't died, my future would have been entirely different. I sometimes wonder what he was like — the mutt who changed my life. It was unlucky that we never met, because at the beginning of this story he was very much alive.

It was August in Falmouth and the place was bursting with flowers, sunshine and reasons to be outdoors. Instead, I was inside fantasising about the five hour train ride away from there.

I fingered the piece of paper again. Was I actually going to do it? I imagined myself on the stage — the audience clapping and begging 'Encore!'; my face glowing with pride; my love in the wings, dressed in a dinner jacket and holding champagne, waiting to kiss a star ...

"Fucking yeah!" yelled Derek, at the television. He was still wearing his boxers and the *Jackass* t-shirt he'd worn to bed, complete with sweat patches because apparently operating a controller was tough work. He absorbed a little dew drop from his nose with the hairy back of a finger, as he watched his computer generated FIFA player star in an action replay.

"I'm going to London," I told him.

"Oh right," he said, not taking his eyes off the television.

"I said, 'I'm going to London.'"

"Cool, see you later."

Something inside me snapped. I stormed over to the television, located the enormous eight-way plug adapter, and yanked it from the wall.

There was a faint electrical hiss, followed by a grating, raucous scream of terror.

"What the fuck Steph?" he yelled, running across the room to fix the problem — the most exercise he'd done in weeks.

"I was trying to talk to you," I explained.

"And you couldn't have done that without unplugging the universe?"

"Apparently not."

"I'm going in the shower," he grumped. Then he grabbed yesterday's damp towel off the floor, and disappeared upstairs.

"But I wanted to talk about London," I said, meekly, knowing that it was already too late.

Gaining an audition in London was no easy feat for a fish waitress from Falmouth. Two nights in a B&B was going to cost more than a dustbin of scallops, and you could feed a sizeable family with halibut for the cost of the train fare.

Still, I had to give it a go. It was my life's ambition to play Madame Offelle in a West End show. It was the meatiest female role in theatre, and not just because she was a cannibal.

I examined myself in the mirror. Was I too short? At five-foot-two, I was hardly intimidating. Did I look devastating enough? I would probably need to dye my hair for the part. Nobody casts a mousette as a flesh-eating whore. No, the casting director would certainly want a blonde. Perhaps a hair transformation was something I could do this afternoon. Counting down the hours would be easier if they were spent preparing for the audition.

Suddenly, the words "Feed me!" resonated around the room. My mobile phone was ringing. My heart leapt, as it had done with every phone call since my profile was added to *Star Now*. Alas, it was not Andrew Lloyd Webber, but Mandy Joy Webster — my mum.

"Hello Steph!" she boomed down the telephone.

"Mum."

"How's Derek?" she asked.

I thought about it. I could hear him upstairs trying to fart the *Mission Impossible* soundtrack. "Same as always," I told her.

"And you?"

A vision of me on the stage flashed into my mind, but I felt my mum probably wanted to know how I was, not how I was hoping to be. "Same old, same old."

"Are you still looking for somewhere to stay in London?" asked Mum.

I instantly brightened. "Yes!"

"Well, how would you feel about house sitting for Myrtle and Ralf?"

"Mum! I don't have a general ambition to visit London, there's an audition!"

"Oh, that's a shame, because Myrtle has had a to-do with the kennels and they might have to cancel Barbados at short notice, and ..."

"Short notice?"

"Yes, they are supposed to be flying out on Monday."

"But that's perfect."

"It is?"

"The auditions start on Tuesday."

"Well, that's great. I'll tell them you're keen. It will be for five days; is that all right?"

Callbacks flashed into my mind. "All right? It's perfect."

What luck! I'd landed right on my feet. It had to be a good omen; Madame Offelle was mine. I imagined lounging in a luxury apartment and catching the tube to the West End every day, for call back after call back.

"Oh Mum?" I asked.

"Yes?"

"Who are Myrtle and Ralf?"

* * *

I looked at my blonde reflection. *Hello!* Why had it never occurred to me to go blonde before? Twenty-six years and I'd never once bleached my hair.

"Oh stop! You're making me dribble," I said to the mirror.

It's not often that a girl judges herself by how much she could charge for sex, but I was delighted to think that the new look must have increased my street value and, therefore, my resemblance to Madame Offelle.

I practised my Offelle eyes — mean and smoking. Admittedly, the eyes needed a little extra work; I looked like somebody who had suffered a stroke. Why couldn't my left eye be as mobile as my right? If I could only arch *both* eyebrows ...

Still, I had two more days to work on the eyes. Right now, I was too excited about my new look to let unpolished smoky eyes bring me down.

Then I had an idea. After tomorrow, I wasn't going to see Derek for the best part of a week. I should say goodbye in style. What better way to part company than with a little sexy time? It would also give me a great opportunity to test drive my new vibrant locks.

It took a little time to find my stockings. I hadn't worn them since the day Derek won his office fantasy football league, two years ago. Damn, I'd forgotten that they weren't hold ups; suspender clips were definitely required. Now I was going to have to wear the hideous teddy that he bought me one Christmas — a crotchless, fuchsia, fishnet number that it was impossible to get into without snagging.

I caught a glimpse of myself in the full length mirror. Was it really me staring back? I couldn't have looked more like a hooker if I tried. I wondered if I should wear this to my audition. Then I looked down at my wiry pubes poking through the crotchless opening, and decided the outfit was best left at home (or burnt).

Still, Derek obviously liked this sort of lingerie, otherwise he wouldn't have chosen it. I smiled to myself as I imagined his face.

Wearing my best heels, I tiptoed down the first two stairs. Derek was on the sofa once again, this time wearing a new t-shirt (*Anchorman*) and boxers that were (hopefully) identical to the ones he'd had on earlier.

When he didn't stop playing FIFA football, I decided to take heavier steps. I wanted him to notice me mid-descent, for maximum effect.

I strutted down two more steps. Still he didn't turn around, so I cleared my throat, as elegantly as I could — it's important not to destroy seductive moments with the threat of germs.

Eventually, when I'd made it to the bottom of the stairs without as much as a glance from Derek, I climbed onto the sofa and attempted to drape myself over him erotically.

The bastard continued playing the damn computer game.

I ran a red nail up his leg.

"Steph, I'm in the middle of a game!"

"Fine," I snapped. However, I reminded myself that causing arguments during foreplay had not worked out well for me in the past. I twiddled my hair in his peripheral vision, hoping that the new colour would capture his attention.

"I'm going to be at least ten minutes, so you might want to get a dressing gown."

"What?"

"And be careful with those shoes, you could do me a serious injury."

If only.

* * *

It was the first time I'd been on a long distance train. Certainly, I knew that you could get trains that had more than three carriages, but I did not know about buffet cars, vestibule areas and toilets with automatic doors that made you feel too vulnerable to undress.

I found myself a seat in Coach E, which was apparently somewhere that I could both use my phone and my personal stereo. The concept of a quiet carriage was alien to me, and perhaps if I'd heard of them prior to my long distance rail experience, I would have chosen my seat more wisely.

All around me, passengers appeared to be having conversations with all manner of absent parties.

"The doctor said I'm probably not infectious," the lady closest to me told her telephone.

One man was on the phone to somebody who needed to ascertain exactly where on the Penzance to Paddington line he was. "The bit with trees either side!" he insisted.

"What?" an older chap asked his mobile, "and then Freud bit him? Good."

I tried to relax by gazing out the window, watching the concentration of buildings grow and shrink, as the train chugged through town and countryside.

A skinhead wearing a wife-beater top got on at St Austell, sat opposite me, and opened what appeared to be a metal suitcase. I watched with interest as he took out what appeared to be some sort of drill. However, when he turned it on I realised, with horror, that it was a tattoo gun. I was immensely concerned; why would somebody tattoo himself on a moving train?

Then a woman twenty years his senior came to join him. "Stop playing," she said.

"Sorry Mum," he snivelled, and put the gun away.

At Bodmin Parkway, the two were replaced by a small family who grabbed the table seats.

"I love Hairy Smith," said a girl of about seven.

"Who's Hairy Smith?" asked her father.

"They're a band," she explained, and began singing *I Don't Want to Miss a Thing.*

After two hours, I'd had enough. I was less than thrilled when the train slowed to a halt just after Newton Abbot. If this was a station, it wasn't marked. There wasn't even a platform. How odd.

The other passengers continued with their

conversations, crosswords and trash magazines, as if nothing significant had happened, but the train had stopped! We were no longer speeding toward our destinations. Minutes went by without any geographical progression. How was I supposed to become a successful actress if the train was not moving?

Having time to reflect on my relationship did nothing to brighten my mood. Derek hadn't so much as wished me good luck. I really wanted to share my excitement with him, but he had no idea who Madame Offelle was, and no desire to find out. Would he even notice if I moved to London for three months?

Finally, the train manager's voice could be heard over the tannoy. At last, an explanation!

"We apologise for the late running of this service. We can now tell you the reason for the delay. This train has been delayed due to a late train."

What? What sort of reason is that to give a train full of passengers? That's almost as bad as my mum's classic response to deep and meaningful questions: "Because it is."

If our train was delayed due to another late running train, then surely we deserved to know what had happened to the earlier train. If my West End career was going to be jeopardised, I needed to know why.

Still, I had ninety minutes to spare. I was meeting Myrtle and Ralf at three for a quick handover before they were to leave to catch their flight. Apparently there was a knack to running the shower, and the back door could be troublesome when it rained. The truth of the matter was that Myrtle was too attached to her beloved dog to go on holiday without personally vetting the person charged with looking after him.

I hadn't had a great deal of contact with dogs during my life, but how hard could it be? I knew the basic commands: 'sit', 'here boy' and 'not the sausages'.

Myrtle on the other hand, sounded insane, and I was glad it was the dog I was going to look after and not her. She'd had Peaches since he was a puppy and had quit two jobs because they wouldn't let her have Peaches in the office. She'd fallen out with three separate kennels because they failed to observe 'Peaches hour' and currently held the record for the most pet food refunds in the whole of Chelsea.

I imagined that Peaches was probably a miniature poodle, or some other funny little dog. He probably had a gold-plated kennel and a yap that sounded like a parrot.

"Feed me!" called a voice from my pocket.

"Yes?" I answered.

"Stephanie, it's Myrtle," said a cutesy voice. If I hadn't known she was sixty-five, I would have sworn I was speaking to a little girl. "I was wondering how long you're going to be, because Peaches needs his nap."

"The train has stopped," I said with concern.

"Stopped?" she echoed dramatically.

"I know, it's stuck behind a late running train."

"How late?"

"I really don't know."

"Oh goodness gracious! We're going to have to cancel the holiday!"

"Well, you could always leave a key under the mat."

"But I need to show you where Peaches likes to be tickled."

"Good Lord," I mumbled.

"Pardon?"

"I'm sure we'll be moving again in no time, but if we miss each other, you can always explain where he likes to be tickled over the phone."

Another passenger gave me a concerned look.

"Oh! The train's moving again!" I told Myrtle.

Alas, the good news was short lived. The train stopped again, twice and then the conductor finally admitted that actually the train was a bit rubbish, and dumped us all at Castle Cary.

We were eventually awarded the generous luxury of a train that was capable of completing a journey. During the wait, Myrtle called me a further seven times.

I eventually arrived at Paddington at five — an hour after Myrtle and Ralf had left for Heathrow.

The phone calls from my hosts had left me rather relieved to have missed the couple. Myrtle was a tiring woman.

Paddington station was incredible. The August light shone through vast, spectacular arches and a beautiful, old-fashioned clock informed me that yes, this really was London.

I stood rotating on the spot, taking it all in. The building was magnificent to look at and what's more — there were hundreds of things to do.

As I ambled towards the ticket barriers, I spotted a pub, shops, stalls ... By the time the barrier drank my ticket, I was desperate for a cookie. However, when I got to the cookie stand, I saw sushi and when I got to the sushi stand, I saw pretzels. Oh my God! There was so much choice!

Why did anybody go out into the rest of London when there was so much to do at Paddington station?

If I was this in awe of a train station, what would the rest of London be like? I could tell it was going to be an unforgettable trip.

* * *

My head was buried in a sweaty man's armpit. I'd never really understood the fashion for waxing, but as stalactites of moist, underarm hair tickled my forehead, I began to wish it had caught on.

Nobody had warned me that 'tube' was a synonym for 'oven'. I felt dizzy and struggled to find air that was fresh enough to breathe. I needed to sit down but there were at least twice as many people as seats. Having a place to stand appeared to be a luxury; some people couldn't get on the train at all. I counted twenty people within my comfortable personal space zone, and it took great skill not to touch any of them.

The tube stopped at Notting Hill Gate and I thought, *Hallelujah! People are going to get off.* But instead, more people packed on. "What are you doing? There's no space!" I wanted to yell, but I was vulnerable and felt frightened.

I wondered, if I reached into my bag, would I be able to find my nail clippers? If I could only *shorten* the man's armpit hair ... Probably not worth it — I might get knocked and end up clipping his flesh. I hadn't been to London before, but I was pretty sure that snipping a fellow underground passenger was a faux pas.

As the train began to accelerate, a few people started screaming. I panicked. Had something terrible happened? Judging by the suits, the brief cases and the frown-line furrows, most of the people around me worked in the city. They must therefore have been familiar with what should and shouldn't happen on the underground. Were the screamers Londoners? Surely, if any bona fide Londoners were screaming, I should be screaming too.

The screeching died down and the carriage was left in eerie silence — so many people, yet so few words exchanged. One man appeared to be balancing a Kindle on another man's head. A business lady read a newspaper. A teenager played *Angry Birds* on his phone. How could people just carry on their lives as if nothing hideous was happening?

Then, I thought of the play and I felt sick. It had been my dream to come to London and play Madame Offelle. However, if this was London, I didn't very much like it. I prayed that the buses were better.

Finally, the tube stopped at South Kensington and I was able to 'alight' — a new word for me. I made a mental note to write it down, if I ever got off this damn train alive.

People began trying to get on before I'd even had an opportunity to start peeling my way through the wodge of bodies. Finally, I realised that the only way off the train was going to be by physical violence. Using my hands like flippers, I firmly guided people out of the way. I could see the door. It was clear. The doors began to bleep. I knew from films that that meant they were about to close.

I dived for the door, but it was too late. I was trapped on the train once more! Forced to continue to the next stop. *No!* I thought, *I was so close.*

* * *

By the time I finally escaped the tube, I felt as though nothing would pick me up, but I was damn sure going to try vodka, Indian takeaway and high cocoa chocolate.

However, when I found the street my mood improved. It was absolutely stunning — Georgian, with tall, elegant cream terraces. "I'm going to stay in a mansion!" I thought. My passion for London started to return. Perhaps if I got the Offelle part, I'd be climbing the opening rung on the ladder that might very well lead me to own, one day, a place like this.

I'm looking forward to this! I thought, as I removed the key from the eye of a dolphin topiary. I opened the front door. I had no idea what I was letting myself in for.

The hall carpet appeared to be a montage of dead leopards. It was made from orange animal-print and had the thickest pile I'd ever seen. However, as I took my first step, I realised that it was soft underfoot. I leant down and stroked the carpet. *Wow.* I quickly removed my shoes, then my socks, and stood on the carpet. It may have looked hideous, but it felt incredible.

On the far wall hung an oil painting depicting a slim lady in her sixties. She was petite and dressed in a white satin robe, and wore enormous hooped earrings. I supposed it was Myrtle.

I followed the hall until it opened out into an enormous living room. "Oh, it's open plan," I thought, but on further inspection, I realised that this was *just* the living room. It was larger than our entire house.

Every wall was glossed a different shade of pink or red, and a foot-thick layer of fairy lights outlined the ceiling. The ceiling itself was textured with an enormous swirly pattern spiralling towards an enormous chandelier.

Looking at the ceiling made me feel dizzy, so I slumped onto the couch to recover my balance. It was a white leather affair large enough for twenty adults. The cushions appeared to have been made from glittery zebras, and at least two of them had photographs printed on one side. 'Myrtle' read the embroidery on one, depicting the lady from the hall painting, riding a horse. 'Ralf' read another, depicting a heavily set man wearing a smoking jacket and holding a hand of playing cards.

As I sat there, taking in the surroundings, I felt perplexed. How could two people make such a beautiful home look so utterly revolting?

It was then that I remembered Peaches. "Hello?" I called. When there was no reply, I started considering other doggy greetings. "Woof?" I barked, hopefully.

When he didn't come running, I decided that I ought to go and look for the little fellow. After all, taking care of Myrtle's precious pooch was the reason that I had the luxury of a six bedroom Kensington house all to myself.

I walked into the kitchen — an enormous monstrosity with pink units. "Peaches?" I called.

No response.

I walked into the second living room (too hideous

to describe.)

No response.

I started worrying that I might have to check all six bedrooms and wished that they'd left me a map of their castle. Then I remembered that Myrtle had said she'd left instructions in the utility room. I went back into the kitchen and walked through to the other side.

The utility room was a kitchen in itself — a fridge, a giant free-standing freezer, a dishwasher and, of course, more units that were as vile as those in the kitchen.

Then, Holy Maloney!

It was the biggest dog I'd ever seen. Peaches was not, in fact, a miniature poodle, but a beast that appeared to be a cross between a Doberman, an Irish Wolfhound and a German Shepherd. He had an enormous head, floppy ears and long, grey-brown fur. His lengthy, floppy tail trailed across the tiles. It was as if the largest dogs in the world had attended an orgy, and Peaches was the result.

I held a new hope for my relationship with Peaches. I didn't imagine that I'd have a great deal in common with a handbag dog, but a big dog and me? Well, we'd have such laughs — we would walk down Kensington High Street side by side, he would fetch logs in Hyde Park, I'd tell little children that he was an elephant.

"It'll be great, won't it boy?" I said, giving him a pat.

He didn't stir. That was odd.

"Come on boy!" I shouted. "Time for some food."

Still, no movement.

"Sausages!" I lied.

I began to panic.

"Wake up, Peaches!"

I poked him, hard.

No, no, no, no!

Peaches couldn't be dead. Myrtle and Ralf had

only left him that afternoon. He couldn't possibly be dead.

I should probably take his pulse.
How do you take a dog's pulse?

I began to panic. I wondered if dogs were heavy sleepers. Looking at the size of Peaches, I can't imagine he was *light* at anything.

Now that I was more than fifty percent certain that he was dead, I didn't very much fancy poking him again, at least not with my hands.

I looked around for something with which to prod him. The first thing I saw was a rainbow feather duster, clipped to the edge of the counter. I plucked it from its holder. It didn't seem like an ideal test of life or death but I wasn't entirely familiar with having to perform assessments of this kind.

At first, I prodded the dog gently, but with each failure to awaken him, I prodded a little harder, until I reached the point where I prayed that he was dead, because otherwise I was going to be in serious trouble with the RSPCA.

I sat down, feeling utterly defeated. I'd failed before I'd even begun. My heart stung for the dead dog. I mourned the moments we'd never share: the walks, the games, the handshakes.

Then suddenly, the most agonising thought so far barged into my skull — Myrtle was going to be devastated.

* * *

It turns out that finding a replica fourteen year old mongrel, is actually impossible. I never had particularly high hopes for the idea, but in my panic, I trawled the internet just in case. There were no dogs that looked anything like Peaches. There was a horse that was similar, but I had a suspicion that Myrtle would detect the difference.

I thought about calling Derek, but he wouldn't

know what to do unless Lara Croft had once had to deal with the discovery of a dead dog. Besides, he'd laughed and said I wouldn't last five minutes in London, so I could hardly admit that there'd already been a death.

In the absence of any way to bring Peaches back, I decided that the best thing I could do for Myrtle and Ralf was to keep Peaches' body safe until Myrtle and Ralf got back from Barbados. The utility room seemed secure enough to me.

Eventually, I felt satisfied that I had done everything I could for Peaches, and decided to allow myself some time to prepare. I had a big day ahead of me.

* * *

When I awoke, a giant china dog was staring at me. It was very similar to the junk that my great aunt used to call an antique, except that it was twenty times as big. I studied the eight foot ornament and remembered where I was — the house of tack.

Of course, the natural progression then was to remember Peaches. I hoped it was a bad dream. I never thought there'd be a moment in my life in which I would hope that a pink, fluffy poodle would run in and lick my face, but if a poodle had scuttled in right then, I'd have licked him back.

But Peaches wasn't a lively, slobbering miniature poodle, he was a giant, dead mongrel.

I checked my watch. It was five in the morning. I knew my audition excitement would make an early riser of me, but this was ridiculous. Still, at least this way I could slip in another quick rehearsal before I left.

Then again, perhaps I should use this advantage to miss the rush hour. The thought of getting back on the tube filled me with terror. Anything to avoid being stuck in a sweaty armpit ever again.

Yes, it was decided, I'd catch the tube to Leicester Square, and then rehearse my lines in a hip, independent thespy café, or Starbucks.

I took a quick look at Peaches before I left. He was definitely dead, either that or the laziest dog to ever live. I would have given anything to discover that he was just habitually lazy.

Checking my reflection in the hall mirror, I decided to have one last go at evil eyes. Nope — I still looked brain damaged. I wondered if I could do exercises to increase control of my facial muscles, and tried a few eyebrow stretches.

I was still exercising my eyebrows as I descended the front steps. I mumbled Offelle lines to myself, testing my memory. "I've got the goods ... that aren't on display," I muttered.

"Morning!" called a husky, cheery voice.

I turned and found myself face-to-face with the sexiest hunk I'd ever seen. Why hadn't I prepared for that? Panicking, I relaxed my facial muscles, wondering how much of the eye-training he'd seen.

"You're an early riser!" I observed, sounding more critical than I intended.

"Been jogging, haven't I?"

He was a toned chap with floppy blond hair and dazzling blue eyes. He reminded me of a surfer. *Hmm, an inner city surfer* ... His post-exercise glow suited him. His voice was deep and chalky. I was in love. I forced myself to think of Derek, but for some reason, the image of my boyfriend slumped on the sofa, with a hairy bollock poking out of his boxers, made the jogger seem even sexier.

"I'm Rick," he told me.

I beamed back at him.

"Are you a friend of the Ducketts?"

"Who?"

"Myrtle and Ralf?"

"Oh. Yes — kind of — by proxy. I'm their dog sitter."

"Ah Peaches! Such a bundle of energy, isn't he?"

"Um ..."

"How is the old boy?"

"Um ..."

"Am I keeping you?"

"I do have to get to Leicester Square. I have an audition!" I told him proudly.

"An audition? How exciting. Film or television?"

"Stage."

"Oh, even better. What's the part? Anything well known?"

"Madame Offelle," I told him.

I saw him look me up and down, and his eyes widened. I knew it! I was too small to play Madame Offelle. If a man on the street could see it, the casting director would notice straight away. Or perhaps I wasn't grubby enough, maybe I should have brought the crotchless teddy ...

"You'll be great!" he said, but the damage was already done.

"Thanks," I said, glumly. Then I turned and hurried out of the gate.

Part of me wanted to catch the next train back to Cornwall. I was going to make a fool of myself. Who was I kidding, thinking that I could play a great like Offelle? The dead dog was an omen. "Go home!" screamed the carcass. "Go home!"

No, I'd wanted this since my auntie had sneaked me into a performance of *Prime* when I was eleven years old. I was going to this audition and I was going to nail it.

* * *

"You're a whore!" barked the director. He was almost as short as I was and sported a toupee that may have matched his hair the last time he dyed it, but didn't now. His voice was humorously deep for such a little man and he spoke with an exaggerated cockney accent.

"Um, right, sorry," I muttered.

"What are you apologising for? You think Madame Offelle would say she's *sorry*?" he scoffed.

My fantasies about the West End were rapidly evaporating. It wasn't the culture I'd imagined, where everybody would tell me I was marvellous, and shower me with orchid petals, but a place where I was subject to ridicule and humiliation.

"You're a twat!" I shouted. That was something Madame Offelle would say, right?

The director, whose name was Bart, looked at me in utter shock. He fanned himself with a hand and sat himself down to recover. I imagined it had been quite a long time since anybody had accused him of being female genitalia, or indeed insulted him at all.

I glanced around the room. The walls were black and littered with photographs. Every square metre was dressed with an enlargement of Bart hanging out with a different actor. There were theatre posters too, but somebody had used a highlighter pen to emphasise Bart's name on each of them. Watching Chantal pout, I had a fair idea who was responsible.

"Brad Pitt," he said, when finally he'd had time to catch his breath.

"I'm sorry?"

"I've worked with Brad Pitt, Ray Winstone, Cate Blanchett ..."

"I was in character," I stuttered.

Over the last few days, my mind had concocted a million reasons why I might not get the part, but none of them involved insulting Bart Fleming. How could I have thought that was going to help my game?

"She's blonde," he told Chantal.

I hadn't quite worked out what Chantal's role was, besides strutting around in designer gear holding a clipboard. She also had a Chihuahua called Whiskey, and I wasn't really sure what his role was either, besides running around trying to trip me up.

Chantal nodded, showing that she definitely

agreed that I was blonde.

"I'm a natural brunette ..." I mumbled.

"She's not right," he told Chantal.

"Not even for a victim?" she asked, and then, tipping my face toward hers, "Or a sewer rat?"

I wanted to fight back, but calling the director a twat hadn't gone down well, so it was probably best to keep it friendly — if that were possible.

"Fine," said Bart. "We'll have her back when we audition the petty roles. Next?"

I grabbed my things together, wondering where I went wrong. Was it my defective eyebrows, my height or, worse still, my acting? Would it have made a difference if I hadn't insulted the director? I tried to fight back tears, but knew I was fighting a losing battle. My eyes searched for the door. I had to get out without crying.

It was too late; Bart had seen me. "What's this? Tears? You have the nerve to come here to audition for Offelle — the most hard-nosed woman in theatre — and then cry?"

"Sorry," I mumbled, forgetting that apologising was outlawed.

"You're from the countryside, aren't you?"

"No! I live in a town."

"A seaside town?"

I looked at the ground.

"Ha!" he beamed. "I thought so. All I see when I look at you is a frightened country girl. I see a virgin, no wait ... you have had sex, only one partner though. I bet he's called Norman and you live together in a house two blocks from the sea. You're not Offelle; you're the *anti*-Offelle!" He chuckled as if he'd made a hilarious joke.

"I can act," I murmured.

"Come back tomorrow after one, I'll get Chantal to audition you for a sewer rat."

Tears were rolling down my face. The anti-

Offelle? But that was *my* part — *the* part. Every actor has one role that he or she longs to play and Offelle was mine. I wanted it more than anything. How could he say that I was the anti-Offelle?

The ride home on the tube was dismal. I should pack my things and go back to Cornwall. If I had any pride then I would. It wasn't as if I could be much use to Peaches now, or anybody else for that matter. Was there any point in going back to audition tomorrow, putting myself through that humiliation again, and probably still leaving without a part? And did I want to play a sewer rat? Sure, I'd have a part in a West End show — my favourite West End show — but would it be worth all the expense, the bullying and spending night after night watching another girl play Offelle?

Perhaps, if I stuck around, the leading lady would suffer an accident, or come down with a terrible illness, and I'd have to fill in at short notice, saving the day. Then, the apparently ad hoc nature of my portrayal of Offelle would make me look even greater.

What was I thinking? Wishing misfortune on another person was not like me. I wasn't mean and sadistic — if I were, the part would be mine.

* * *

The house was scorching when I arrived back. I knew the cause — the hideous three storey conservatory. As I walked into the kitchen, I was struck by a horrible smell — *oh no, Peaches!*

"Get off! Go on! Shoo!" I shouted at a collection of blue bottles buzzing around his ear. *Jesus.*

It was then that I realised that I'd made an error of judgement — I couldn't leave Peaches' body on the utility room floor. He was going to decompose in the heat. His death was going to break poor Myrtle's heart as it was, without her having to see his rotting carcass. I had to dispose of the body.

I looked around me, what options were there? I

looked into the yard — an audacious affair with ornate pillars that lead nowhere, a water feature that centred around a pissing cherub, and a patio scattered with plastic flamingos. In the mid-summer heat, a dead dog was unlikely to fare well out of doors. It would be fine if I could bury him, but the whole of the outdoor space was paved.

Perhaps the basement would be cooler. I decided to go downstairs to investigate. Oddly, unlike elsewhere in the house, the door was locked. I felt that perhaps I shouldn't pry, but then I thought of Myrtle returning to find blue bottles chewing off Peaches ear, and decided that needs must.

I knew that the keys to the shed were in a drawer in the kitchen. I'd been gifted such knowledge in case the water feature tripped a fuse — apparently the property's wiring objected to pissing cherubs too.

When I found the key, it was, as I had hoped, on a bunch with a selection of other keys. With any luck, one of those would open the cellar door.

Had I known what I would discover, I would never have set foot on those brass-plated stairs. Oh my God — I was not prepared for what I found.

The door to the cellar was clunky and heavy, like that of a dungeon. It took a lot of force to open it, and when I finally did, the room inside was pitch black. My arms searched the wall, hoping to find a light switch, but I failed.

I should have left there and then, but the room was lovely and cool, and felt suitably chilly for the preservation of a dead body. I ventured in a little further.

The door slammed shut behind me. "Dammit!" I cursed. I reached for a handle without success. I began to panic. I fumbled around, once again searching for the light switch. There was clearly nothing at arm height, so my hands searched further down. Finally, I found a plug just above ground level. I flicked the switch, but what occurred? Not a plethora of light, but an unsettling grinding noise.

What an earth could there be in the cellar that might make a grinding sound? I thought of Derek's computer games and my blood ran cold. I was too afraid to investigate, and stood rooted to the spot for some moments.

The darkness, unidentifiable echoing sounds and my vast sense of panic rendered me completely disoriented. I could no longer remember the direction to the door. I crept forward, using my hands to feel the way.

My legs bumped against something soft but solid. I found myself falling forward onto what felt like upholstery, but it was moving. I dropped myself back onto the floor, but had no idea where the moving sofa might have taken me, or why a sofa might move. I staggered backward and my elbow fell on something metal. *Ouch.*

Suddenly, the room filled with light. What luck! I'd landed on a touch lamp. *Luck* is a funny way of putting it. What I saw before me was not a sofa, but a revolving bed!

The walls were lined with mirrors, allowing one small lamp to illuminate an entire room. Naturally, the bedding was hideous — black satin with a zebra trim, and the bed itself seemed to have loops and cuffs attached. I'd never seen anything like it in my life.

Surely Myrtle and Ralf had no idea that this was here — they were in their sixties, and friends with my parents. Admittedly, I'd never met them, but they certainly didn't sound as though they were into bondage — whatever bondage fiends might sound like.

Just as I thought it couldn't get any worse, I saw a large, framed picture on the back of the door, or should I say *photograph.* Bloody hell! Myrtle Duckett *did* know about the sex dungeon, and what's more, she used it.

The photograph was the nastiest thing I'd ever seen.

I wondered if scooping my own eyes out would require a spoon, or whether my bare hands would suffice?

At least now I knew where the exit was.

The cellar was the coolest room in the house and no doubt the temperature would be perfectly suited to preserving the body of a dead dog. However, if I brought Peaches down here, then the Ducketts would know I'd been in their cellar. They would know that I knew what they got up to.

Facing the Ducketts was going to be hard enough as it was, there was no way I was going to add discovering their kinky sex life to the list of revelations. No, as much as I wanted to keep poor Peaches' body intact, it wasn't worth setting foot in this room, ever again.

* * *

The only viable option was the freezer. Towering above me, rivalling my arm span and reaching two feet deep, it was massive. It could easily accommodate even the most whopping of dogs.

I opened the freezer door with trepidation — after what I had found in the cellar, I couldn't rule out anything. Fortunately, it just contained shelves of frozen fruit and neat little rows of broad beans. I retrieved a jar and saw that it wore a handwritten label, 'From Ralf's allotment, July 2011.'

Which is worse, letting a couple's home-grown raspberries defrost, or letting their dog decompose? It was an age-old quandary.

I decided that the fruit had to go, and began removing the bags and jars one by one. The shelves were going to have to go too.

Eventually, it was time to move Peaches to his new home. I didn't very much fancy the job, but it had to be done. I found a pair of Marigold rubber gloves, thankfully not stumbling on any more bondage gear during my search.

Peaches was heavier than I could have ever imagined. I'm not a large woman, but I'd like to think I could handle a dog. I was going to need to put my whole body into this.

Clad in rubber gloves, a gingham apron and a pair of Ralf's wellies, I grabbed Peaches upper body, pulled it in against my chest and began to drag.

Just then, I saw a face at the window.

Fuck.

It was Rick.

Double fuck.

There was no disguising what was going on. When a woman is surrounded by thawing fruit and handling a dog with rubber gloves, it can only mean one thing.

Peaches' body was in the way of the door. However, I had to talk to Rick. I had to explain.

I scurried toward the window and opened it as wide as I could.

"Rick?"

"I was about to knock, but I can see that you're busy."

"You startled me!"

"Sorry, I usually use the back door when I pop in." As he peered over my shoulder, I moved my torso to try and block the scene that lay beyond, but I knew it was too late. "Is that Peaches?" he asked.

I gulped, then nodded, glumly.

"What happened?"

"Long story. Would you like to come in for a cuppa?"

"Um ..." He surveyed the utility room. "Ordinarily, I would say yes, but ..."

"I tell you what, why don't I come out?"

And so I climbed out of the window and faced the

sexiest man in the world, wearing oversized wellies, a frilly apron and rubber gloves. I patted my head; just as I thought, sweat held my fringe in a bizarre quiff.

It was the first time that I noticed that Rick was holding flowers. "I wanted to see how your audition went," he began, "I'm hoping these are congratulations flowers."

"Make that commiserations."

"I'm sorry to hear that. What went wrong?"

"I called the director a twat."

"Ah."

I began telling Rick about my day. I wasn't sure whether it was because he was exceptionally easy to talk to, or because my throat was overflowing with words, but when I'd finished explaining my day, I began on the day before that. I told him about the frustrating journey, finding Peaches dead and the hideous audition. I cunningly left out the part about the mortifying failed seduction of my own boyfriend and the cellar that would haunt my nightmares for the rest of my life.

"It sounds as though you're better off without the part. That Bart sounds awful."

"But I don't care. I want to be pushed."

"Do you want to be humiliated?"

"If it makes me a better actor, then yes!"

"Why don't I cook you dinner tonight? I'll come around the front in a minute, and help put Peaches in ..." He paused and looked at the freezer. "... A more suitable resting place. Then, I'll cook you a tasty meal."

"That sounds ..." *Absolutely bloody perfect.* "... nice. Thank you."

I climbed back in through the window, and realised, with horror, that I'd chipped the magenta paintwork. *How did I do that?* There was now an obvious gash in the plaster. I frowned.

So far, I'd let blue bottles eat their dead dog's ear, destroyed the fruits of their gardening efforts and dented the paintwork. I wondered what the baseline wear and tear was for house sitters, was I doing better or worse than average?

I let Rick in through the front door, taking care to remove my dead-dog-handling accessories first.

God — he was gorgeous. I found it much easier to enjoy his beauty now that he'd offered to cook for me. A gorgeous man is an annoying reminder of your own inadequacy — unless he's yours!

Could he be mine? A man who offers to cook after he's seen you trying to freeze a dead dog has to be at least a little bit keen.

My mind flipped back to Derek. I'd never cheated on him before and I wasn't prepared to start now, but dinner was only dinner. The fact that my dining companion happened to be a mighty fine example of man, whilst my boyfriend back home was a gorilla with a driving licence, was neither here nor there.

"I'm not sure that we're going to get Peaches into the freezer," mused Rick, after taking a look. "I mean, the volume is fine, but he's the wrong shape."

"The wrong shape?"

"Well, you won't get him in there unless we ..."

"Unless we what?"

Rick looked sullen, and bit his lip. He inhaled through his teeth and then offered, "Unless we break a bit off."

"Break a bit off? We can't do that! I'm supposed to be protecting the body, not massacring it."

"Well surely it's better if he has a broken leg, than he starts to decompose."

Perhaps if I had a large pet of my own then "Snapped bone or rotten flesh?" would be an easy question to answer, but I'd only ever had a fish. The hardest decision I'd had to make was "To flush or not to flush?" which wasn't really applicable here.

Certainly a broken leg sounded less grisly, but were these my decisions to make? I wasn't the decomposition God.

I contemplated calling Myrtle and asking what she would like me to do. However, nothing ruins a holiday like being asked to give permission for the house sitter to snap off one of your beloved's limbs. She wouldn't even have gone if I hadn't assured her that Peaches was in safe hands — oh, what a foolish optimist I had been.

Even though Peaches' death hadn't been my fault, I had to wonder — if I was this bad at looking after a dead dog, could I really have taken care of a live one?

"When did you say they're coming back?" asked Rick.

"Friday."

"We can't leave him here until Friday."

"We can't break off a leg."

"Legs."

"What?"

"We'd have to break off more than one."

Argh! I tore at my hair. The entire trip was turning into a nightmare. I mean sure, I was excited about the upcoming dinner, but no date could be hot enough to compensate for having to saw the legs off a domestic animal. There were certainly more romantic ways to start an evening.

"Nobody is breaking any legs," I said.

"Well, what are we supposed to do? Aren't there pet cemeteries for this sort of thing?" Rick suggested.

Yes! Why didn't I think of that?

In a flash, I was upstairs on Ralf's computer. Apparently, there was a pet cemetery in Hyde Park. Perfect — we could even carry Peaches from here.

My delight was short-lived. Alas, the cemetery was no longer open to new burials. For a crazy moment, I considered climbing the iron gates and sneaking him in anyway, but then I imagined telling Myrtle what I'd done. From what I'd seen in the cellar, it was clear that she liked pain. However, having an iron spike up her bum every time she wanted to pay her respects to her dead pooch was probably not the sort of pain that she enjoyed.

Next, I found a cemetery that was still in use. Each dog got its own patch, a deluxe doggy casket and a tombstone.

"This is perfect," I told Rick.

"How much is it?"

I swallowed hard. "Whoa!"

"How much?"

"Three thousand pounds!"

"Where is it, Buckingham Palace?"

"Zone three."

"Well, there's your problem. You need to look outside London."

"Do you have a car?"

"No, but I'm sure we can sort something out."

I continued looking: Berkshire, Essex, Kent — they all wanted at least a grand to bury a dog. As much as I wanted to grant Peaches a deserved resting place, I was just a fish waitress from Falmouth. The train fare up here had left me bankrupt.

"Cremation ..." I muttered. It looked more reasonably priced, but was still unaffordably high, and there would still be the problem of getting him there.

"If you want cremation, try a vet," Rick advised.

After a little more surfing, I found a vet in Highbury that would cremate Peaches for less than fifty pounds, provided that I could demonstrate that I was on a low income. *Perfect*. I'd been demonstrating that I was on low income for years.

"So what's the plan?" asked Rick.

"I'll take him to Highbury tomorrow."

"And how will you get him there?"

"I dunno, I'll get a cab or something."

"And what are we going to do in the meantime?"

"Have you got a tarpaulin or anything like that?"

"I'm sure my dad's got something in the garage."

"Where does your dad live?"

"Next door."

"Oh."

Suddenly, I wondered how old Rick actually was. From his appearance, he could be anywhere between eighteen and twenty-eight. I desperately hoped it was twenty-eight.

I decided that subtlety was a must. "How old are you?"

He laughed. "Twenty-seven."

"And you live with your parents?"

"Why do you think I offered to cook here, and not at mine?"

"I couldn't stand living with my parents now."

"If you were living in London and saving for a house deposit, you might feel differently."

* * *

Sitting down to dinner with a lifeless corpse on the other side of the wall was not as bad as I thought. Rick was excellent company and kept me entertained with tongue twisters and jokes.

I found out that he was an English teacher at a fancy private school. He liked French films, archery and tennis. His life's ambition was to do up a run-down house in the south of France, and his dream theatre role was Macbeth.

"Macbeth, really?"

"He's great."

"Isn't that a bit cliché for an English teacher?"

"What wouldn't be cliché?"

"Hedwig."

"Hedwig and the Angry Inch?"

"Yeah, I'd love to see an English teacher from a poncey school singing *Wig in a Box*!"

At once Rick jumped up onto his chair and burst into song. "On nights like this, when the world's a bit amiss ..."

It was absolutely hilarious. I watched him with admiration, wishing more than ever that I'd got the part in *Prime*, so that I could move to London and be nearer to Rick. Perhaps it would be worth auditioning for a sewer rat after all?

"So, what made you want to audition for Offelle?" he asked.

"She's great."

"She's a murderer."

"Yeah, but she's strong. She goes out and gets what she wants. She's only a cannibal because of the environment she's in."

"So you're saying, if she lived in a different time, she'd be prime minister or something, like Maggie Thatcher?"

"God no! I'd never say that."

Later on, while we were enjoying coconut ice cream with the sort of chocolate sauce that sets when it gets cold, the dreaded moment arrived.

"So do you live on your own?" he asked.

I needed to think carefully about my answer. Up until this point, we were just two new friends having dinner. If I lied about Derek, I was taking a step towards making this into something more.

"I have a housemate," I said, telling half of the truth and therefore avoiding having to make a decision.

"Oh right."

I felt instantly guilty and began to panic. I wasn't the cheating type. No matter how much I wanted Rick to take me right there on the revolting leather couch, it probably wasn't a good idea.

My mouth opened and words started spilling out. "I have a boyfriend. He's called Derek. We're very happy together — some of the time — all of the time. I love him. He's my boyfriend."

I looked at Rick. Had I blown it? He seemed more amused than anything.

Right on cue, my phone exhorted, "Feed me!"

"It's my boyfriend," I explained. "Hi Derek!" *Boyfriend*. "How are you? The audition? Yeah, it went fine ... I have a call-back tomorrow at one. It went really well."

"Apart from that *twat* part," laughed Rick.

"I called the director a twat but ..."

"Who was that?" demanded Derek.

"Who was what?"

"I heard a man talking in the background."

"No."

"He said, 'Apart from the twat part.'"

"Oh *him*."

"Oh him! So, who is he?"

"He's just a neighbour."

"Where are you?"

"At Myrtle and Ralf's, where else would I be?"

"Well, what's a neighbour doing there?"

"Oh, grow up Derek," I snapped, and hung up the phone.

If Derek were the sort of boyfriend that worshipped me, if he were somebody who paid me bucket loads of attention, if he were somebody who noticed when I entered the room wearing lingerie, I'd have had more sympathy for him. However, since he was a self-obsessed, lazy prick who turned his attention on and off at will, I didn't have a great deal of time for him right now. In fact, his jealousy was driving me dangerously close to straying.

"Where were we?" I asked

"Here," said Rick, grabbing me unexpectedly. Then before I knew what was happening, he planted a kiss on my lips.

"What are you doing? I have a boyfriend. We're happy."

"It didn't sound like it to me."

"Well, we're a rare sort of happy. You wouldn't understand."

"But I think I do understand," he said, putting

both arms around me.

"Don't," I said, using every cell in my body to conjure up the strength to resist him. If I was going to end my relationship, it shouldn't be like this.

"Come on, be naughty, I thought you wanted to be Madame Offelle."

"*Play* her Rick. I want to *play* her."

"Play her tonight."

"No."

I was grateful for his persistence, because it gave me something to dislike — something about which to get angry. His pushy, arrogant behaviour made it easier to say no. Mind you, is it really 'arrogant' to think that somebody who wants to get sexy with you, actually wants to get sexy with you? No, I had to believe he was egotistical — it was the only way to save myself from a ... perfect night.

Perhaps, if he'd taken things more slowly, if I'd had a couple more glasses of wine, or if he hadn't brought Madame Offelle into it, things might have turned out differently. However, instead, I ended up with enough willpower to kick him out.

"Look Rick, you're a great guy and I'm really thankful for all of your help with the dead dog and everything, but this isn't what I want. I'm sorry."

"Okay, I'll behave."

"No, you should leave."

"Why?"

I said nothing.

"It's because you don't trust yourself around me, isn't it?"

Yes. "No, it's because I have a sewer rat audition to prepare for."

"Are you sure you want me to leave?"

No. "Yes."

He frowned and began collecting his things. "I'll pick up my chopping board tomorrow."

I put the chopping board in his hands, along with

the other three items that he strategically tried to leave behind.

When he got to the door, he turned back. "Just a little kiss?"

It wasn't really a question. His lips met mine for just a second — an electric second. I felt even more certain that he needed to leave.

I showed the sexy neighbour to the front steps, our eyes locked for a brief moment, and he held my hands. Then, thinking of the dead dog to quash my sexual appetite, I finally had the strength to close the door. I sank down into the leopard print carpet and wondered when my medal would arrive.

Then, suddenly, a single unpleasant thought occurred to me — I was going to have to wash all of the dishes by myself.

* * *

As it happens, taxi drivers are not fond of having dead animals in their boot — not even ones that are relatively fresh.

"No," said the driver, firmly. "I've a good mind to charge you for wasting my time."

"He's wrapped up in a tarpaulin!"

"Still no."

"I'll pay extra."

"How much extra?"

"A fiver."

He scrunched his eyes into wantons and scoffed.

"Ten?" I offered.

"If you stink out my car, I won't be able to work for the rest of the day. I might have to get a professional cleaner in. You're looking at five hundred quid."

"Five hundred quid from South Kensington to Highbury? You must be joking."

"It is you who's taking the piss," he said, getting back into his cab. I heard a painful screech as he accelerated and then sped away.

I was not to be defeated. It would take more than one cab driver with cleanliness issues to stop me. Having woken up to eau de dead dog, I was determined to unite Peaches and a furnace as soon as possible.

"Hello?" I began, trying a second taxi company. The operator on the switch board had a fun and fruity voice. I was sure my luck had changed. "Can I have a cab to Highbury please? Where from? South Kensington. Perfect. There's just one more thing: you're okay with dead dogs, right?"

She dropped the receiver.

I decided to try a different tack.

"Good morning. Are you a dog lover?"

Click. Another one cut me off.

"Oh, hello there. Let me tell you an interesting story. No, I'm not selling insurance. No, I really do want a cab. I'll get to that if you let me speak ..."

Click.

"Good morning. I don't suppose you want to do a dear little old lady a massive favour? Yes, I know you're a cab firm. No, I don't want to speak to Bertie. He does *what?*"

This time, it was my turn to hang up the phone.

I had to face facts — no taxi firm in London was going to want a two-day old dog carcass for a client.

I felt defeated. Highbury was many miles away. I hated London and missed Falmouth, where you could reach any part of the town on foot. Getting to the vet's was impossible without a vehicle. If only I'd finished learning to drive, then I could hire a car. For a crazy moment, I considered trying to hire a car regardless, but I soon came to my senses.

What was the matter with me? Just a week ago, I hadn't known that Peaches existed and now I was prepared to break the law for him. I was losing the plot.

Back in the house, I could smell the carcass from the hallway. The stench was getting worse. I decided I'd better air the utility room and braved going in there. The stench was rotten. Even if I did manage to talk a taxi driver into letting me take a dead dog in his car, one whiff of this and he'd soon change his mind.

Yet for some reason, I felt compelled to look under the tarpaulin. I can't explain it. I knew that the results would be bad, but I felt a morbid necessity to quantify how bad.

Gingerly, I pulled back the tarpaulin. Peaches didn't look much different from the way he'd looked when I first saw him, but his scent suggested otherwise.

As I went to open the window, I was reminded of yesterday's damage to the plaster. Well at least that was something I could fix. After grabbing the keys from the drawer, I climbed out the window and headed for the shed.

Just as I'd hoped, the shed contained tins of paint. Surely the utility room shade was among them. I was amazed by how many different varieties of pink one couple could acquire: lily pink, bacon pink, flesh pink, flamingo pink ... Flamingo pink looked like the best bet.

I climbed back inside and caught another whiff of the nasty smell. However, I was surprised by how quickly I got used to it. I surveyed the damage. Yes, there was a little dent in the plaster, but painting over the crack would probably mask it.

Naturally, the paint lid was jammed and I had to find a spoon handle to loosen it. Just as I was taking off the lid, a shrill ringing sound made me leap out of my skin. Consequently, the lid came flying off the paint tin, flew across the counter, bounced off the back door, and landed somewhere near Peaches.

My main concern was getting to the phone. The Ducketts' landline continued its urgent ring. Perhaps one of the taxi firms had changed its mind.

"Hello?" I panted, holding the receiver with the clean backs of my painty hands.

"Oh Steph, it *is* a relief to hear your voice!" It was Myrtle. "I've been trying to call, but the line has been engaged for ages. There's no problem with Peaches is there?"

I turned and looked at Peaches. It was then that I realised that the paint lid had given the dog's coat a light splattering of flamingo pink emulsion, before finally sticking itself to his ear.

"Define problem?"

"Well, he's not missing me too much, is he?"

"No, he's not missing you too much."

"And he's not over-eating? I know how greedy he can get?"

"No, he's definitely not over-eating."

"Oh good! Well, I shouldn't stay on the phone because it's costing me a fortune, but as long as everything's all right, I'll let you go."

I had to tell her. Letting her believe that Peaches was alive and well was dishonest, and would only store up problems for the future. The Ducketts had put their trust in me and I had to prove that I deserved it.

"Myrtle?" I asked.

"Yes."

"Have a nice holiday."

"Thank you Steph, and thank you so much for looking after my baby."

As I hung up the telephone, I felt worse than ever. Not only had I lied to Myrtle, but I was causing a traumatic scene for her to return to.

I looked down at Peaches, half covered in a tarpaulin, half covered in paint. How could one lid have caused so much spoilage? I peeled the lid off Peaches' ear. Myrtle Duckett seemed like the sort of woman who appreciated dogs dyed pink, but I doubted that having her pride and joy doused in emulsion would qualify.

Well, I had to dispose of the remains now that they were covered in paint. If I didn't, the Ducketts would think I cared nothing for the body of their deceased pet, or perhaps they'd even think I'd killed him! Is it possible to kill a dog with a paint lid? The flamingo paint told a vicious lie, but it was one I would have to live with.

What would Myrtle and Ralf say when they saw the body? What would they do to me? Would they believe he was dead when I found him? Is it illegal to kill a dog? Would it go to trial?

I had to get to Highbury, whatever it took. I could think of one way to get there, but I didn't very much like the idea of doing it alone, let alone with Peaches in tow — the London Underground.

No girl expects that her trip to London will result in taking the body of a dead dog on the tube, but I was rapidly running out of other options.

It wasn't an ideal plan, but was it workable?

Certainly, Peaches was too large for my little trolley bag, but surely a suitcase would not be too difficult to come by. Perhaps there was one in this very house. I mean sure, Myrtle and Ralf were on holiday, but they seemed like people with more than one of everything. I imagined it now, a glittery silver suitcase covered in sequins. Ordinarily such an object would be easy to find, but in a house that resembled the interior of a Christmas shop, it could be somewhat harder.

I began searching the spare rooms. I wasn't happy about it, but whatever I might discover could not be worse than the bondage cellar.

It's incredible to see what rich people keep in their cupboards. One room had a cupboard full of diving equipment that had never been used — labels and shrink wrap remained intact. In another, there were no fewer than seventeen ball gowns, all encased in dry cleaning packaging. Another cupboard was dedicated to death; it contained black outfits, a bulk pack of sympathy cards and a collection of prayer books. Finally, I found a cupboard that appeared to be designated for holidays. It contained ski wear, sleeping bags and, mercifully, suitcases!

I withdrew the largest case from the cupboard. It was surprisingly quite pleasant — a brown, flowery affair, which appeared to have gold-plated clasps. It seemed like a worthy carrier for man's best friend.

Lugging the suitcase down the stairs, I wondered if I'd be able to manage it with Peaches inside. Thankfully, it had well-oiled wheels but even so, Peaches was a big dog. I had no other choice. I had to try.

When I put the suitcase next to Peaches, I was pleased to see that it did look large enough for the giant dog. Now, *where did I put those rubber gloves?*

Eventually, after much heaving, the body was finally in the suitcase. All I had to do was zip it up and we could be on our way. Alas, that was easier said than done.

Peaches' legs were not happy about being packed into a suitcase; they kept springing upwards, making the case impossible to close. I needed to strap them down somehow.

Then I remembered that there was somewhere I'd seen straps recently, but was I ready to step back into the cellar of terror?

Realising that I had no other choice, I made the journey down to the basement. I snapped on the lamp and shuddered when I was reminded of what was down here. How do you have sex on a revolving bed anyway? Surely you'd get dizzy. I'm not an expert on sex, but surely a steady dick is essential.

I started searching. At first, the only restraints I could see were built into the bed, but on further investigation, I managed to find two pairs of handcuffs and a leather strap. Handcuffs were not plan A, but they would have to do. I was itching to get out of the dungeon.

Back upstairs, I cuffed Peaches legs together in pairs, and used the leather strap to tie them to his body. The strap had a hefty metal clasp and I felt sure that it was up to the task — those Ducketts didn't take bondage lightly.

With his legs strapped down, I started zipping from the head end. However, when I got to the end, the tail popped out. So, carefully, I unzipped the case and started from the tail end. However, when I got to the top, the head popped out. I repeated this process several times, before realising that it would not be possible to accommodate both the head and the tail at once.

Nonetheless, I'd got this far and I was not going to be defeated. I am not one of those women who gets beaten by a hairy tail. I scanned through the drawers until I found a bin bag. I wrapped Peaches' tail in a black sack, and zipped the case from the head end.

I stepped back and looked at the case. Was it obvious that the trailing appendage was a tail? Perhaps I should add a hook, so that it looked like a hockey stick ... No, the tail would be fine as it was. After all, how many people would even consider that somebody might board the tube with a dead dog in her luggage?

* * *

I rolled the suitcase toward the tube station feeling as though every single person within eyeshot was staring at me. I tried to smile politely at passers-by, but this seemed to irritate them, and people rapidly averted their gaze.

In Falmouth, if one trundled a dead dog down the high street with its tail hanging out, people would no doubt intervene. However, Londoners seemed determined to ignore me. I began to realise that if there were ever a place to get away with committing a heinous crime and parading down the street with one's ill-doings branded on a t-shirt, it would be London.

The stress of the last forty-eight hours had left me in need of cocoa. It seemed unhygienic to roll a dead dog into a supermarket, but I was desperate for the good stuff. Besides, there were no signs prohibiting deceased animals.

I quickly located the darkest chocolate I could find — Green and Black's eighty-five-percent dark. Once I'd grabbed three bars, I made a beeline for the tills. Ordinarily, I avoided self-service checkouts like the plague, but today I felt it would be best to have contact with as few humans as possible.

Leaning the suitcase down beside me, I began scanning the first chocolate bar.

"Unexpected item in bagging area!" shouted the checkout.

"It knows!" I thought. I dropped the chocolate, grabbed the suitcase and ran — literally *ran* out of the shop.

I stood outside for a few moments catching my breath. I realised I was becoming hysterical, but I defy you to show me one woman with a corpse in her suitcase, who isn't at least a little frenetic.

After a few moments, I managed to compose myself and recommenced trundling Peaches along the road.

Abruptly, a smartly dressed gentleman reached for the case. "Here, let me help you with that."

"It's fine, there's no need," I replied, tightening my grip.

"Nonsense, we're going in the same direction."

I resigned myself to the fact that he was not going to take no for an answer.

"Blimey, this case is rather heavy. What have you got in here, an elephant?"

I glanced at the tail and managed a weak smile.

The experience was excruciating. With every step, I expected the man to stop and make a citizen's arrest. Surely, he must have noticed that something was awry.

Finally, we reached the tube station and the man gently set the case upright. "Well, it's been lovely to meet you Miss ..."

Better use a false name. "Offelle," I offered.

"Offelle, like the ..." I could tell he wanted to say prostitute, but he was polite enough to trail off. "Lovely name."

"Thanks for your help," I said, begrudging every agonising second of it.

I watched him walk away. When he was finally out of sight, I let out an enormous sigh of relief. That was way too close for comfort. It just goes to show where complacency can get you. I wouldn't be assuming that I was invisible again.

Finally, when I got inside the tube station and onto the escalator, I felt a little less conspicuous. I began fantasising about lifeguards, and was unsure why, until Rick's face popped into my mind. He did look a lot more like a lifeguard than a teacher. I wondered what his pupils thought of him. I imagined sitting at the back of the class daydreaming ...

The escalator ended and deposited me on solid ground. It took me half a second to remember where I was.

Then, to my horror, a hoody stopped me. He grabbed my arm roughly, and yanked me off to one side. He was younger than I was and wore a sweatshirt with its hood pulled up over a baseball cap. I experienced an extremely unsettling vibe and my heart started to race.

"You got a tail hangin' out!" he said, in a faux black accent.

I blushed, and was about to deny it, when he continued.

"It nearly tripped me up! You better be careful."

My eyes began to well up. I'd had a horrendous morning, and couldn't see any way for the day to improve.

"Don't cry, lady."

"I need to get him to the vets for cremation. I

tried to get the tail in, but I couldn't."

He looked at me for a few moments, before stepping forward. "Let me."

Before I knew what was happening, the boy got out a penknife and began sawing — yes *sawing,* at the tail.

I wanted to tell him to stop, but at the same time I realised he was actually doing me a favour. Besides, you don't interrupt a hoody with a knife.

Suddenly, he stopped. "It is dead, right?"

"Yes!" I said, stifling a laugh. "It is dead."

The boy continued, until finally the tail was off. "Here you go madam," he said, passing it to me. Then, as quickly as he'd entered my life, he was gone.

I stared after him, wondering if that had really just happened. Just when you think you've found the most unfriendly place on the planet, a kid chops off a tail for you.

With Peaches' tail now tucked safely inside the suitcase, I could finally zip it up to the max. For the first time since I left the house, I looked like an ordinary traveller. There was no reason for anybody to suspect that there was anything dodgy, or indeed doggy, about my luggage.

I caught the Piccadilly line northbound. It wasn't nearly as busy as it had been when I first arrived. I was finally beginning to master the tube.

As I sat on the train, counting stops, I recommenced daydreaming about Rick. It was a long time since I'd felt this way about anybody. A large part of me wished that I'd let things go further. Yes, it would have been cheating on Derek, but Derek had been having an affair with his games console for months. Perhaps I hadn't blown it. Perhaps I'd get another chance with Rick.

I was just remembering his lips touching mine, when I became aware that the train had stopped — not problematic in itself. However, after the train had been at the station for a while, suddenly the man opposite grabbed my suitcase — grabbed Peaches — and stepped off the train.

"Hey!" I yelled, and sprang into action. I leapt through the double doors onto the platform, just before they kissed together, sealing the train from the villain forever. Thank goodness I'd got off in time.

I gave chase, amazed at how speedy I felt without the weight of the suitcase to carry. "Come back!" I yelled.

The thief took the stairs. He was already some metres ahead. The escalator had to be an advantage, even if it was crammed with people.

"Excuse me," I called, expecting to have to meander in and out of passengers. However, incredibly, everybody politely shifted to the right.

I scurried up the escalator. After not much time at all, I was level with the thief.

"Hey!" I shouted again.

At soon as he saw me, he turned and began heading back down the stairs. To my horror, he released the suitcase from his grip and it began to roll.

I watched in terror, imagining it hitting the bottom and springing open, depositing bits of dead dog all over the tiled floor, in front of hundreds of people.

Quickly, I climbed onto the partition between the stairs and the escalator and began to slide, being careful not to bruise my fanny on the 'Stand right' signs.

Everything appeared to happen in slow motion. I slid — he ran — the suitcase toppled. By this point, a number of people had gathered around and were watching — an audience to my disgrace.

Finally, the suitcase reached the bottom, and, in a rather anticlimactic finish, simply flopped onto its side.

The thief rushed off into the tunnel, leaving the dog and his packaging alone. I wanted to follow him, to have him punished for frightening the life out of me, but it was more important to stay with Peaches. There was no way I could pursue him with a miniature horse in tow. It is a sad fact that a giant dog thief will always get away, either with the dog, or without.

I sat down and took check of what had just happened. If the fiend had got away with the suitcase, I would have been in serious trouble — my story would have been too incredible to trust. Who would believe that a thief had run off with the remains during an essential underground journey?

If it weren't for the pricey suitcase and its ridiculous gold-plated clasps, the theft probably wouldn't have happened. I imagined the man's face if he had opened the case, expecting it to be full of jewellery or expensive clothes, only to discover a decaying mammal. Perhaps that would have served him right, but it wouldn't have helped me.

I still needed to get to Highbury, but after the panicked pursuit, I needed some fresh air. I remounted the escalator, this time satisfied to ride on the right, with the people who were not in hot pursuit of a carcass.

"He had it coming," sang my phone — ah, a voicemail. As I hit play, I prayed it wouldn't be Myrtle, again.

"Stephanie, it's Chantal. Be here at twelve, or don't bother coming at all."

What? But the call-back wasn't supposed to be until one. I looked at my watch, it was gone half eleven already. Perhaps I could ring and beg for more time, but that was not something Madame Offelle would do.

I thought to myself, "What would Offelle do? What would a scheming, flesh-eating, murderous whore do?" Well, she'd go and get what she wanted with no consideration for anybody else. She'd drop Peaches and dash to Leicester Square.

Of course I couldn't do it. I couldn't leave poor Peaches in a suitcase on the streets of London for just anybody to find. He might end up as some poor tramp's lunch, or sold to a glue factory — or was that horses? I didn't care. I was not going to abandon Peaches, especially not now, after everything we'd been through together.

However, neither was the audition something I was prepared to miss — perhaps today's sewer rat was tomorrow's whore — and there was no time to go via Highbury, or even back home. No, there was no alternative — I would have to take Peaches to the audition.

There were other considerations too. My makeup bag was back at the house. I couldn't audition bare faced, even for a sewer rat. I needed to show that I took care of myself. Nobody would cast somebody who left the house without straightening her hair. Ordinarily, I would not have left the house looking at all sloppy, but mornings when you've accidentally splattered a carcass with pink emulsion are not ordinary.

"Come on boy!" I said to the suitcase, and set foot back inside the tube station praying that this time, it would be crook free.

* * *

I arrived at the theatre sweating and panting. There was a mirror in the foyer, but I was too afraid to look.

"Well, you certainly smell like a sewer rat!" chuckled Chantal. She was wearing heavy blue eyeliner and carrying her Chihuahua in a baby sling.

You know your life's gone peculiar when you start seeing animals in terms of their disposal potential. I have to confess that my first thought was not, "Why is there a Chihuahua in a baby sling?" but "What an easy dog to bury." If Myrtle had owned a small dog, as I first imagined, my life would be so much simpler right now.

Whiskey started yapping, so Chantal put him on the floor. He made straight for the suitcase. I tried to pull it away from him, but he followed keenly.

Bart appeared from the audition room and addressed Chantal, "The Scot is too Scottish — can't understand a word and neither would anyone this side of Dundee."

A small, freckled lady followed him out of the audition room looking devastated. I recognised that look. It was the one I'd been wearing the day before. Her hopes and dreams had been squashed under the weight of the smallest man in show business. It was not a pleasant feeling.

Without even looking at me, Bart went back into the room. I wanted to speak to the girl, but felt that I shouldn't. I watched her leave, wondering if I really wanted to work with somebody who made people feel like that.

Whiskey started biting at the suitcase. I tried to lift it up onto the chairs, but it was too heavy. Eventually, I got down on the floor, to give myself a better angle. It was then that I realised that the suitcase was leaking.

Thick, brown fluid seeped from around the zip.

No Whiskey, don't... Oh God, Madame Offelle was not the only cannibal in the theatre. Whiskey lapped up the brown sauce.

"Whiskey! No!" I scolded.

"Don't talk to my dog like that!" snapped Chantal. Then she saw what he was doing.

"Whiskey! No!" She picked him up and, looking disgusted, stepped away. "It looks as though something in there is leaking," she told me.

I arranged my facial muscles into what I remembered to be a smile.

"Well, aren't you going to see to it?"

I grinned back, not really certain what else I could do.

"What have you got in there anyway?"

I put my arms around the suitcase defensively.

Whiskey started whining.

"Have you poisoned my pup?" she demanded.

Suddenly, Bart appeared in the foyer. "What is going on?"

"It's Seaside Girl. She's poisoned my Whiskey."

"What?" he asked, looking confused. Then he turned to me, "What is she on about?"

"I don't know, sir," I replied. *Sir?* What was I thinking? Yesterday I called him a twat and today *sir?* When was I going to learn to address this man properly? Well, I didn't suppose it would matter. It seemed unlikely that I'd even be auditioned for a sewer rat, now that Chantal thought I was a dog killer.

"Something dripped out of her suitcase," explained Chantal. "And she won't tell me what it was."

I decided that it was time to leave. Although my departure would completely destroy any chance of getting a part in Bart's production, staying might prevent me from getting a part in any production ever again. If the suitcase was opened, I'd become a laughing stock. My reputation would spread far and wide, I'd be known as *Mad Dog Seaside Girl* and no director in the world would touch me.

I scurried out of the door, hoping that they wouldn't follow. I may have won one chase today, but I was at a severe disadvantage now that I was the one with the dog.

"Leave it," I heard Bart say.

"But ..."

"It was probably just shampoo or something."

"Shampoo?" she wailed, as if that was the worst news imaginable. If only she knew ...

* * *

Forty-five minutes later, I was sitting in Starbucks, nursing a cappuccino. My résumé had no doubt been put through the shredder, along with my dreams and ambitions. Dog sitting was supposed to facilitate the audition, not blow it.

To think that just days ago, having mousy hair had seemed like a problem. What a sheltered life I'd lived. Without hope of a part, I would return to Cornwall and my boring life with my boring boyfriend and his boring computer games.

"Feed me!" came a muffled voice from within my handbag. "Feed me!" it repeated. I naively hoped it would be Rick, until I remembered that he didn't have my number.

It was Derek. *Great.*

"Where are you?" he demanded.

"What do you mean? I'm still in London, obviously!"

"Well, you're not at your audition!"

How did he know?

"I'm at the theatre now and you're not."

"What?"

"I'm at the theatre. One o'clock you said."

"You're at the theatre?" I asked. I was stunned, and not sure whether to be annoyed or impressed. Had the man who couldn't get off the sofa to blow his nose, really come all the way to London?

"You're with him, aren't you?"

I wish. "Who?"

"You know who! That guy you had dinner with yesterday."

"I've told you a dozen times, there is nothing going on between me and Rick."

"Oh, so you're on first name terms."

"Of course we're on first name terms, it's the twenty-first century."

"Well, where are you, if you're not with him?"

"Starbucks. My audition was moved forward."

"Oh!" he said, breathing a sigh of relief. He let out a little chuckle. "I didn't know what to think, when I got here and all I could see was a mad Chihuahua and some blond bloke holding champagne."

"Wait, there's a blond bloke?" My heart leapt.

"Shall I come to Starbucks then?"

"No, wait exactly where you are."

Excitedly, I downed the dregs of my coffee. Then, Peaches and I set off once again, bounding across Leicester Square. I smacked my lips a few times, hoping that the increased blood flow might resemble lipstick.

Could Rick be the champagne bearing blond? Had he come to the theatre to wish me good luck in my audition? It seemed likely, after all, yesterday he gave me flowers. All my life, I'd wanted a dishy man to meet me at the theatre carrying a bottle of fizz. Had that day finally come?

Hang on a minute, Derek had just travelled all the way from Falmouth, and I was excited about a virtual stranger who'd travelled five stops on the tube? There could be something wrong with my relationship.

As I neared the theatre, I hoped I wouldn't have to face Bart and Chantal again. They couldn't have gone far if Whiskey was still running around causing havoc.

By the time I neared the theatre, I was almost running. I was just about to walk into the foyer, when the automatic sliding door slammed shut on the suitcase. Derek spotted me and immediately came over to help.

Stuck outside on the pavement, I peered through the gap in the door. Where was the blond carrying champagne? Then, I saw him — gorgeous Rick. He stepped out from behind a vending machine. I felt all fuzzy in the belly.

Derek began tugging at the suitcase, which was jammed in the door and clearly going nowhere.

"Let go!" I shouted, certain that the doors would soon open of their own accord.

"It's all right, I've got it."

"Hey," Rick joined in, "the lady said leave it."

"Who the hell are you?" demanded Derek.

"The lady said let go."

Through stubborn refusal to ignore the guy who was clearly stronger, sexier and better spoken, Derek continued tugging at the suitcase.

"Let go, Derek!" I shouted.

The suitcase had taken quite a bashing already today, and I could tell it was on its last legs.

"Let go, Derek!" echoed Rick.

Suddenly, there was a low splitting noise. The corner of the zip had given in.

I stood, motionless, as if watching a car crash that I couldn't prevent. I prayed that the gold clasps would stay fastened. Indeed, the clips did themselves proud, but alas, the broken zip was a liability in itself.

A fuzzy leg flopped out.

"What the ..." began Derek.

"I'll take it from here," said Rick.

"No, actually, I'll take it from here," asserted a rumbling voice. It was Bart.

Right on cue, the sliding doors retreated.

"Open the case," Bart ordered.

"I really don't think that's a good ..." began Rick.

"Shut it, Norman."

I was going to point out that technically, Derek was Norman, but decided it was neither the time nor the place to be discussing the particulars of Bart's mockery of my romantic situation.

"Right," snarled Bart, "if you won't open the case, I'll do it myself."

He was too fast for me. He grabbed the suitcase and dragged it into the centre of the room. Impatiently, he wrestled with the gold-plated clasps.

Eventually, the last of the clasps popped apart and the lid, which had clearly been under a great deal of strain, sprung open.

Everybody staggered backward with disgust. A female scream came from the corner of the room; Chantal was back. Derek looked peaky too and even Rick, who had known what to expect, looked horrified.

How bad was it? I peered inside to survey the damage. Oh dear, it was as bad as I feared. The monstrosity before our eyes was not just a lifeless shaggy dog, but a lifeless shaggy dog with a hacked off tail. And, not just a lifeless shaggy dog with a hacked off tail, but a lifeless shaggy dog with a hacked off tail and handcuffed legs. And not just a lifeless shaggy dog with a hacked off tail and handcuffed legs, but a lifeless shaggy dog with a hacked off tail, handcuffed legs and a splattering of flamingo pink paint.

I wondered if there was any way that the contents of the suitcase could be mistaken for anything other than a lifeless shaggy dog with a hacked off tail, handcuffed legs and a splattering of flamingo pink paint. There wasn't. There was absolutely no way that I could come out of this without looking utterly sick in the head.

"I can explain," I explained.

"It looks like ... a dead dog!" observed Bart.

"She moved the audition!" I cried, pointing an accusatory arm at Chantal.

"You mean if the audition hadn't been moved, I would have never known you carry a dead dog in a suitcase."

"I don't carry a dead dog in a suitcase! It's just today!"

"Well Chantal," he called, "what do you think?"

"Get her out of here!" she screamed, grabbing Whiskey, who seemed to take a less than healthy interest in the contents of the case.

Bart looked at me and squinted his eyes, then nodded a few times. "I think we've found our Madame Offelle."

"What?" exclaimed everybody, including me.

"But you thought I was terrible!"

"But she's disgusting!"

"I didn't think you were terrible, I just couldn't see you as Offelle. I've had a change of heart."

"You are not casting her!" shrieked Chantal. "She might kill Whiskey!"

Bart ignored her.

"So that's it? I've got the part!"

"Yes."

"Yes!" I screamed and began dancing on the spot.

"Are you sure you want to work for this guy?" asked Derek. "I mean, you did say he was a twat."

I glared at him.

Fortunately, Rick stepped in to rescue the situation. "Congratulations!" he sang, offering me the champagne.

"Hey! If anyone's going to give her champagne, it's me!" cried Derek, trying to grab the bottle.

"Oi! Get off!"

When Derek and Rick started battling for the champagne, I knew bad things were about to happen. I watched in horror, waiting for the bottle to smash. Some seconds later, Derek wrestled it out of Rick's grip, without having the forethought to prepare to hold it himself. There was a loud shattering sound and I felt liquid slosh over my ankles. The floor was covered in champagne and broken glass.

Furious, Rick grabbed Derek in a headlock. Then, to my horror, he punched him hard in the face!

"Hey! Get off him!" I yelled sternly.

Rick thumped him again, with force.

"Stop!"

Somehow, my voice got through and Rick let go of Derek, who promptly fell to the floor.

"What the bloody hell do you think you're doing?" I yelled at Rick.

"Who the devil are these men?" demanded Bart.

"I'm her boyfriend!" announced Derek.

"And I'm ... what am I, Stephie?" Rick cooed.

"I was wondering that too," frowned Derek.

All eyes were on me, waiting for an answer. I wasn't really sure why I needed to explain myself to any of these people, except perhaps to Derek who, despite being a prat, was still technically my boyfriend, if only for a few more seconds.

"Which of us is it going to be?" asked Rick, looking confident.

"Yeah!" demanded Derek, trying to size up, but failing miserably.

"Derek," I began, "I'm afraid it's over. You didn't pay me any attention until you were worried that somebody else might."

"But babes ..." he said, reaching out to me.

"Don't 'but babes' me. I know that your Sims 3 wife is a towering red head."

"But that's just fantasy, babe."

I tutted, rolled my eyes and turned away.

Rick shot Derek a smug grin.

"And Rick, you just tried to punch someone's lights out over a bottle of champagne."

"I was fighting for you. Come on, you know we'd be good together."

"I barely know you from Adam."

"But I could make you happy ..." he stuttered.

"I am happy. I'm going to play Madame Offelle!"

I smiled to myself, realising that despite everything, I was, actually, happy. I mean sure, I still had a dead dog to cremate, had just broken up with my long-term boyfriend, had nowhere to live, was about to work for a monster, and had to tell a woman that her cherished pet was dead, but all things considered, this was a brilliant moment. I was going to play Madame Offelle in a West End show. It was my life's ambition. I glanced down at the lifeless shaggy dog with a hacked off tail, handcuffed legs and a splattering of flamingo pink paint and smiled. *Thank you, buddy.*

* * *

The ornate brass urn took centre stage on the dining table. Thanks to Bart, his car and his chequebook, Peaches was now a respectable collection of ashes in a suitable ornamental container.

I dressed the Ducketts' giant table in a black lace table cloth, bought especially for the occasion. Then, I found Myrtle's funeral dress and one of Ralf's suits in the death cupboard, and brought them downstairs where I draped them over the table. Then, I picked a suitable prayer and marked the page in the hymn book with a doggy biscuit, and left it on the table. I collected photographs of Peaches from the shelves and scattered them around the table.

A car pulled up outside. My breath was barely present as I waited for Myrtle and Ralf to enter. I heard the key turn in the lock and then the soft sound of footprints on the leopard carpet. *This is it.*

"Hello?" they both called, merrily.

"Peaches!" called Myrtle.

Ralf entered first. He looked at me, noted my stern expression and followed my gaze to the table, until his eyes rested on the urn.

"Oh no," he mumbled.

Myrtle came in next. "What is it? What's the matter?" Suddenly, a loud, blood-curdling cry echoed through the room. I thought the chandelier might shatter, but apparently it was Myrtle-proof. "Peaches!" she wept.

"I'm sorry," I said softly.

I recognised her from photos. She was small, with silver hair and was dressed in a leather jacket and gold leggings. She had vast hoop earrings and a necklace made from glitter-dusted shells. I thought of the photograph on the back of the cellar door and shuddered.

She rushed over to the table and wrapped her

arms around the urn. She grabbed it from the table and collapsed on the floor, hugging it against her body. "No, Peaches. No, Peaches," she repeated.

"What happened?" asked Ralf.

"He was dead when I got here."

Ralf nodded.

"What have you done to my baby?" sobbed Myrtle.

"Now come on love," said Ralf, putting a hand on his wife's arm, "you know that Peaches has been poorly for a very long time."

"He has?" I clarified.

"Yes, the poor thing had cancer."

"Oh thank goodness!"

They both stared at me. It was awkward.

Obviously, I wouldn't wish a painful illness on any creature but, given that Peaches was already dead, I was delighted to have an explanation that got me off the hook. I hadn't killed him, and now, thanks to cancer, there was a way for the Ducketts to see that. Cancer doesn't often do people favours, but when you're suspected of killing a precious pet, it can be of assistance.

"I mean, thank goodness that he's no longer in pain," I added.

Myrtle embarked on a new burst of sobbing.

"Don't worry," said Ralf, "she'll be alright in a … year or two."

"I've taken an extra day off work," I explained, "so that I'll be here for the funeral tomorrow."

"You organised a funeral?" squeaked Myrtle.

"It was the least I could do."

A doggy funeral wasn't usually my thing, but after everything that Peaches and I had been through together, it felt only right.

"Thank you," said Ralf, with an appreciative nod. "It will mean the world to Myrtle."

* * *

The next day, as I packed my things together, I reflected on the week. It had been the most frantic of my life, yet somehow it had turned into one of the most successful.

The funeral was more enjoyable than I had expected. It was clear that Peaches had had a long and happy life, despite his troubled transition from death to his final resting place. I was amazed at how many people turned up to celebrate the life of one dog — at least forty. He was clearly a remarkable mutt. Myrtle's poem, "Without my baby" was a little embarrassing, but all things considered, it was a very moving occasion.

I found myself rather sad to leave London, but I would be back in three weeks for the first read through. Myrtle and Ralf said that they'd be happy to put me up until I found permanent accommodation.

The lead role in a West End musical, new digs, a new start ... Somehow, I knew that, from now on, life was going to be fantastic. I'd had my share of bad luck for one year.

Suddenly, I heard Ralf's voice echo up from downstairs, "Myrtle! Why is the cellar door unlocked?"

Introducing Boris

Boris Something-Or-Other sits on the page, waiting to be understood, waiting to be described. Only the twitching of his left foot shows that his veneer of patience is just a ruse. Like all protagonists, he aches to be introduced, yet is thwarted by the intimidating barrier of appearing on the first page.

I watch as his weathered hand adjusts the position of his water glass, only to pick it up, take a gulp through his chapped lips, wetting the tip of his unruly moustache, and return it to its original spot, off-centre on the mat.

A more forthcoming character, such as the flirtatious minx Jenny Thingybob, may have jumped out of the page and forced me to describe her showy cheekbones, but not Boris.

Boris is silent. He hopes that his patience alone will earn him the description that he so craves. Ironically, his lack of oomph drives me straight to Jenny, who can no longer be confined to a passing mention.

Jenny, thirty-one, has the perfect balance between experience and youth. Her large brown eyes have a childish shape that will never be lost with age. Only the three fine lines joined to her right eye, and the two by her left, show that she's a day over twenty-one. The tip of her nose curls up slightly, away from her glossed pink lips. She has a round chin, like a young girl. Facially, it's her high cheek bones that differentiate her from her younger self; emotionally, it's her ability to judge the exact moment to stop flirting with a man before he becomes clingy.

Boris often finds himself idly wondering what life would have been like if he hadn't married his second ever girlfriend. Certainly, he would not trade twenty-nine years of marriage and their three beautiful children for anything, but if, God forbid, anything had happened to Linda, where would he be now?

He has a sneaky suspicion that his market value has increased over the last three decades — once a geeky student, now a celebrated businessman. He knows that age had brought with it money, success and a moustache, which he is certain makes him look irresistibly distinguished.

Had he met his first girlfriend later in life, would she still have left him to chase her Hollywood dream? He finds it interesting that in all the years that have passed, he's never once seen her in a film or even an episode of *The Bill*. He often finds himself wondering what happened to her.

I catch Boris taking a sneaky glance at Jenny. Surely he doesn't think he could get this dazzling brunette? He may be solvent, he may have won one or two business awards, but his moustache really isn't sexy, and Jenny really isn't that shallow. Or is she? I watch as she pretends to attend to an itchy chest, letting her fingers caress her left breast as she gently scuffs. She's certainly no stranger to manipulation.

As I speculate, Jenny pretends not to notice Boris's increasingly frequent glances, and I wonder what sort of tale I'm about to write. The fact that there are two heroes suggests a romance, and their mismatched natures suggest comedy. Jenny looks up and catches Boris's glance with a faint smile. Surely I'm not about to narrate an affair? I find nothing more tedious than reading about a middle-aged man torn away from his family by a young seductress.

I always cringe when authors fall over themselves to justify the sexual indiscretions of their protagonists. "His wife didn't like blow jobs", "Her husband didn't appreciate Mozart in the way that the handy man did." The rules of fiction seem happy for a married person to have multiple orgasms with his or her spouse's sibling, so long as the spouse has initiated at least one conversation about tax returns.

I study Boris. Does he look the type to cheat on his wife? Not at all. He looks earnest, like a man who cares deeply about his family and his responsibilities. They say never to trust people with eyes that are too close together. Are Boris's eyes too close together? They look fairly average to me. In fact, Boris's eyes are very average in many ways — pale blue, neither large nor small, not slanting in either direction, neither bloodshot nor tired, but no sparkle to speak of either. It is his eyebrows that are extraordinary — giant, bushy, grey caterpillars. Jenny is quite slight; I imagine she could easily get lost in one of those eyebrows.

Jenny is aware that she's being watched. She twiddles her hair and uncrosses her slender legs, only to cross them again ten seconds later. It seems unlikely that this display is personal — not exclusive to Boris — far more likely that she's on a mission to be fancied by every man on the planet. A psychotherapist might say it's because she never knew her father, but Jenny doesn't care for dwelling on the past.

Boris's glances morph into a sustained stare. At first I'm embarrassed for him, but then I realise that it's not lust in his eyes; it's discomfort. I was mistaken. I've let Jenny's beauty cloud my judgment. It is I that is shallow, not my protagonist. Boris doesn't fancy her at all.

Jenny notices that he looks uncomfortable too, and she stops flirting with the atmosphere around her. She returns to reading her book. Boris is noticeably more relaxed by this.

Yet his interest in her continues. I start to respect my protagonist. He's visibly put off by Jenny's flirting, yet his interest does not diminish. His concern is with some deeper aspect of Jenny.

Boris touches the floor with the toe of his brown polished shoe — the very beginnings of getting up from his stool. Just as he prepares to transfer his weight to the foot, Jenny touches her breast once again. Boris quickly averts his gaze to the bar. He is greatly deterred by her displays of sexuality. His stern expression conveys appalled disapproval.

I'm a little disappointed by the false start, and can no longer wait to find out what their connection is. Apparently, neither can Jenny.

"Do I know you?" she asks.

At last Boris steps down from the stool and embarks on a brave journey across the floor. He sits opposite Jenny and studies her. Up close, he can see the similarity to his first girlfriend, to her mother. He searches for a resemblance to himself. Could she really be his daughter? A mixture of emotions knocks him backwards.

"No, not yet," he says.

On the Rocks

"Why are you up here when it's getting dark?" I heard. It was a deep, intriguing woman's voice, but I didn't turn to face her. Stubbornly, I looked out to sea.

Admittedly, there wasn't much of a view. In the distance, the vibrant cliffs of Exmouth were now a grey blob merging with the horizon, and the ships were starting to scatter stars across the water. The voice was right; nighttime was creeping in on me.

"Let's go and get some coffees," the voice continued.

"Who are you?" I asked, too afraid of eye contact to seek an answer to my own question.

"I'm Poppy," she told me.

Poppy was a sufficient answer. It informed me that she was not somebody I knew. Beyond that, what did I care?

"Leave me alone."

"I'm not going to do that."

I said nothing. Red Rock was mine. Perhaps I had no exclusive claim in the daytime, when it was littered with picnickers, or early evening when the more energetic teenage couples climbed up for a quick smooch against the sunset. But after dark, this cliff top was mine.

"Please let me get you a coffee, or a cup of tea. You look like you could use a hot drink. It's getting chilly up here."

Silence.

"What's your name?"

Silence.

Poppy sat down next to me on the grass. I wondered if she could tell that I'd been crying for many hours. I was not happy to have my quiet place invaded by this caffeine addict, but in a funny way, I welcomed the interruption to my own miserable thoughts.

"Shall we sit up here together?" she asked. "One

troubled young woman on a cliff at night is dangerous. Two is company."

* * *

The TV had definitely gone. I lifted an eyelid with a finger and then blinked a few times. My head was throbbing. Where was Biff? Was he gone too? Ouch! My head! If the TV was gone, then the most likely explanation was that Biff had stolen it. Poppy was going to kill me.

I thought back to the night before at The Amber Rooms. So much had changed in the six weeks that I'd known Poppy. I was no longer taking midnight walks so that I had the privacy to cry — I was rarely crying at all. I had friends. I went to pubs. It was almost like term time again, except without the study guilt.

Poppy was a striking woman with a perfect, shiny, jet-black bob that looked like Lego hair. Her tall, slender figure lent itself well to the skinny jeans she usually wore tucked inside knee-high boots. One eyebrow sat higher than the other, which gave her resting expression an amused quality.

In stark contrast, I had long shaggy fair hair and liked to wear tatty clothes from the grunge era, which I was never part of. My brows were scruffy and already had worry wrinkles between them. I thought about smartening myself up, but what would the point be? You cannot polish a turd.

Nevertheless, I wasn't short of male attention. My friendship with Biff had begun so well. We were out in Exeter. Poppy was outside the bar, taking a call from Nick, when a burly, stubbled chap strolled up doing the smug swagger that told me he knew he was in with a chance. I felt flattered that that was something that pleased him, and fluttered my eyelashes. The words that came next were just packaging.

"Can I get you a drink?"

"Vodka and Coke please."

"That your usual?"

"Yeah."

"I'm having JD and Coke."

"That your usual?"

Our scintillating conversation was interrupted by a pat on the shoulder. "I'm going to head home," explained Poppy.

I looked at Biff.

"This is ... er ..."

"Biff," he explained.

"Biff," I agreed, as if his name had been on the tip of my tongue.

"You don't have to come back with me," she said, with an awkward glance at Biff.

I took Poppy to one side. "Are you sure? I mean, I don't want to wake you later on."

"You won't wake me. Here, take my key, I'll get Nick to let me in. The bed in the spare room is already made up for you."

"Are you sure?"

"Of course!"

Staring at the empty space where Poppy's television had once been, I willed that the spinning sensation in my head was time rewinding. I longed for the chance to stop myself sharing the steamy kiss that led to bringing Biff back to Poppy's house, where he could steal her television and ... Oh my God, wasn't there once a stereo too?

My head fell into my hands. Poppy, although ten years my senior, was my closest — possibly my only — friend in Devon. How could I have blown it so badly, and so quickly?

I felt the kebab from the night before rising in my throat and rushed for the bathroom. Adding a spoilt carpet to the carnage would certainly not improve the situation.

The seven and a half hours between discovering the theft and Poppy's return from work were my only chance. I had to find Biff. It was ten o'clock now and the earliest the robbery could have taken place was eight thirty, after Nick left for work.

I had the dreaded cocktail of a ripping hangover combined with remaining slightly drunk. It was not a good time to face sunlight but I had little choice. I opened the front door and allowed a little of the morning to rest on my face. I felt like a vampire starting to sizzle.

Stumbling along the road, I had difficulty remembering the route back into the centre of Exeter, let alone any factoids about Biff. I knew not where he worked, where he lived, nor even his real name (assuming he wasn't christened Biffofer or Biffrey). Aside from his preference for oral sex, the only thing I knew about Biff was where he liked to drink.

The Amber Rooms pub was not yet open. I decided to kill the time in a nearby Costa Coffee, where I slumped into a wooden chair and buried my head in my hands. I was nineteen and already a screw up.

Why couldn't I be more like Poppy? She would never get herself into a mess like this. Poppy had a severe mental health problem, yet she had her own house, a part-time job and the wonderful Nick, a damn hot charity guru. I was healthy, yet living with my parents, facing a definite threat of getting kicked out of uni, and was too lazy to get a summer job. My love life consisted of one-night stands with wankers called Biff or Skip or Daz or Plonker. It certainly wasn't my golden era.

If there was ever a good time to buy an Yvonne Coomber painting it was now — lovely bright fields of flowers, just innocent splashes of colour without a hint of impending doom. I'd wanted a Coomber since I'd first clapped eyes on her exhibition at the Paragon Gallery.

It was then that it struck me. What better way to make amends with Poppy than to buy her a cheery, uplifting painting? She was a manic depressive after all. Didn't they love to be cheered up? I got out my phone. Could I order one online?

No, an online delivery would not be fast enough. I needed the painting by five thirty today. It needed to scream, "Yes! Your telly has gone, but look what I got you instead!"

* * *

As I navigated Poppy's narrow front gate, carrying two thousand pounds worth of painting, I got the sinking feeling that she was already home from work. I had hoped that I would have the chance to hang the Coomber in her house before she got back, so that she had minimal time to hate me. But alas, it was not to be. I felt my heart pounding in my chest. I needed to get the peace offering to Poppy as soon as I could.

The front door opened as I approached it. The painting obscured my view but I saw parts of Poppy's shadow escape onto the front path beside me. As I climbed into the hall, she definitely noticed the metre square painting, but she didn't say anything. Didn't she like it? She showed me into her bare living room and helped me place the painting against the left wall.

"It was Biff," I stammered, "he stole your television, stereo and possibly ... but I got you a painting. This painting! Do you hate me?"

"No Meg, I don't hate you," she said softly, but I knew she was disappointed. Her eyes were welling up. "Please let me take you to see the doctor."

* * *

What my mother called an artistic temperament; two doctors, a psychiatrist and a professor, called bipolar disorder. Apparently I was having a hypomanic episode, which as far as I could tell, meant NHS-prohibited fun. Poppy assured me that that was not the case.

So there we were, Poppy and me, two friends with matching diagnoses. I'd have rather had a band or favourite TV show in common.

I wondered how long it would have taken to put a name to my mood swings without Poppy. A lifetime of unexplained rages and eight months of depression alternated with unfocussed frustration, financial indiscretions and spontaneous sexual disasters, had been explained with two simple words: bipolar disorder. I hated those words.

The summer was drawing to a close and I wondered how in the world I was going to face going back to university in light of these new circumstances.

Bipolar disorder was a lot to take in and whilst I welcomed an explanation, I was not fond of the prognosis. Therapy? Possibly having to take medication? I hated doctors. I wasn't a self-aware, confident woman like Poppy. I was just a kid. A kid who hadn't had a clue that this was coming.

Poppy — the very name spoke confidence and fun. What did *Meg* say? Nothing positive. Who called a baby Margaret in the twentieth century? I sounded like a witch.

I hadn't told my parents about the diagnosis, or even mentioned to them that I'd seen a doctor. It had only been a matter of weeks since I'd accused them of wishing I was dead so that they could devote all their time to my superior younger brothers. Parental relations had never been worse. Added to which, I didn't want to hurt them. I wasn't ready to tell my mother that her artistic only daughter was actually just plain mad.

Poppy suggested some alternatives to the word *mad,* but I was far from receptive. I was now a bona fide loser. What more was there to say?

The only thing that gave me comfort was the knowledge that Poppy, a brilliant, successful woman, also had bipolar disorder. I didn't think that she was mad or freaky or, in any way, a loser. However, I couldn't shake the sense that I was somehow different, that I lacked the ability to comprehend whatever stability secrets Poppy knew.

She told me to stop beating myself up over Biff. The insurance company had paid up and the police were doing their job. How do you stop yourself feeling guilty about something when you're to blame? At least if Biff turned up, there would be somebody more culpable than me in the picture. If he was punished, I might be able to stop torturing myself.

I sat on Poppy's sofa, watching the new television provided by her insurance company, and wondering if I'd ever find a boyfriend as incredible as Nick.

"You might be interested in Therapies for Devon," he told me, gambling that I was ready to hear the "T" word.

Together, Poppy and he were raising the money to start a charity that provided affordable Cognitive Behavioural Therapy for people who couldn't face the NHS waiting list.

They first met at a support group for people with bipolar disorder. Nick, a healthy chap, had shyly approached them, seeking greater understanding of the condition. He wanted insight so that he could be there for his little sister, who had attempted suicide on Christmas Day.

Poppy and Nick recognised their shared desire to improve access to therapies and, whilst working together to found Therapies for Devon, had found themselves falling in love.

He was quite a stringy man, even taller than Poppy, but with much less width, and the lankiness added a charismatic edge to his otherwise classically handsome features. He had a strong jaw, intense brown eyes and thick chocolate-coloured hair.

Nick was everything I wanted in a man — gorgeous, funny, caring and nuanced about mental health problems. Would I ever meet somebody who understood what I was going through well enough for us to have a real relationship?

"Thanks, but I don't need therapy," I told him. Poppy looked up from her laptop and I saw her exchange a nervous glance with Nick.

"Maybe dreckly," he added.

Suddenly Poppy exclaimed, "Bloody hell!"

"What is it?" we replied in unison.

"There's six thousand pounds in the Therapies' account!"

"What?" cried Nick, leaping across the room to view the computer. "Where from?"

"I ... I have no idea."

"Well doesn't it say?"

"It just says cash deposit — five thousand pounds."

Poppy and Nick had held a charity fundraiser the week before — a buffet at The Thistle. The event itself raised only eight hundred pounds, but they had been hoping the raised awareness would lead to later business donations.

"Perhaps a letter will follow," I offered.

"I certainly hope so," said Poppy, "I need to know who to thank!"

"It's funny; we're on the hunt for two people, one who stole from you, and one who gave to you."

"There is a somewhat amusing symmetry to it," agreed Poppy.

"Forget about Biff," Nick added. "What's done is done."

* * *

"Where have you been going?" asked a voice from the stairs. I was somewhat startled, having been home for less than three seconds.

"Mum! You mustn't sneak up on me."

"I didn't."

"That's the third night in a row that you've stayed out. Who is he?"

"I told you, I've been staying with my friend Poppy."

I knew there was more to come, but there was a brief questioning ceasefire. My mother guided me into the kitchen, where the kettle was full of lukewarm water. She discarded it and began again with fresh water. She remained silent during the entire tea-making process.

Once the teas were made, Mum thrust a mug into my hands and gently prodded me towards the living room. I sat down wondering why my mother was being so solemn. Did she know that I was sick? Had somebody told her?

"Are you and Poppy ..." she began, "Are you ... Is Poppy ... Are you both ..."

Bipolar?

"Lesbians?"

"What?" I couldn't help but laugh. "No. We're friends. Poppy has a boyfriend — Nick. He's usually there too."

"Then why do you spend so many nights there? Is it like a ... Do you three ... Do you all ..."

"No! I told you, it's expensive to get back to Starcross by taxi."

"Meg, is there something you're not telling me?"

Yes. "No."

"Are you sure?"

"Everything's fine."

"You would tell me if there was a problem?"

"Look!" I shouted, standing suddenly and spilling tea all over the canvas sofa and surrounding carpet. "Get off my fucking case!"

I'd like to say my mother looked alarmed, but actually she looked petrified. I felt instantly guilty. I wanted to tell her I was poorly, I wanted to tell her that I needed help, but I didn't know how. They would be devastated and it would be all my fault.

Besides, how could they understand what I was going through when they were healthy? To them, being content was the easiest thing in the world.

If they weren't able to help me then they'd feel the same hideous, frustrated anger that I felt, I couldn't put them through that.

I made a dash for the door.

"Where are you going?"

"Out!"

"Out where?"

"Anywhere away from here."

Slam.

* * *

"I hope you didn't use my scissors for that!" joked Poppy with a cautious smile. I looked at my lacerated arms, feeling ashamed and stupid. How could Poppy take such a thing in her stride? How could she be so comfortable with self-harm that she could make such a casual remark? Nevertheless, I was grateful that she did. The last thing I needed was another scene.

"Can I stay here tonight?"

"Of course."

"How come you don't cut?" I asked Poppy.

"A number of reasons I suppose."

"Tell me!"

"Meg, you need to sort out the underlying problem, not the symptoms. You have bipolar disorder — that's a big deal! It's about your whole lifestyle. You need to accept every form of support you can find. You need to go to therapy. You need to try medications. You need to tell your parents."

"I'll tell them when I'm better, like you are."

"But you won't get … You'll find it easier to get better with their support."

"I'm not ready for that."

Poppy nodded and picked up my glass.

"More orange juice?"

"Have you got anything stronger?"

"Not today, hey Meg?"

Poppy had had a good day, a much better day than I'd had. She had found out that the mystery donation had come from a local estate agent. A further four local businesses had made generous donations and they had received three enquiries from trained therapists. Also, Nick had found potential premises for the centre.

The things Poppy did, the things that she achieved, they weren't because she took meds, or went to therapy, or had an honest relationship with her parents, they were because she was naturally stronger than I was.

Sometimes I woke up with a crushing feeling in my chest and getting out of bed wasn't even a possibility. I just wasn't equipped to deal with that degree of pain, like she was. No amount of therapy, drugs or support from anybody would ever change that.

Poppy was strong enough to fight her highs. She nipped them in the bud with her relaxation techniques, anti-psychotics and lifestyle management. I was greedier than she was. I welcomed the highs — the feelings of invincibility, the sexual arousal, the energy ... Medication wasn't going to help me, because the overriding factor was my own greed.

Speaking of greed, I was desperate for a drink. Poppy was trying to help me stay away from alcohol, but she had no idea how much I needed it. She had no idea how painful it was to be me, or how friendly a shot of vodka could be.

"I'm going to nip out for some chocolate. Would you like any?"

"There are bourbons in the cupboard if you want some?"

"Thanks, but I'm having a craving for Cadbury's."

I hated lying to Poppy, but disappointing her was

worse. I slipped into my shoes and hurried across the playing field towards the Co-op. Would I have time to drink the vodka? Perhaps I should have made up a lie that allowed me to be out for longer.

In the Co-op, I felt too guilty to make eye contact with anybody. Perhaps I should have gone further afield, to ensure that I was not recognised. I felt as though I was sixteen trying to buy cider with fake ID.

"Excuse me?" asked a man.

I almost jumped out of my skin.

"Your shoe lace is undone."

Instead of replying, I hurried out of the shop, carrying a bottle of vodka by its neck. I clutched it tight against my body and made a dash for the park.

Beneath the shelter of a sycamore tree, I enjoyed the friendly click of a Smirnoff cap breaking its seal and smelt the uplifting aroma of spirits. I was just about to take my first swig when I heard a loud rustle behind me. Feeling like a child caught stealing sweets, I hid the bottle inside my coat.

"Meg," sounded a familiar voice.

"Nick?" I swung around. Was the vodka well hidden?

"Let's go to the pub."

"The pub? Really? Are you sure Poppy would approve?"

"Well, you've got a bottle of vodka hidden up your shirt anyway, haven't you?"

* * *

"You didn't use our scissors did you?" asked Nick.

"Poppy said the same thing."

"Great minds ..." he winked.

"Yeah, you two."

"And you."

"I'm not brilliant." I mumbled, twisting my arm to give him another brief flash of my freshly cut flesh.

"Well, you're not well."

"Neither is Poppy, but she manages not to mutilate herself."

Nick took a deep breath and studied me for a moment. "You think she was always like this?"

I shrugged.

"You think she was diagnosed and it was suddenly, 'Right! Health kick for me then!' do you?"

I didn't reply.

"She was hospitalised three times before she agreed to get any help whatsoever."

"What? Seriously?"

"She's not holding down a job, a relationship and a home because she's any more brilliant than you, she's just had more time."

It was hard to imagine that Poppy was ever in the state I was in right now — lonely, frightened, possessed ...

"She was sectioned once and she overdosed more times than she can count."

"Poppy has never overdosed!"

"She has."

"But she seems so together!"

"She is now. My point is, Meg, you need to play the game. The doctors, the drugs, the therapies, they're not there for a battle."

"My doctor doesn't take me seriously."

"Why has she prescribed lithium then?"

Obviously, I could see what Nick was trying to do, but it wouldn't make any difference. I wasn't well enough to respond to treatment.

Some days my depression was so bad that I couldn't face asking my mum for a cup of tea. How was I supposed to talk to a therapist about difficult issues?

Then there were the overwhelming urges to do something, or to be somewhere. When those happened, I could not rest until the urge was satisfied. I wouldn't be able to commit to treatment when I was a slave to such intense impulses.

As for the highs, I didn't want to give them up. Certainly, some parts of hypomania were destructive and frightening, but at other times, it felt amazing. I saw hypomania as compensation for my depressive spells. I wasn't going to allow a doctor to take it away from me.

* * *

"I'm sorry madam, but your credit card has been declined."

"Seriously?" sighed Poppy.

"I'll pay."

"No you won't!" she insisted, and disappeared to find a cash point.

Sitting in Wagamama's, surrounded by chopsticks and edamame skins, I cursed being alone with my brain. Some days, every thought brought with it a new wave of pain. Today was one of those. I had no idea why I felt so shocking. I had just woken up with an unbearable feeling that hadn't gone away.

That morning I had put on my prettiest item of clothing, a custard-yellow sundress, in the hope that it would make me feel better about myself. But I felt like a hippo in a tutu — a big, ugly, stupid hippo.

It's safe to say that the last thing I expected was for Biff to swagger in. Yet in he walked, with one hand in his pocket and the other attached to a blonde lady wearing a silver Primark party dress.

At first, I just stared, rooted to the spot, but then I recognised the necessity to act, and to act fast. I needed to call the police.

Before I could reach my phone, Biff turned and looked straight at me. His eyes lingered for a moment, until they flickered with recognition. I leapt up to give chase, but to my astonishment, he just nodded politely, and turned his face away. His feet didn't move.

What?

"Hey!" I cried, hurling myself towards him. Had

he forgotten that he was wanted for theft?

"Hey Meg, what's up?" he asked, in the manner that somebody might enquire about the weather.

"What's up? *What's up?* I think you know what's up!"

"Can we talk about this another time? As you can see, I'm with a friend."

"No, we bloody well cannot talk about this another time!"

Biff yanked me by the arm and dragged me away from his date. That was odd, why was he moving *into* the restaurant and not running out the door?

"Look," he began, "I know I shouldn't have left without saying goodbye, but what was I supposed to do?"

"What?" I could not believe what I was hearing.

"You should have told me you were married. Even if you did think he was away."

"*What?*"

"Sprung, Meg, sprung!"

"I'm not married."

"Oh give it up Meg, I met him."

"Who?"

"Your husband. I went downstairs to get a drink, and there he was, in the kitchen."

"You must have met Nick, Poppy's partner!"

"Meg ..."

"Anyway, even if I had been married, that doesn't give you the right to steal stuff!"

"What? Oh look Meg, it's lovely to see you and everything, but you're starting to piss me off now."

"No please," I begged, desperately catching his arm. Something didn't add up, and I had to know why.

"What is your problem?"

"Tell me exactly what happened."

"And then can I get back to my date?"

I rushed a nod.

"I went into the kitchen. He was there. He asked

me who I was. Then, he told me he was your husband."

"He said those words?"

"More or less."

"Did he say those words?" I bellowed.

"He said he was your husband, yes."

"What did he look like?"

"I can't remember."

"Well try!" I cried, shaking him.

"Tall I think. Yes, he was very tall ... and thin! He was like a stretched man."

Shit.

"Can I go now?"

"One more thing: what happened after he said he was my husband?

"I got out as quickly as I could. What else would I do?"

"You didn't ... *take* anything?"

"Oh piss off Meg. Of course I didn't."

* * *

By way of settling the bill, I poured the contents of my wallet onto the table, euros, buttons and all. Then, I rushed out into the street. I felt dizzy, I felt sick. The last thing I could deal with was noise, crowds, and the aroma of spicy food.

I propped myself up against a wall, trying to make sense of it all. Was I starting to suffer from psychosis or was the world actually turning upside down?

If Biff hadn't stolen the things, then there was only one person who could have. What was more likely: me imagining things, or lovely Nick being a fraud?

"Alright Meg!" called a deep voice.

I turned to see Nick standing beside me. Automatically, all of the hairs on the back of my neck stood on end.

"What are you doing here?" I shrieked.

I studied him. He looked harmless enough, but I

couldn't shake the feeling that he was up to something deeply disturbing. Was this what full-blown mania felt like?

"I'm meeting Poppy and, apparently, you," he explained. He went to put a friendly arm on my shoulder. He was still dressed in his sincere-looking shirt and tie from the office. I wanted to believe that Biff was lying, but if that was the case, why was he enjoying a date at Wagamama's, instead of fleeing before the police had a chance to arrive? Nick's fingers touched my arm and I leapt.

"Get off me!"

"What's the matter? Are you depressed again?"

"Seriously, let go of me."

"Where's Pops?"

"Where's her television?"

His micro expression said it all — a brief moment of horror, before he replaced it with a false look of bemusement. "What *are* you talking about?"

"I know it was you."

What happened next happened so fast it was hard to know exactly how it came about. One moment I saw Nick reach into his pocket, and the next, I felt cold metal against my back, chilling me through the thin cotton of my dress. "We're going to my car," he told me, "and you're going to get in it."

I was poised to object when I identified the object now digging uncomfortably into my spine. It was the blade of a knife.

* * *

"You know she hates you," laughed Nick as he drove. "She used to think it was endearing, your little girl crush. But now, she just hates you."

"No she doesn't."

"You're around our house all of the time. She can't breathe."

"It's her house, not yours," I told him. I tried to

sound brave, but I was petrified. I had no idea where Nick was taking me, or what he planned to do with me. At least however, being kidnapped at knife point put paid to any suspicions that my concerns about Nick were simply paranoid delusions. This was clear-cut badness.

I felt comforted by the fact that the roads were familiar, but how long would it be before he took me out of Exeter and towards somewhere more deserted? Would I be stabbed and buried on Dartmoor?

"You'll go to jail for this," I mumbled.

"Who's going to believe a word you say? You're a mentally unstable alcoholic."

My phone started to vibrate in my bag. I was too frightened to answer it. Perhaps my fate depended on how well I behaved. I tried to stifle the vibrations with my arm. The last thing I wanted was to remind Nick that I had a phone, in case he took my one lifeline away from me. I had to cancel the call. I pushed my bag to the edge of my chair and reached into it. The phone slipped through my fingers and fell beneath the seat.

"Shit," I mouthed.

I was relieved to find that this animal had brought me straight to Poppy's house. It seemed unlikely that he would bring me here if he planned to stab me and leave me in a ditch.

"Your sister didn't really try to commit suicide, did she?" I demanded.

There was no reply.

Nick parked his Astra beside Poppy's Micra. I wondered how long it might take her to get home from town without a car. Half an hour, forty-five minutes?

As soon as the car stopped I grabbed the car door handle. It was locked.

Nick climbed out of the car and casually strolled around to my side, where he unlocked the passenger door. He helped me up in a manner that may have looked gentlemanly to a passer-by. I wondered if I should bite his hand.

"Don't scream," he whispered in my ear, holding the knife so tightly against my side, that it broke the surface of my skin. I didn't *think* Nick would stab me, but I hadn't thought him capable of theft or kidnap either.

He guided me into the garage and slammed the heavy metal door behind us. It made a loud noise that echoed around the small, unplastered room, deafening me and adding to my terror.

The garage was dark. I could only just make out the shape of Nick, as he paced around, apparently looking for something.

"I don't want to hurt you," he explained. "I just need some time to get my affairs together, before you go squealing to Poppy."

I wasn't going to die! Thank God. However, could I really trust him? He'd lied about many things. Were his intentions towards me another lie?

Eventually Nick found a length of rope. "Get down!" he ordered. I fell to the floor and let him tie my arms by my sides. The rope scratched and I wished I was wearing more than a light cotton sundress. I wanted to struggle. I wanted to scratch and claw at him, and perhaps I could have done, but what then? I would not win a fight with a man of six foot four.

He removed his tie and used it to gag me. It tasted of nothing and its texture was kind to my tongue, but being gagged instilled an even greater sense of helplessness.

Nick disappeared through the door connecting the garage to the house and there was nothing I could do. I couldn't move. I couldn't speak.

* * *

After what seemed like hours, I finally heard Nick's car pull away. I did not feel as relieved as I had expected.

He was the only person who knew I was here. With Nick gone, when would I be rescued?

Being bound and gagged was more painful than I could have ever imagined. The rough texture cut my elbow. The back of my neck itched and I couldn't reach it. My shoulder ached from its awkward positioning. My mouth was dry and my throat started to ache. However, the worst part was being alone with my thoughts and having no idea when relief might come. My mind was a dark enough place when there were no problems; with the new material it had been given to churn over, I was in agony.

How was I going to tell Poppy? How would she ever be able to hear that her boyfriend was a thief, a con-artist and a kidnapper? What else had Nick stolen? Had he planned this all along?

Nick's car had only been gone for five minutes when I heard a key in the front door again. My chest tightened, fearing that he had come back to hurt me, but the facts did not fit. There was no engine this time. Whoever opened the door had arrived on foot. I prayed that it was Poppy.

How long would it be before she looked in the garage? During the many weeks that we'd been friends, I'd never known her to use this room. Her car lived outside on the drive and she suffered chronic arachnophobia.

In sheer frustration, I wobbled my body, trying to scratch an itch but failing miserably. Wait! Was it my imagination, or did the ropes feel slightly looser? What would happen if I did that again? I shook my torso once more. It hurt, like sandpaper. Had I made my bindings any looser? It was difficult to tell when there were so many sensations rebounding around my body.

Some minutes later, the rope had definitely loosened. Just a little more squirming and I'd be able to release an arm. Once an arm was free, I would have a tool.

After what seemed like an age, I freed an arm. The first thing I did was attempt to remove the gag, but my arm just flopped beside me like a useless, dead appendage. I tried to lift it once more, but it didn't budge. The frustration was intense.

Impatiently, I waited for the blood to spread back into my arm, and once it did, I struggled to free the rest of my body, allowing each part a few moments to adjust to its freedom.

It took several attempts to muster a sound. "Poppy!" I squeaked, bursting through the garage door and into her house.

She didn't reply, but I could see that the living room light was on. I felt cramp rising in my left leg and the other felt like jelly. Like a drunk, I stumbled into the living room.

Poppy was slumped on the floor, surrounded by dirty tissues that illustrated a hefty episode of tears.

"Are you having an affair with Nick?" she wept. Her face was red, wrinkled and angry.

"What?"

"I saw you two together, leaving Wagamama's."

"We did leave Wagamama's together, but not because ..."

"It looked very cosy to me."

"Believe me Poppy, it was anything *but* cosy," I tried to explain. I sat down next to her on the floor, so that she could see my eyes.

"Well then how do you explain this?" she demanded, thrusting a piece of paper at me.

I read its contents aloud. "Sorry Pops" it said.

"I know you're having an affair!"

"We're not!" In many ways, I would have preferred it if we were. "I'm afraid it's worse than that," I explained.

"You're pregnant?"

"No!" I couldn't believe I was hearing this. I thought Poppy believed in me as much as I believed in her. I thought she was rational and sensible. Why was she saying these ridiculous things?

"Why are your arms bleeding on the outside? Where's Nick?"

"I think he's gone Poppy."

"Gone where?"

"He left. I'm sorry."

"He wouldn't just *leave*."

"Poppy, did you manage to take any money out of the bank?"

"No. What makes you think Nick would leave me?"

"What happened with the bank?"

"I rang them. They said my credit card limit had been reached. Another mistake. Where's Nick?"

"Another mistake?"

"My bank's been rubbish lately."

"Poppy ... Poppy, I don't know how to ... I think Nick has been stealing from you. Well, I know he has."

"What?" she scoffed. "No, the bank just messed up, that's all."

"I saw Biff."

"Biff? When?"

"Today. Poppy," I began softly, "Biff didn't take your things."

"Of course he did. Who else did?"

"Nick. He took them and made it look like it was Biff."

"Why would he do that?"

"Because he's been playing you all along. I'm sorry."

"I think you should go now," she told me, looking fierce.

"Poppy ..."

"You've always been jealous of me. Now you're trying to break up my relationship."

"I do envy you, you're right, but that's not what's going on here. Poppy, he kidnapped me and tied me up in the garage. Look at my arms!"

"I know you're going through a difficult time Meg, but please don't take it out on me and Nick. We're your friends ..."

"Look, just do one thing for me, log onto your bank account, and if everything's all right, then I'll leave, I promise."

* * *

"It's all gone! All of the Therapies money is gone!" wept Poppy for the seventh time. I had no more responses left in me. I'd said everything I could say, and I suspected that none of my clichés had really helped anyway.

"And my credit cards!" she continued. "He's been buying things on my credit card."

"I know," was all I could offer.

"I'm sorry I accused you of having an affair behind my back."

"It's OK, you were upset."

Poppy was quiet for a few moments and then she surprised me with, "I think he still loves me."

"Er? Really?"

"His note. It says 'Sorry Pops', *Pops*! His nickname for me! He must still love me or he wouldn't have left a note."

For the first time, I realised that Poppy, whilst undoubtedly incredible, was not invincible.

* * *

As somebody suffering from a severe mood disorder, I was not unaccustomed to waking up to a feeling of dread. However, on the morning of September 2nd, the sense that something terrible was happening was not an illusion.

I wriggled in Poppy's spare bed. Something didn't feel right. The shiny sheets, which usually slipped readily along my silky skin, dragged against my arm. I looked down and saw the skin damage from the ropes. I recalled with shock the events of the previous day.

The reality seemed so unlikely, that for some moments, I was convinced that I'd just had a bad dream.

Nick had made a very convincing liar. His knowledge about bipolar disorder was second to none. He had certainly done his homework before turning up at Poppy's support group looking for a vulnerable victim.

I had never thought of Poppy as vulnerable before. She was my hero, and heroes always seem to have superhuman qualities. I wondered how she was feeling this morning.

It was the first time I'd ever been up before Poppy. I was torn, should I take her a cup of coffee to help prepare her for the day, or leave her to sleep?

When another half hour went by, I decided to go for the hot drink option. I boiled the kettle, smiling to myself as I imagined how proud my mother would be, knowing that I was investing in the uplifting powers of the hot drink.

Gently, I knocked on the door. When there was no response, I was about to go back downstairs, but something stopped me. I knocked again, no answer. Carefully, I placed the tea tray on the landing carpet and opened the bedroom door ever so slightly.

"Poppy," I whispered, "Fuck! Poppy."

I threw the door open. My best friend was slumped over the edge of the bed, her short, black hair trailing on the floor. When I saw that her eyes were wide open, I knew that she was dead.

* * *

I had often compared depression to finding out that somebody had died, over and over again. However, depression is lazy, it sucks the motivation out of you, it confines you to your bed. Poppy's death fuelled me with energy and determination. It had been thirty hours since discovering her body and I had never felt so active in my life.

That bastard Nick had killed her. The police were waiting for the coroner to confirm that it was suicide — a lithium overdose. But it didn't matter who fed her those pills, Nick was to blame.

Poppy had been so stable, so sorted, so calm. She wasn't a volatile teenager struggling to come to terms with a new diagnosis or a long-term sufferer worn down by years of sickness. She was a champion. If it wasn't for Nick, she'd still be right as rain.

I told the police everything I could about Nick, but I knew they wouldn't find him. They hadn't even managed to find Biff, who may well have been in Exeter the entire time that they were searching.

Nick's phone was found discarded in a litter bin and there had been no sightings of his car since the initial police report. Nick could be anywhere in the world by now. He could be on some tropical island, living off the funds that had been raised to save the lives of people who desperately needed help.

He deserved to be jailed for life. His actions murdered Poppy as certainly as holding a gun to her head and pulling the trigger.

The police asked me for details about Nick. Where did he come from? What did he do for a living? Where had he lived in the past? I couldn't answer any of them. I wracked my brains. I had the vague sensation that Nick was Cornish, but no idea what had given me that impression. I stared at the wall of my bedroom, willing myself to remember details about Nick.

My mother brought me up cups of coffee. I didn't tell her what was going on, but I stopped pretending that there was nothing to worry about — my red, streaming eyes betrayed my desire for secrecy. My mother didn't ask any more verbal questions, but she often hovered by the door, hoping that answers would come.

When Nick killed Poppy, he didn't just kill a remarkable woman, but my hope for a strong future. When I had a successful, bipolar role model, I felt that there was a chance that I would be able to build a life alongside my health problems. My role model had killed herself. The strongest woman I knew, had killed herself. What hope was there for me?

Still, it wasn't just my bleak future that tore me apart; it was the knowledge that I'd never see Poppy again. Already, I missed her more than I thought it was possible to miss a person. Although we'd only known each other for a few short months, she was my best friend in the world. I missed mocking bad soap operas together, I missed ridiculing clothing fashions, and I missed baking cookies at her house on a Sunday afternoon.

How was I supposed to deal with grief? I couldn't even cope with day-to-day life. How could I deal with my best friend dying? Well, simply put, I couldn't.

With tears streaming down my face, I tucked my toes into my sandals. Why hadn't I accepted lithium when my doctor had offered it? That way I would be able to die right here, right now. Still, Red Rock wasn't very far away.

* * *

I sat on the edge of the red sandstone cliff, with my legs slung over the side. There was a bittersweet symmetry to it, dying at the place in which Poppy and I had met.

The sepia, sandy ground wasn't very far below, but distant enough to make my stomach stir whenever I looked down. I'd have to dive headfirst to ensure death. A broken neck was a necessity if this was to be my spot. I gulped and shuddered.

"Why are you up here when it's getting dark?" she had asked. I remembered how resentful I had been at the time. How opposed I had been to her interruption. Now, I would give anything for her to intrude on me one more time.

Why hadn't I saved Poppy? I'd known how upset she was that night when she went to bed. Why hadn't I taken her lithium away from her? Why hadn't I insisted on staying with her? Why hadn't I called for help? Instead, I'd left her alone in her bedroom to die. What sort of friend was I?

I should have seen through Nick sooner. Poppy was smarter than me, but I had the upper hand when it came to Nick because I was not in love with him. I had the clarity of thought to see through him, but I hadn't.

Death was something I dreaded, but the pain I felt was too ghastly to bear. I needed these vile feelings to stop and I was willing to take any action to make that happen.

What options were there besides suicide? What else would stop the pain with such precision and speed?

I wondered what other people did at moments like this, to get them through to the next. There are suicidal people who don't die, but how do they bring themselves back from the brink of death? Somewhat unexpectedly, a school social education class burst into my mind.

Perhaps the Samaritans could help, but how could I call them without my phone? Another thing for which Nick was to blame — it was probably still under the passenger seat in his car, where I had dropped it.

Then it struck me — if my phone was in Nick's car, then perhaps the police could locate it.

My heart pounded in my chest and I realised that life was claiming me back. I wasn't going to die here tonight on the rocks. I had important business to attend to. My existence did have a point after all, even if my purpose was brief.

Of course, there was no certainty that my phone

was still in Nick's car, or that Nick's car was anywhere near Nick. Even if they were, the battery could be flat by now. However, there was still a significant chance, that my phone would lead the police straight to Nick.

Being careful not to slip as I pulled my legs back onto the grassy surface of Red Rock, I hurried towards the narrow steps back to the sea wall. Poppy had been right, it was not a sensible place to be at night. I slipped and skidded. One of my ankles twisted but I didn't have time to attend to the pain. Using a conveniently placed root as a handle, I swung my body from the final ledge onto the footpath. I rushed back to The Boathouse as fast as I could.

"I need to use your phone!" I spluttered, and collapsed against the bar.

* * *

After calling the police, I rang my parents. I hurried outside The Boathouse to wait for them, but my energy levels and the pain in my ankle threw me to the floor.

The next thing I was aware of was my mother pouring out of her car and dropping to the ground beside me. My father followed.

"Meg!" My mother placed a finger under my chin and tilted my face to hers. "What is it darling?"

I sobbed for some time, before stuttering, "The doctor said I've got bipolar disorder."

She took a moment to absorb the information. There was a flicker of recognition, as if something had fallen into place in her mind.

"You mean you're poorly?"

I nodded and turned away.

"And you've been going through this on your own?"

"No, I had Poppy."

"You *had* Poppy?"

"She's dead," I stuttered, in little more than a whisper. "She killed herself."

* * *

Twelve months later, I am almost ready to return to university. I'm not a massive fan of my new drugs — quetiapine makes me sleepy and sodium valproate makes my hands shake occasionally. But the mood swings have largely subsided, which means that my life is my own once again. I am on the waiting list for cognitive behavioural therapy and I've reduced my drinking by half. It has been seven months since I last cut my skin.

I have joined a support group and met other people with bipolar disorder. Some are living relatively ordinary lives, others face constant obstacles. Three members knew Poppy and I find it comforting to be around people with memories of my friend.

The last year has been difficult for my family, but my parents and brothers support me wherever they can. We are still adjusting to the diagnosis and what it means for us all.

Mum has risen to the challenge spectacularly. She took over from Poppy and founded Therapies for Devon. The new centre is due to open in three week's time.

The police found Nick's car in a garage at his mother's house in Newquay. As a result they now know his real identity, but have yet to catch him.

I think about Poppy every day. Sometimes it hurts, sometimes it makes me smile. I have realised that the best way to keep her memory alive is to live my life the way she lived hers, but without the fatal lithium overdose, obviously.

Will I finish my degree? Will I be able to hold down a job, a house or a relationship? Will I grow old? I don't know, but I am going to give myself the best chance that I can.

The Selfish Act

'Every year around 200 people decide that the best way to go is by hurling themselves in front of a speeding train.

'In some ways they are right. This method has a 90% success rate and it's extremely quick. However, it is a very selfish way to go because the disruption it causes is immense.

'The train cannot be removed nor the line re-opened until all of the victim's body has been recovered. And sometimes the head can be half a mile away from the feet.

'Change the driver, pick up the big bits of what's left of the victim, get the train moving as quickly as possible and let foxy woxy and the birds nibble away at the smaller, gooey parts that are far away or hard to find.'

— *Jeremy Clarkson, 2011*

It felt like the longest wait for a train in my life. Balanced on the railings in my apricot, polkadot party dress, I felt detached from the previous night. I could not comprehend that I could be the same person.

Yesterday's me had felt happy and free; today's appreciated the reality of the situation: I was pointless. I cursed the clear December sun. I willed for it to set so that I could be alone in darkness. I was tired of the hypocrisy of my environment. I wanted it to match the way things really were — I was isolated.

* * *

"To Morwenna and Steve!" boomed Dad, raising a glass.

"To Morwenna and Steve!" came the echo, then an orchestra of clinks. The parroted toast contained an interesting blend of accents — Cornish, Yorkshire, Scottish, French ... I hadn't expected so many people at an engagement party held in the depths of Cornwall. There were friends and relatives from age three to ninety-three.

My eyes met Steve's. Neither of us could hold back large toothy grins. We were doing it! We were fucking doing it!

He put an arm around me and we beamed at the crowd. Annie caught my eye. She made a cheesy thumbs-up gesture. I felt my eyes welling up — how embarrassing!

"Bugger!" I thought. "If I can't get through an engagement party without weeping, how will I ever get through my wedding?"

It was all rather overwhelming. I hadn't thought I'd ever get married. I had more private ambitions, like directing a film adaptation of *George's Marvellous Medicine* and planting my own orchard. Yet here I was at twenty-six, in front of all my friends and family, celebrating the fact that Steve Harris had proposed to me.

When I first met Steve, he was a singing crocodile, covered from head to toe in green paint. I volunteered for a charity that he ran called Child's Play UK. We brought theatre to children in hospital. Even without the snout and tail, he was clumsy looking — six foot five with curly hair, massive ears and droopy, brown eyes. I could never look at him without smiling.

I knew that he adored me just as much. He was kind, honest, and all that important jazz, but with the added virtue of being absolutely hilarious. He was not the first boyfriend to have me in tears on a daily basis, but he was the first to cause them with laughter.

However, on this occasion, I did not want to cry. Being drippy was not part of my image. I needed to stop those tears.

"Can you stop being precious and start the chocolate fountain?" I demanded, disguising a soppy sob for a chuckle. I think I got away with it.

* * *

Reflecting on the party from the grey metal bridge, I felt foolish. The event had been little more than an elaborate fancy dress party. I'd dressed like the normal people, I'd bumped elbows with the normal people, but I was not one of the normal people.

I was bad news, I always had been. Why had I allowed myself to believe that things had changed for me? Why had I allowed myself to think I could be happy and healthy? I was still the same destructive and hopeless person that I had ever been. Sure, I could pretend to be normal for a while, but any happiness I experienced was accompanied by a ticking bomb. It wasn't a case of *Will I fuck this up?* It was a case of *When?*

The worst part of this situation was that I'd managed to convince Steve that I was normal. I'd allowed a decent, wonderful man — the CEO of a national charity — to believe that he'd met a good person. In fact, he'd actually met a disturbed creature with the potential to destroy lives — his life! I'd known full well what I was when I agreed to marry him. Accepting his proposal was a self-centred, cruel gesture, and if I had really cared about him, I would have politely declined and allowed him to move on.

* * *

Billy Joel flooded the atmosphere and electrified two hairless uncles. Were they flirting with each other, or was I beginning to feel the effects of those two glasses of champagne? That's what happens when you restrict drinking to special occasions.

Annie spun me around on the dance floor, moving with elegance in her blue trousers. Her tidy, fair ponytail flapped as she danced.

"I'm so happy that you agreed to be my bridesmaid!"

"What did you think I'd say?"

"Well, I know you're not a great fan of dresses."

"Wait? I'm going to have to wear a dress?"

I'd known Annie since we were eleven. She'd approached me carrying a pencil case shaped like Feathers McGraw and set it down on the desk next to my Wallace and Gromit folder. From that moment, we became firm friends.

We tackled acne together. We overcame the rumour that Annie was carrying an alien baby. We mastered tampons. We fended off an angry boy with a stick. We were solid.

There was no greater mark of friendship than Annie Robbins agreeing to wear a dress. She had been a tomboy when we climbed trees as children, a tomboy when she took up rugby as a teenager, and was a tomboy now, working as the head gardener on a large estate. Bows, ribbons and tiaras were foreign to her.

I wondered how long I'd keep this up before telling her she could wear a trouser suit. I wanted my best friend at my wedding, not a processed version of her.

* * *

The following day, I knew I had trapped Annie into agreeing to become my bridesmaid. My poor friend had had to deal with tricks like that for fifteen years. Admittedly, I was almost normal for the first seven. However, I was not normal now. If, on the first day of secondary school, she had known that I would become so damaging in later life, she would not have chosen to sit next to me.

The first time I was truly sick, was the day of my second geography A-level exam. I was walking along the road towards college. With every step, I felt more and more dread. I tried to push myself forward, but although my legs worked, my head said no. It didn't make sense — I usually thrived on exam pressure.

Eventually I had to stop; I let myself fall to the pavement and just lay there, not speaking, for many minutes. Annie should not have had to find me like that.

It was time to give Annie a break. I owed it to her to get away, to give her a chance to have a normal life, free of sickness.

* * *

The Village People were playing. It's hard to find music to please guests spanning a ninety-year age-range, but a startling variety of folk were dancing.

After discovering that my dress swished beautifully when I moved, I spent two minutes spinning. After finding that I was dizzy, I tried to initiate a conga. However, people were surprisingly wrapped up in trying to spell Y.M.C.A. whilst holding drinks.

I felt a long, gangly arm grab my waist and sweep me off the dance floor.

"Do you think, perhaps, it's time I took you up to our room?" whispered Steve.

"Nah, it's OK. I'm fine." I tried to grab his back — a conga of two was better than no conga at all.

He spun around to face me. "You don't understand," he said, pulling me close and looking at me with a sensuous intensity, "I *want* to take you up to our room."

I felt his breath on my forehead and felt a twinge a few inches below the naval — you know the spot ... I rose to tippy toes and stretched. I put my arms around his neck to bring his lips closer.

"All right," I smiled. "Just let me say goodbye to everybody, and then we can go."

"Do I get a dance first?" he asked.

I grinned. "Of course you get a dance first."

With that, he grabbed me around the waist and lifted me high into the air. One of my white shoes flew across the room, but I hardly noticed, I was too busy laughing and protesting.

* * *

Now, contemplating my death, I understood that I had wanted to fail. If I had truly wanted to succeed, I wouldn't have had two glasses of champagne when I know I shouldn't drink. I wouldn't have stayed at the party until one, even though Steve had urged me to leave at eleven. I wouldn't have had a massive party, when I know that overexcitement can trigger my mood swings.

No, I had brought this on myself. I'd tempted my inner monster, and here it was, taking me onto a railway bridge, to end my life.

The doctors never made their mind up about what was wrong with me. A bundle of diagnoses had been thrown around — bipolar disorder, borderline personality disorder, obsessive-compulsive disorder. I had my own theory about what was wrong — too many thoughts.

New thoughts liked to begin before old ones had finished. Dozens of thoughts would arrive at once, often conflicting with one another. Whenever I tried to focus, unrelated thoughts found their way in.

I knew what caused the thoughts — dark moods. Great cannonballs of despair flattening everything in their path, creating gaping holes for armies of thoughts to flood in.

* * *

"Morwenna! You-hoo!" sang Mum. "We're off now!" She was already wrapped in her long, red, winter coat, complete with enough accessories to brave the Antarctic.

This announcement stole me from the dance floor, which I'd been sucked back to by The Beatles. My parents were going already? Then I realised that it was rather late, and I was supposed to heading back to the hotel room with Steve.

"You are coming to ours for brunch tomorrow, aren't you?"

My mum loved her brunches. Rather than a cross between breakfast and lunch, they tended to include everything anybody could possibly want for breakfast, plus everything anybody could possibly want for lunch. Massive menus of pancakes, cereal, toast, baked potatoes, baguettes, scrambled egg, sausages, bacon and scones would spread across the dining room, covering every surface. I knew, as soon as she offered to throw us an engagement party, that it would be followed by some sort of elaborate morning meal.

"Of course I'll be at the brunch!" I felt my mouth water as I imagined buttery scrambled egg. Mmm, pancakes ...

I gave my mum a long hug. Both my parents loved Steve almost as much as they loved me. They'd liked him from the word go, and had actively campaigned for him to become a permanent part of the family. As a big chap with a tiring job, Steve was a big fan of enormous meals in the morning — this certainly didn't hurt their relationship.

* * *

It was the day after our engagement party. I woke up with the usual level of blank bafflement. A few seconds later, I was punched with a burst of despair. Frantically, I searched my memories from the day before. Did I have some reason to be depressed? Had somebody died? Had Steve broken up with me? Had I had a fight with Mum?

As I neared the end of my worst case scenario list, I concluded that there was no reason for me to feel disgusting, I just did. If my brain had stopped there, everything would have been fine, but no, it had to continue searching. It had to continue trying to destroy me. Thoughts, nasty, malicious, little thoughts, began eating away at me.

Steve wasn't in bed next to me, or indeed anywhere in our hotel room. Was that the problem? Was it upsetting to wake up and find myself alone? Certainly, it was something that had never upset me before, but perhaps our recent engagement party called for Steve to stay in bed until I woke up. After all, it wasn't often that we got to stay in a hotel.

Thoughts — too many of them — stoning me to death, before I even had chance to get out of bed.

Stop! I yelled in my mind, as loudly as an inner voice can. I let the vowel stretch for many seconds, blocking the thoughts for as long as I dared. I marvelled at the three seconds of peace that followed, but then the thoughts came flooding back.

The more thoughts that splattered in, the more abhorrent it seemed for Steve to have gotten out of bed before me. Was he having second thoughts about the wedding? Did he not care about me and how I felt?

Tears ran down my cheeks. Less than ten hours after our engagement party, cracks were already beginning to form. How could Steve, who had seemed so lovely and kind, be so callous?

The sound of the rain was the only soothing part of the situation. I listened to water patter down, and imagined that it was washing away my pain. It appeared to be a beautiful day out. Sun streamed in through the white curtains.

Something didn't add up. How could it be raining heavily if it was such a bright day? I paid more attention to what my senses were trying to tell me. It was not rain I could hear, but a shower.

Steve had gone no further than our ensuite shower room. Surely that made his disappearance acceptable. Surely it was all right for my fiancé to take a shower while I was asleep. Yet, I still felt devastated.

I heard the water stop. I wondered if I had time

to get up, out of bed, and away from the hotel room, before Steve returned from his shower. I didn't want him to see my tears. I didn't want him to know how stupid I was being, how unreasonable and unstable. Admittedly, he'd seen my illness many times before, but I didn't want him to see it today, not straight after our lovely party.

I folded the top half of my body over the edge of my bed, looking for my clothes. My early morning torso was not ready to be stretched. My back and my shoulders ached, while my stomach crunched like a concertina.

I heard the door of the ensuite open. It was too late to get away.

"Morning!" he beamed, with a level of happiness that irritated me. Could he not see that I was in pain? How dare he show such indifference to my plight?

"We can't get married." I heard myself speaking words that I hadn't instructed my brain to say.

He froze.

"We can't get married," I repeated.

This time he looked at me with infuriating insight. He gently took a spot next to me on the edge of the bed. "Hug?"

"No!" I cried. "I'm leaving you! A hug isn't going to make any difference."

"Nothing has changed since yesterday."

"Yes it has!"

"What has changed?"

"I've changed."

"You've just woken up."

"Well, I've woken up to some truths I was burying. I can't make you happy."

"You already do!"

"You're mistaken."

I tried to get out of bed quickly, but my joints were stiff. It was like trying to ride a bicycle with a rusty chain. My shoulders protested as I reached for my clothes. The only thing I could see was the dress I'd been wearing the night before. Polka dots hardly reflected my mood, but I needed something fast.

As much as moving hurt, continuing the conversation would be worse. I needed to get out of the room, away from Steve, away from this hideous break-up scene.

"Don't go," he begged. "I don't think you're feeling very well. Please stay."

"Don't patronise me!" I screamed. On some level, I knew that he was right, but I despised him for having clarity when I did not. I despised being ill. I hated being a slave to a disease with the capacity to override my actual feelings.

Nevertheless, my brief moments of perceptiveness were not enough to stop me going. Something indescribable was driving me to leave. Still buttoning up the white fastenings on the front of my apricot dress, I hurried out of our room. I slammed the door, for speed rather than impact. I wanted to tone down the drama as much as I could. I wanted to fade away, unnoticed. If only Steve had stayed in the shower a few moments longer, then there would have been no scene at all.

Knowing that it wouldn't take Steve long to pull on some trousers, I broke into a run. However, as I reached the staircase, I experienced a painful moment in which I entertained the notion that I was ill, and could be helped. My thoughts were determined to isolate me from Steve, but I might be able to seek support elsewhere.

Distraught, I hammered on the door of Annie's room. I hammered for some time before finally the door opened. I saw Annie's expression change from curiosity to alarm.

"Wait a sec!" she said and closed the door. I felt a desire to run, but forced myself not to. I felt light-headed and wasn't entirely sure that I could run even if

I tried. I leant against the wall for support.

A few moments later Annie returned. She was wearing a hotel dressing gown. I expected her to invite me in but she moved out into the corridor instead.

"What's up?"

"I've left Steve."

"What?"

"I've left him."

"Are you feeling poorly?"

"No! I've left Steve."

"What? Why?"

"I just know I can't make him happy."

"We've been through this before. It's not true!"

Suddenly, I heard a male voice from inside Annie's hotel room. "Annie?" it called.

"Who's that?"

"Tristan," she admitted, trying to suppress a guilty smile.

"My cousin Tristan?"

"Yeah."

I suddenly became aware of what I was doing to Annie. I was putting a strain on her yet again. I was letting my screwed-up love-life stand in the way of hers. She deserved to be having fun, not listening to me repeat a conversation we'd apparently had before.

"I've got to go," I said.

"No you don't."

"I do."

"I'm worried about you."

"I'm fine," I said, with as much sincerity as I could muster. I tried to smile but my facial muscles dragged the corners of my mouth back into my chin, as if they were on elastic. I walked away.

"Morwenna?" Annie called, urgently.

"I'll be fine," I sang. More tears were already preparing to escape. I must not look back.

* * *

I walked for a long time. It was the only thing that seemed to stop me from breaking down into a hysterical pile of bones. I needed a purpose. It didn't matter if it was just getting from A to B, I had to be doing something.

At first, my mission was to get from the town to the first field. The next mission was to get to a stile that I could see in the distance. The third was to cross a railway bridge.

The sun was too low in the sky to provide any warmth. One only had to look at the bare branches of the trees to see that the world had long since been separated from the kinder months. My cotton dress was not suitable for outdoors, and I trembled as I took the strides that were the only things stopping me from freezing altogether.

My heart beat painfully fast, my empty stomach growled, and the crisp air nibbled at my skin. However, my physical discomfort was nothing compared with my mental torture. Acknowledgements of my bodily sensations were quickly replaced by thoughts of my bleak prognosis.

I should have foreseen this fated, inevitable decline. It was not the first time it had happened. It would have been easier to simply accept that I was sick, and just live the life of a sick person. By constantly trying to live in the healthy world and repeatedly failing, I was just torturing myself and those around me, over and over again.

Even though the thoughts in my mind were repetitive, each recurrence stirred the same intensity of emotions as it had on its first presentation. Rather than become desensitised to the rapid-fire self-accusations, the thoughts became increasingly real. Eventually, I could see no possible alternative to the theory that I was rancid to the core.

This wasn't the first time I'd tried to free Steve of me. I'd told him over a dozen times that I was too sick to make him happy. However, each time I'd weakened, and gone back to him.

So far today, I had twenty-one missed calls. It pained me to ignore them, but I had to do it. Annie wanted to hear that I was all right. Steve wanted to hear that I could marry him. I couldn't please either of them. Words could not reconnect me with yesterday's world — that illusion had passed.

I hadn't even stopped to think that Annie might be with a lover when I had barged in this morning. I'd been too wrapped up in my own life. Now she was worried and anxious and it was all my fault for attention seeking, instead of just leaving the hotel straight away.

I tried to occupy my brain with thoughts that couldn't hurt, such as numbers. I started counting backwards in threes.

Time slipped away from me, as I let numbers replace my thoughts as often as my polluted brain would allow.

My phone rang again — Mum's ringtone. My stomach lurched. I suddenly remembered brunch with my parents — I'd missed it entirely.

How could I have been so careless? I knew how important brunch was to Mum, and I hadn't given it a thought. No doubt she had wasted food. I was a cunt.

I'd treated my parents appallingly. It was unforgivably greedy to let them throw me a party when I was inevitably going to break up with Steve.

My life was an earthquake with me at the epicentre, and those closest to me kept getting hurt the most. The worst part was knowing that I might not be strong enough to walk away from Steve even now. Even though I could see so *clearly* that I could not make him happy, I still felt a greedy desire to be with him. How could I put a stop to these self-centred whims?

The subject wasn't one that I could approach without agony. When I tried to think of a solution my mind locked, like a busy road junction with vast quantities of angry traffic coming in from every direction.

I needed a proper break from my thoughts. Still, even if I could make another hour pass, it would only postpone the problem. In an hour's time, I would have to face it again. Best not to allow myself a moment's peace, because plummeting back into the gritty depths of depression was worse than staying at rock bottom.

Suddenly, all of the clashing strands of thought twisted into one coherent thread — a *permanent* solution. I gulped. There was only one permanent solution.

I felt myself begin to tremble, and was engulfed with a sense of tragedy. I remembered who I had been at seventeen, and felt sad for the life I might have had. Nevertheless, it was a life I did not have. There was no use grieving for the pointless person I'd become.

The realisation that I had to end my life brought with it some comfort. I'd always known that suicide would be my cause of death, I just hadn't known when it would happen. It was a relief to know that the pain would soon be over. What's more, I once again had a purpose: to find a way to die.

* * *

The air held a pleasant hint of soap. It was a very pleasing hotel room — lavender, with an indigo bedspread and white curtains. I hoped that we'd soon become more closely acquainted with the blue bedspread.

"Alone at last," I whispered to Steve, with my best naughty grin.

To my surprise, he pulled away from our embrace. "I got you something," he explained and his head vanished into a rough leather suitcase. I decided that giving me a present was one of the few acceptable reasons to delay sexy time.

A few moments later, his curly head emerged and he held up a lumpy gold parcel secured with what appeared to be an entire roll of Sellotape.

"What on earth...?"

"Open it!"

"Give me a chance!" I laughed. It was a very peculiar present. It felt like a net of tennis balls, but Steve was usually spot on with presents. I pulled back a shred of paper and was none the wiser. I kept unwrapping.

"Apples?"

"Apples." He was smiling, so I knew there must be a good explanation.

I searched for one, but couldn't find it. "Go on then, explain."

"They're not for eating."

"What else do you do with apples?" I asked. Then I caught on. I clutched my chest and then threw my arms around him.

I imagined the empty lawn outside the kitchen window, scattered with apple trees. I'd always wanted an orchard! I wondered how long they'd take to grow.

"I've bought some young trees as well, so that we can start harvesting fruit next year," he explained, as if he knew what I was about to ask.

"Yay! And how long before we can harvest these?" I asked, tapping the apples.

"Four, maybe five years."

"Yay!"

I imagined what our lives were going to be like by the time these apples could produce fruit of their own. I'd have definitely dug our pond by then and probably finished my *George's Marvellous Medicine* script. In five years time our lives might have changed entirely. Perhaps there would be more than two of us ...

Steve gently pulled me onto the bed.

"Are we definitely at the sex part now?" I asked.
"Yes!"
"Excellent!"

* * *

I looked around. What fatal tools were to hand? Certainly, I had no pills or blades, and there were no shops nearby. There were no buildings at all, let alone tall ones. In fact, the only man made structures I could see were fences, roads and the bridge over the ... wait! Railway line!

My heart thrashed. I had to get back to the railway bridge, and I had to get there fast. This moment of enlightenment and strength might not last long. I had to kill myself before the coward in me had time to object.

As I sprinted across fields, over styles and across lanes, I heard my phone ringing again. It stung me not to touch it.

My contaminated brain throbbed. This wasn't a feeling like sadness or fear. This was something entirely different — a super-emotion, with the power to wipe out everything else. I no longer had a mind containing a myriad of different feelings, but a skull that was stretching and splitting, in an attempt to accommodate one thing — raw pain.

I got to the railway bridge and began walking very slowly across the tarmac, as though balancing on a beam.

When I got to the heart of the bridge, I looked down. I felt afraid — afraid! It was a wonderful feeling and it threw me back to life. I burst into deep, grateful sobs. There was something in my mind besides destruction. A part of me still wanted to live! I let the warm feeling of relief pulse through my body.

* * *

Lying on the indigo hotel bedding, I felt content. Life was pretty damn good, and it wasn't just the effect of my post-coital buzz. I had a fiancé that I loved to bits, an occupation that delighted me, and a big bag of apples. Naturally, I was excited about our wedding, but mostly I looked forward to the rest of our lives.

"Can I turn the light off?" asked Steve.

I looked at him, draped naked on the bed. "Do you have to?"

"It's just for a few hours," he chuckled, "I'll still be here in the morning."

* * *

I lay on the pavement crying hysterically. It was a mixture of laughter and tears. I was amused by how wrong I'd been. I'd thought I was ready to die, and I wasn't.

However, time passed and the horrible blackness began to creep back into my brain. I realised that I could not stay on a railway bridge forever. I had to go somewhere else; I had to continue with life. It was an utterly terrifying moment and I felt paralysed once again.

Part of me wanted to go back to the hotel, but another part of me knew that if I did, we'd go through this whole process again. Perhaps not today, perhaps not tomorrow, but one day in the not-too-distant future, I'd realise *again* that I had to leave my fiancé.

There was really only one way out — only one way to prevent the cycle recurring. I needed to get onto that track.

Tentatively I raised an ankle over the blue railings. Then I realised that there was no point in being half-hearted. The last thing I wanted to be was half dead. Adding physical disabilities to my wretched existence would not help anybody. I used my hands to lift me up. I wobbled a little and felt myself slip.

When I managed to steady myself, it wasn't relief I felt this time, but disappointment. If I'd fallen, it might all be over by now.

As I sat, balanced on the railings, I pictured the scene. I saw myself diving down onto the track. The driver sees me too late to stop. The brakes screech, but I'm already dead — my body torn in half.

I felt sick, imagining how my body might look. My once-beautiful engagement dress shredded and blood stained, covering multiple chunks of my diced torso.

Suddenly, an excruciating thought burst through the others — what was I going to put the driver through? And what of the people who would find my broken body?

The thoughts maximised my self-disgust, and I was even more certain that I deserved to die. The planet did not need somebody who was prepared to torture others with her violent demise.

I needed to get off the bridge. I needed to find a way to kill myself that wouldn't traumatise anybody.

However, just as I was about to drop back down onto the road, my phone played music to me once again. I recognised Steve's ringtone. I longed to answer the call. I wanted to tell him that I still loved him and that I needed his help.

Instantly, I felt appalled by my cowardice. I had resolved to end Steve's suffering, yet there I was, weakening again.

No, I couldn't risk taking any more time over this. Walking back to the nearest shop would take at least an hour. The universe needed me to die now.

Jumping onto the tracks would cause an ugly scene, but it would be nothing compared with the destruction that my vile character would cause if I were allowed to survive the day.

I tried to reason my way out of the situation, but

faced gridlock once again. A thousand thoughts smashed together. A sharp stabbing spasm shot through my skull.

All of a sudden, I was painfully aware that I was hungry to the point of severe stomach cramp, and so cold that my teeth were chattering. My muscles ached as I trembled. My heart rate accelerated, and the world started to spin.

Then the thoughts started flying once again, like a swarm of bluebottles trapped inside my skull. The hopeless scenarios zoomed in from all directions, stacking up in my mind like toxic waste.

I'll break Steve's heart over and ... I'm putting a strain on my ... I'm stopping Annie ... I only call my friends when ... I'm a terrible ... I add nothing to this ... I'll pass my disease to my children ... I'll be abusive to ... I'm a burden ... I'm a burden ... I'm a burden ... I'm a burden ...

I heard a train in the distance. This was my one chance to cleanse the world of my poisonous existence. I had to take it. The thoughts drifted away and I was left with a numb bliss.

It felt like the longest wait for a train in my life. It wasn't, but it was the last.

Is He Going to Kill Me?

A snotty tissue sticks to my hand. A hairpin pricks my fingers. My car keys — all I want are my car keys.

I'm thinking about aubergine lasagne and getting some winter tights — those thick ones, what are they called? Bamboo legs or something.

Suddenly, a weight pushes me against the car. It takes me a few seconds to work out what's going on. Then I realise it's a man. Fuck. There is a man pushing me against my car.

I try to scream. A leather-gloved hand covers my mouth. I panic — do I have the full function of my nostrils? I breathe in fast. The air seems to snag on catarrh. I'm going to suffocate.

He loosens his grip. I guzzle as much air as I can. When will he next afford me the luxury of inhaling?

There's something smooth against my forehead, like satin. Don't gag me — please! My nostrils aren't working! Without the use of my mouth I'll die!

Perhaps that's the plan.

The satin finds its way to my eyelids. He's not robbing me of my breath, but my sight. He wants me alive — yes! At least, for now ...

"Get off me!"

I feel prickles all over my skin and it's as though I'm scared, but the emotion isn't there. My heart rate tells me that I'm frightened. My skull feels like a cave, with violent waves crashing around inside.

"I said, 'Get off me!'"

Before I know what I'm going to do, my elbow lashes sideways. He dodges me and I end up thrashing thin air.

I hear him wet his tongue, as if to speak, but nothing follows.

He prises the car keys from my fingers.

He drags me around to the passenger door and awkwardly pushes me inside. At first, I resist, but then

I realise it might be less dangerous to comply.

"Who are you? What are you doing?"

I can feel something spongy against my wrists. I can't quite identify the material. Oh Jesus-shitting-Christ — it's some sort of restraint!

He gets into the driver's seat. I'm thankful for the sticky clutch. I've been on at Mike to fix it for weeks, but now I'm grateful that my boyfriend is lazy. Perhaps the kidnapper won't be able to start my car.

I feel a lump in my throat when I think of Mike. What would he do if anything happened to me? He can barely even cope on my Zumba nights — living on baked bean scones.

"Please, just let me go."

Then, I hear the last person I expected to hear — Paul McCartney. The bastard kidnapper is only bloody playing The Beatles. I'm not impressed by the choice of track — 'Magical Mystery Tour'. What a wanker.

Well, I'm glad *he* thinks he's got a sense of humour. I bet he's congratulating himself on his hilarious joke right now, wobbling up and down as he does a silent chuckle.

I realise that I've stopped feeling numb. I'm getting angry. The kidnapper brought his own soundtrack — this was clearly pre-meditated. I'm more tense than ever.

"You won't get away with this!"

I can feel the car moving. Shit, the bastard has mastered the clutch.

The drive is excruciating. I'm terrified to the point of passing out, but I don't. I'm still painfully conscious. The journey doesn't take long, which is reassuring because, when I feel my car come to a halt, I know we must still be in the city.

I hear him get out of the car and my relief is short lived. For all I know, he could be taking me into a deserted warehouse or an empty garage.

However, when I get out of the car I can feel the

crisp outdoor air on my knees and when I tilt my bandaged eyes toward the sky, I detect a strong increase in light. We are definitely outdoors.

He puts an arm on my waist and tries to drag me along. I'm tired of being compliant.

"Help!" I cry at the top of my lungs. "Help!"

The gloved hand is over my mouth again, but this time, I'm ready to take him on. I ram an elbow sideways, ploughing it into his ribs.

He cries out in pain. Then, he grabs me and I feel him pulling at the blindfold.

"For heaven's sake baby!" he cries.

Oh God! I think I've already identified the voice. I pray that I'm wrong.

Suddenly, my eyes are free and they sting in the sunlight, like nothing I've ever felt before. I wince and look down, away from the source of light. Slowly, I begin to get a hazy picture of my surroundings.

I'm in a park! I can see a man's legs. I look up.

"Surprise!" Mike cries, with a stupid grin on his face.

I hate him more than I've hated anyone or anything in my life. I know that I will never be able to look at that grin again without wanting to chop his fucking head off. I lose my temper. I begin hitting him, smacking him on the chest with the palms of my hands. "You fucking animal."

"Chill, Jill!" he says, still using an obnoxious level of joviality. "Look!"

My eyes try to follow his arm, but they are still struggling to cope with the light. There appears to be some form of banner tied to some trees.

Oh God, no.

"Will you marry me?" he cries, with that enormous grin. The hideous, tacky banner asks the same question.

"You scared the living crap out of me!"

"To make the surprise even better!"

"You're insane. I thought I was going to die. There is no way in the world that *any* self-respecting woman would *ever* marry a man who would put her through that.

"You're a monster. No, you're worse than a monster. You're a psychopathic, steaming cauldron of sadistic excrement.

"Look at you grin, like you think it's funny, like you think that this is a hilarious story that we'll tell our grandchildren. Well, I've got news for you — nothing on this planet would urge me to procreate with an irresponsible, pathetic pile of phlegm such as yourself.

"And while I'm on the subject, blowing your nose on dirty boxer shorts is vile. Also, Manchester United are just a bunch of morally bankrupt, overpaid, sportsmen corrupted by the pedestals that they're put upon by *you* — their moronic fans; Jack Black is not God, Adam Sandler is not Jesus and Owen Wilson is not the holy-fucking-spirit.

"My breasts aren't stress balls, believe it or not. How would you like it if I grabbed your bollocks and had a quick squeeze? And, just so you know, being woken up by a cock trying to tease its way into my mouth is not my idea of a perfect weekend morning. And let's clear up another thing, singing 'Hallelujah!' during sex is never acceptable, not even on a Sunday.

"In fact, I want to thank you. Thank you so much for crossing the line, because if you hadn't, I might still be under the illusion that your titanic inadequacies were things I could live with. A jail full of evil gorillas with salmonella could not produce a rotting pile of diarrhoea more putrid than your stupid, smug, grinning face."

"That's a no, right?"

Lipstick and Knickers

What is that on the floor between the painful source of light and the route to my toilet? If only the room would stop spinning long enough for me to focus. It looks like a ... No, it *is* a thong!

Shit, this sort of thing doesn't happen to me! And, *wow*, this sort of thing doesn't happen to me. But mostly, *shit*!

Hang on ... What sort of thing doesn't happen to me? How did that thong get there? What did I do?

"Hello?" I call hopefully into the bathroom.

It was the worst possible Saturday morning — the most terrible hangover of my *life*, coupled with the knowledge that once one feeling of death subsided, my girlfriend was going to dump me.

My predicament was even worse than your regular drunken one-night stand — my memory had been pulverised. I couldn't even remember getting home, let alone a memory of the act that I had clearly deemed worthy of ruining lives over. Yet the thong was proof that I had strayed.

Why, why, why, did I go to a party without Lizzie? It was just asking for trouble — or at least, it would have been, were I James Bond and not a smaller than average, slightly spotty twenty-three-year-old with ginger facial hair.

No, it was fair to say that nine-hundred-and-ninety-nine times out of a thousand, Ross Turpin could be relied upon to get drunk without messing up anybody's life.

So what went wrong this time?

If only I knew!

I crept closer to the edge of the bed, moving slowly through fear of the vomit monster. I reached out an arm and tried to grab the thong. It was more slippery than I expected. Satin, hey?

But every burst of momentary excitement was

followed by a bout of self-loathing. The more exotic the panties, the greater the betrayal.

Unable to face the overwhelming power of a bedside lamp, I used my phone to light the thong. It appeared to be of a greenish colour.

Luxury lingerie was a novelty for me. Lizzie's ladybits preferred to hang out in stretchy black shorts. She said they were seamless, which — I'm told — is a good thing. Looking at these green knickers, I observed that a black lace trim was a good thing too. Agh! There it was again: self-loathing.

How was I ever going to tell Lizzie? How would the conversation even begin? It wasn't a scenario I'd envisaged needing to prepare for.

"Hey darling. I've got something to tell you. I probably cheated on you, but I'm not exactly sure."

And what if I confessed, then found out that I *hadn't* cheated on her? Then I'd put us both through a hellish ordeal for nothing. No, I needed answers; answers first, confessions second.

My head felt as though an expanding chisel had been wedged inside its core. It was hardly a time for sleuthing. Still, the task at hand couldn't be that difficult given the small number of thong-wearing suspects. I only really knew four women: my mum, my gran, Lizzie and Nina.

Dammit. If I was going to sleep with Nina, I would have liked a memory of the occasion. Nina and I had been friends for over sixteen years, which meant I'd imagined her naked at least one thousand times, from the innocent curiosities of boyhood, to the more shamefaced urges of blokehood.

I told myself not to jump to conclusions. The presence of a thong on my bedroom floor did not necessarily mean that Nina had been here. There were other possibilities. Perhaps it had been a flirtatious gift. Perhaps I found it on the way home. Perhaps one of my housemates put it there for a laugh.

Yes! That was it. Gerry must have seen me come in drunk and thought to himself, "I know what'll really get Ross going, I'll put a woman's thong on his bedroom floor."

Ah, good old Gerry, always the prankster. Well, it hadn't worked this time. *Nice try though*, I chuckled to myself.

It turned out that chuckling was more than my tender belly could handle. I leapt out of bed and sprinted toward the bathroom. I felt gunk rising in my throat. I wasn't going to make it! I lunged forward just arriving at the toilet on time.

A combination of red wine, Baileys and stomach acid splashed back into my face. I wiped something solid off my nose. Alas, the toilet lid was down.

However, it wasn't the vomit dripping from my chin that concerned me the most. Why was the lid of the toilet down? I *never* put the toilet lid down.

"Get a grip!" I told myself. "You don't remember getting home. Who knows what adjustments of habit you might have made."

My mouth tasted of puke, as mouths often do after you've been violently sick. The taste made me feel as though I might throw up again.

I was sweating, shivering and struggling to stay vertical, yet I was determined to make it to the sink. I needed that fresh supply of water.

With all the energy I could muster, I dragged myself to the washbasin.

Slumped on the floor, my hand grappled for the tap. I felt something plastic against my fingers. Without thinking, I flicked it out of the way and by chance, it landed on my lap.

When I saw what it was, I leapt with terror. As my eyes focussed, I felt a shiver down my spine. Its colour was like blood, and its meaning more sinister still. I felt chilled to the core. How did a bright red lipstick find its way into my ensuite?

* * *

To somebody who didn't know Nina, her bedroom could have easily been mistaken for an amateur porn studio. The bed was dressed in pink satin and a large corner of the room was devoted to computer and camera equipment. However, when you added the fact that she was a technology-obsessed virgin who lived with her parents, it was all quite innocent.

"You should come on my podcast. You could have opinions about golf and share prices," she enthused, massaging a webcam with her big toe.

"You don't already have that covered on 'Lambrini with Bikinis'?"

Nina was smart, yet seemed determined not to realise her potential. She could be a serious writer, like me, but instead she wasted her talent podcasting and doing something called Twitter. Still, her weird social networking enterprises were always beautifully presented. Her self-portraits successfully captured her girl-next-door beauty: brown, slightly wavy hair; big eyes and cheeky dimples when she smiled. She had a light, airy voice which was pleasant to listen to, even if the content of her podcasts was less appealing.

If I wasn't so madly in love with my girlfriend, then I'd appreciate having momentarily trespassed into the garden of Nina. However, I was in love with Lizzie, and that was that. *Put that big toe away my bare-footed friend.*

I had to stop this now. I felt certain than Nina's naked feet were trying to flirt with my eyes.

But how would I bring it up? Maybe Nina really liked me. Maybe she'd be devastated when she heard that our night together was a mistake.

Still, I had to say something. I had to say something decisive, honest and to the point.

"Nina, do you always wear that shade of lipstick?"
"Not always."

"What other shades do you have?"

"What? Since when were you interested in makeup?"

"Do you ever wear a green thong?"

"What? No. What sort of question is that to ask your sister?"

"You are not my sister!"

"As good as."

"Really Nina, I think it's a good time to stop using that word."

"What's going on? And why do you want to know about my knickers?"

"Okay, let me put this another way. You were at the party until quite late, weren't you?"

"Yeah."

Just ask her Ross! Ask her! "When did you leave?"

"Er ..."

Just say it! Ask her if you had sex together. "Nina, did we ..."

"Did we what?"

Fuck. "Make the four legged monster."

"What?"

"Play hide the mighty sausage."

"Huh?"

"Get in touch with our inner Sir and Lady Humpalot?"

"You've lost me."

"Did you have sex with me?"

"What? I can't believe you need to ask!"

Her large eyes were like little pools of sadness and I wondered if she was going to cry. I'd handled this really badly. I should never have let her know that I couldn't remember. Her sorrow seemed to be rapidly turning into rage. Dammit. But who could really blame her? I'd taken her virginity, stamped around on it and then forgotten all about it.

Why did I have to go and let her know that I

couldn't remember? How hard would it have been to guess how a liaison went with a virgin who was also my best friend?

"I'm sorry," I said, taking her hand.

She roughly shook me off. "Ross, seriously! What's wrong with your head?"

Oh, that sounded like a good get out clause! Pretending I'd sustained a head injury. Yes! That would get me off the hook. No, it was Nina. We'd been friends for sixteen years; I owed her the truth.

"I didn't *forget* as such. I knew that we did. I just ... had to check — not because I couldn't remember — sometimes when I'm drunk things, *great* things, can seem a little dreamlike and I have to check, just to be sure. It was a great night though Nina, hey?"

"It wasn't me."

"What?"

"It wasn't me."

I looked at her suspiciously. Was she lying? She no longer looked like she'd just had her virginity whipped away from her by an amnesiac. In fact, she was fiddling with her laptop in a semi-distracted fashion.

"Are you serious? It wasn't you?"

"Wait? You cheated on Lizzie?"

"Well, I found lipstick and knickers in my house."

"Doesn't Lizzie wear lipstick and knickers?"

"Not like these," I said grimly, removing them from my pocket.

"Oh Ross!" Nina stretched the elastic between her fingers, looking intensely entertained. It wasn't quite the reunion I'd been expecting.

This was even worse than I could have imagined. I'd always known that cheating on Lizzie was a mistake, but sleeping with Nina seemed like the loveliest sort of blunder. She would have been like consuming the whole of a naughty box of luxury chocolate truffles. If it wasn't her, then it was like drinking an unmarked sample from a test lab.

"I really hoped it was you," I said.

"Did you?" she asked, showing a little softness amongst the disdain.

"Well I wasn't likely to catch anything from you, was I?"

There was nothing soft about Nina's glare now. The central edges of her eyebrows were half way down her face. For a brief moment, I understood why she was still a virgin.

Then I remembered that I was the one in the wrong, and that Nina had every right to use her angry eyebrows on me.

"I'm sorry Nina. It's just that ever since I found these, I haven't known what to think."

"I imagine there was quite a lot of booze involved."

"Boozematic," I confessed, bowing my head in shame.

"You might not have had sex," she offered. Typical Nina, naïve as always.

"Oh come on, why else would a woman leave makeup and lingerie at my house?"

"If you were too drunk to remember, perhaps you were too drunk to ... perform."

"*Me?* I don't think so." I couldn't believe that my best friend was accusing me of erectile dysfunction. Did she really say *perform*? Still, she hadn't slept with me. She didn't know about the raw power of Ross Turpin Jr.

"How can you be sure?" she asked.

"Well ..." How could I put this without seeming bigheaded? "It's *me.*"

"Well that's my point. You're not exactly the cheating type."

What did she mean, *not the cheating type*? Did she think I was physically incapable of consummating a cheat? Bloody hell, I knew she was a bit annoyed with me, but this was brutal! "What do you mean?"

"Well, you're ..."

"What?"

"Never mind."

"What?"

"Well you're very ... agreeable."

"What do you mean by that?"

"Well, you're not the type to make an impulsive mistake."

"I'm a very passionate person! I'm a writer!"

Bloody hell! When I put it like that, it didn't seem too bad after all. My indiscretion was a part of my author mystique, just like Charles Dickens and Richard Madeley. I hadn't cheated on Lizzie because I was a bad person; I'd cheated on her because I was a wild and creative person, too fiery to be caged in. After I died, my biography would say that Elizabeth was my great love, but that I was cursed by an artistic temperament that led me into temptation.

Oh, who was I kidding? I was a run-of-the-mill knob end.

* * *

Twelve months earlier ...

The leaves of a yew tree rose self-importantly above me as I sat with my back against the grave of Walter Baggins. An owl hooted, completing the creepy atmosphere. It was dark, chilly and a little bit macabre, but when a graveyard is the only spot that you can pick up an unsecured wireless internet connection, a man's gotta do what a man's gotta do.

I rather enjoyed the tranquility. Here I was in the middle of Exeter, and I'd found a spot out of doors, where I was completely alone. The autumn would no doubt trash my working environment, but at the moment, it had a pleasant, summer charm.

A young woman started calling for her cat. At least I hoped that was what she was doing.

"Muddles!" she sang. "Muddles, are you out here?" She had the sort of voice that made me hope that I had seen her pet — rich and fruity.

"Not guilty!" I called.

The girl jumped. "I didn't see you there!"

"What? You didn't expect to see a man sitting on a grave, cradling a laptop?"

"I'm just trying to find my cat," she said, wandering away.

"Wait!" I shouted, because I already adored her. She had big brown eyes and a slightly discerning look, which I found sexy. Dammit, now I needed to think of something to say. I had about three seconds before she would realise I was bluffing, and leave forever. "I'm writing a book about a cat!"

I'm writing a book about a cat?

"That's nice," she said, politely.

"If I find your cat, who shall I say is looking for him?"

I saw her eyes sparkle, and her dewy pink lips peeped up at the corners. Incredible — she thought I was funny.

"I'm Lizzie," she told me.

"I'm Ross," I said, preparing to stand up, but to my astonishment, she sat down on the grave next to me.

"What are you really writing?" she asked.

"You knew the cat story was a lie?"

She nodded. I noted that her eyes crinkled when she was amused. I liked a charismatic face. Of course, it helped that she was also drop dead gorgeous.

"It's a bit of a dark tale I'm afraid. No furry animals at all."

"Excellent!" she said, "I like dark."

As the last shards of sunlight disappeared behind the hills, I reflected on the weirdness of it all. We were within half a mile of pubs, nightclubs and all the usual spots where boy meets girl, yet the grave of Walter

Baggins was the setting for our tryst.

"You're not a vampire, are you?" she asked.

* * *

Sam Belinda was a human hurricane. She tended to drop sweet wrappers, hairgrips and bus tickets as she scurried along. Her blonde ringlets had minds of their own, like Medusa's snakes. In addition to this, she never stopped talking, and making sense wasn't a priority. Which begged the question: why did I sleep with her?

I sat at my table in a pub called The City Gate, not knowing what to hope for. I had previously thought that sleeping with Sam was impossible but then Nina had pointed out that I didn't necessarily have to have liked the owner of the knickers, especially not with the high prescription beer goggles that I'd donned that night. Sleeping with a maniac didn't sound like something I would do, but I had already eliminated all of the women who weren't clinically insane.

Any moment now, Sam would arrive and I'd find out the truth. However, I didn't know what I wanted to hear. On the one hand, I hoped to God that I hadn't slept with Typhoon Woman, but on the other hand, if it wasn't Sam, then I was still clueless as to the identity of the thong owner.

Suddenly, the door crashed open, and in tumbled Sam. Her inordinate number of bags smashed against the walls, as her stick-thin body wobbled from side to side.

She dropped her bags about four feet away from the table, and then rushed forward and grabbed my arm, urgently.

"Ross, do I look like somebody who would steal a babygro?" she demanded, her voice its usual shrill and grating tone.

"What?"

"Do I? Do I look like a babygro thief?"

"I don't know what a babygro thief would look like."

"Plump, maternal ... Do I look maternal?"

I studied Sam, noticing that when it comes to eyes, there is a fine line between twinkling and crazed. She smelt faintly of broccoli and looked like the last person I would ever want to leave a baby with. I decided it was not a good idea to tell her that.

"I don't look maternal, do I?" she whined.

"No of course you don't," I said, thinking it was what she wanted to hear.

She immediately switched from looking annoyed through her right eye, to looking annoyed through her left. "You don't think I'd make a good mother?" she cried, looking genuinely hurt.

A terrifying thought suddenly occurred to me. "Why do you ask? You're not pregnant are you?"

"God, I hope not. I've only had sex once in the last six months, and I tell you, the way we did it, I'd be pretty unlucky ..."

"There wasn't protection?"

"That's the man's responsibility," she said, with a private smile. Before I had a chance to ask why contraception was a source of personal amusement, she got distracted. "What's that? Is that a cappuccino? I've fancied a coffee the whole way here on the train. The journey was a nightmare," she told me. Then, suddenly, she shouted at great volume, "Don't ask!"

Of course I wasn't going to ask. Three years of Sam had taught me not to make enquiries into the nature of her personal disasters. There simply weren't enough hours in the day.

Nevertheless, she decided to enlighten me. "There was a cow on the line. Such a tragedy. If farmers invested more in the mental health of their livestock ..."

Oh good God, it was a story that involved a bipolar cow. *Not another one.*

"As I sat there, waiting for them to wipe poor

Daisy's hooves off the window, I weighed up my options: lattes, cappuccinos, mochaccinos, Americanos, filter coffee, tea, fruit infusions, hot chocolates ... But now that I'm here, I can't drink a thing."

"You're not feeling sick are you?" I asked, more alarmed than ever. If I *had* slept with the batty woman, then the one blessing was that it was over now. If it turned out that she was pregnant, the nightmare was only just beginning. I felt my breakfast mixing with my cappuccino, somewhere worryingly north of my belly.

"Who wouldn't feel sick if they knew that cattle were being denied access to crucial psychiatric treatments?"

Over the last few years, I had often wondered whether Sam's character was largely put on, in order to entertain people. However, at moments like this, I could see that she was genuinely barking.

"Hey Ross!" sounded Lizzie's voice. Ah, lovely calming Lizzie ... Hang on? *Lizzie?*

I spun around and saw my girlfriend standing just a few feet away from the woman who might very well be incubating an insane, frizzy-haired mini me.

"What are you doing here?" I demanded, much more defensively than I had intended.

"I just popped in to look for my jumper," she explained.

My God, she looked gorgeous. Was this intentional, to make me feel as bad as possible? Looking at her perfect cheekbones and her cute hips ... All right, I mean bum. Looking at her perfect cheekbones and her cute bum, I felt the strongest sense of torture any man has ever experienced. That girl, that lovely piece of perfection, might never kiss me ever again. We might never go on another date. We might never watch another movie huddled together under the duvet. We might never ...

Oh hell, these might be our last civil moments spent together, and here we were in the company of

Sam Belinda, a nut job who I may or may not have slept with.

The sense of wanting to relish every last moment of Lizzie was vastly offset by the fear of her finding out about my infidelity. *Not now, not here, not like this ...*

"I haven't heard from you for a couple of days," said Lizzie.

Of course you haven't. I can't look you in the eye, knowing what I know, and not knowing what I don't know.

Sam rescued me with, "Did you get that top from New Look? I had the exact same one, but it got wrecked in the wash. Never put a Primark pillowcase in with anything else! All my delicates are now green — a pleasant shade of green, but green nonetheless. Who wants to dress their privates in green?"

It was a very good question.

"Lizzie, have I ever told me how much you remind me of Cameron Diaz? Different hair of course, and face, and build ... I think it's more of a mannerism thing."

"Er ... thanks."

Lizzie was a patient soul, but everybody has their limits and Sam is usually one of them. If I was lucky, Sam might irritate Lizzie out of the building before she could do any real damage.

"Don't eat the ham and cheese!" Sam shouted, inexplicably.

"What?" Lizzie and I asked in sync.

"Sandwiches. Their pigs are grown in Spain."

"Is that a problem?" Lizzie asked.

"Well it's hot in Spain isn't it? Pigs like a lot of mud to roll around in. I can't imagine that there's much runny mud in Spain."

"Maybe they get it shipped in?" suggested Lizzie. I caught the sparkle in her eye and had to hide a smirk.

"Shipped in?" cried Sam, clearly outraged. "Don't those Spaniards care about their carbon feet?

Purchasing a ham and cheese sandwich is like a vote for the apocalypse!"

"I'll bear that in mind," said Lizzie, through gritted teeth.

I decided that my nerves could stand it no longer. "So Sam, I suppose you'd better get back to your cat?"

"Are you kidding? I spent *forty-five* minutes getting here. I'm jolly well going to get my cappuccino!"

Fortunately, Lizzie inadvertently rescued the situation. "Do you know what Ross? I think I do have to get back to the office after all. I've just remembered I told Kelly I'd do a … thing."

I watched with bated breath, as my beautiful girlfriend walked away with our relationship still intact. Finally, when the door of the pub closed behind her, I let myself exhale.

Apparently Sam felt the same. "Wow. That was awkward!" she whistled.

So it *was* Sam that I slept with! Shit, really? You think you know yourself and then you find out that your inner alcoholic is attracted to maniac frizzballs. Bloody hell, at least I had much better taste when I was sober.

Remembering, with shame, my earlier conversation with Nina, I decided to handle this moment with more sensitivity. I wheeled out voice number three: soft but firm.

"Look Sam," I began. I was momentarily distracted by the sight of her licking condensation off the outside of a glass. *Come on Ross, focus.* "About that night: you're …"

I stuttered, struggling to find a pleasant adjective that wasn't a lie.

"… *lively* …"

Well done Ross!

"But I love Lizzie. She might not be as ham and cheese savvy as you, but she is caring in other ways, she's beautiful and … well, she's my Lizzie."

I studied her reaction. What was going on now? Was she actually ... Oh my God, she was actually crying. She didn't even try to dry her eyes. She just let big, frightening tears run down her face, each one reflecting a little piece of her weeping face. Dammit, I thought I was doing so well.

Surely she hadn't thought we were going to be together? We had nothing in common. Although it hardly surprised me that she didn't know that, having rarely ever let me speak.

"Come on Sam, don't be upset."

"I'm not upset!" she blubbed. "I'm touched. It's so refreshing to hear that there's love like that out there! I hear fucked up stories every day — lies, infidelity, murder ..."

"Murder?"

"Of hope."

"Oh."

"It's a fucked up world out there Ross. You and Lizzie, you have to cling to love like that!" Her blue eyes gazed off into space and she rested her lips together as her nose ascended towards the sky.

"So you understand why we need to keep the other night a secret?"

"What other night?"

"It was you that I slept with?"

"What was?"

Oh bugger. *Not again.* I really needed to start establishing the definite facts before doing *the talk.* There are only so many women a man can let down gently in one week, without losing his grip.

But on the bright side, I didn't sleep with a lunatic — *score!* Whatever maternity and nausea issues Sam was experiencing, they had nothing to do with a little Ross Turpin growing inside her new age, fair trade womb.

Hang on, something didn't add up. "Why did you find bumping into Liz awkward?"

"Pigs!" she said, as if it should have been obvious. "I could tell she is apathetic to pig living conditions."

"Shit. Who did I sleep with then?" I asked myself aloud.

"You cheated on Lizzie?" she hooted.

I felt something hard smack against my brow and I was knocked backwards. Warm pain spread throughout my face. Sam had thumped me!

"What was that for?" I asked, clutching my forehead.

"Taking away my last shred of faith in humanity!" she said, tossing her snakes. Then she rose, grabbed her handbag and strutted out of the pub.

The gesture would have been a lot more effective had she not returned thirty seconds later, to collect her shopping.

* * *

Ten months earlier ...

"Do not worry madam. I shall have your keys out of the drain in no time," I assured the silver-haired lady, wondering how the hell I was going to get an enormous set of keys through a very small grating, using just a stick.

"A lot of young men wouldn't help an old lady in need," she said, beaming from shrivelled ear to shrivelled ear.

"There was an old lady in need? I didn't notice. I must have been too busy talking to you."

The lady blushed a little. I commended myself on my charm. Elderly folks loved me.

"So what is it that you do?" she asked, propping herself up against an ivy covered wall.

"I'm a writer," I told her.

"Oh, very creative. What sort of things do you write?"

"Fiction, mostly."

"And does that pay the bills? Sorry. Force of

habit."

"Habit? Have you got children?"

"Yes, two sons, and a granddaughter."

"A granddaughter? Never!"

She blushed again and tucked a strand of white hair behind her ear. "So, do you think you'll always live in Exeter?" she asked.

It was like the Spanish Inquisition. I began to wonder whether the drain incident was a plea for company. She had quite sturdy hands, not the sort with large key-shaped gaps between the fingers. Still, perhaps easing somebody's loneliness was as important as trying to rescue her personal effects.

I still had no idea how I was going to retrieve the keys. Fortunately, Lizzie would be here soon. Perhaps she'd have some bright ideas.

"I don't want to be any bother," the lady said.

"Not at all Mrs ... Um ..."

"Mrs Um is fine."

"I'm going to give my girlfriend a call," I explained. "I think she has a fishing net."

"Aye, she does."

"Sorry?"

"Aye hope she does."

"Do you know Lizzie, Mrs Um?"

The old lady looked guiltily into space and clutched her handbag. It looked as though she might be about to whistle.

"Are you Lizzie's grandmother Mrs Um?"

"Oops!" she chuckled.

It was difficult to be annoyed with somebody who had such an enigmatic giggle. "Why didn't you just introduce yourself?"

"You might have put on a show. I wanted to see what the man my granddaughter is in love with, is really like."

"Wait? Lizzie's in *love* with me?"

* * *

Hamish was a short, stocky Bristolian, prone to angry outbursts and random acts of violence against inanimate objects, usually wheelie bins, traffic cones and signposts, but occasionally fire hydrants and hanging baskets too. He was jealous, possessive and a little condescending to women. He was also one of my mates.

You don't stay in a friendship for ten years without a good reason. The truth was that Hamish's good qualities outnumbered the bad; they were just exceptionally well disguised, especially if you got on the wrong side of him.

In fact, it was safe to say that my harmonious relationship with Hamish was a direct result of having never done anything to piss off the angry ginger fist fighter. Which is why I'm sure you'll understand my sheer terror, when I realised I might have accidentally slept with his girlfriend.

Obviously, I was going to avoid jumping to any more conclusions. I was going to establish the facts before embarking on any more speeches or confessions. However, my panic reflex was not so patient. I was rapidly running out of options and unless I was missing something *really* obvious, I had to consider that having betrayed Hamish was a possibility.

What if I had slept with Linda? Hamish pinned the last guy who looked at her up against a lamppost. Who knows what he would have done to the poor chap if Gerry hadn't thrown a bucket of cold water over him. What he did to Gerry is another story ...

I needed to ask Linda what happened. The problem was she might tell Hamish. Then, even if I *hadn't* slept with her, Hamish would know that I considered myself capable of betraying him.

Nevertheless, if I didn't ask Linda, then I might never know. I might always be waiting for a tearful call from Lizzie or a ferocious head butt from Hamish. Linda was my only hope.

Fortunately, I had Linda's number. She thought that we were friends, having no idea how different 'friend' and 'girlfriend of a terrifying mate' actually are. Our relationship was entirely dependent on Hamish. If, God forbid, anything happened to their romance, I would not only never speak to her again, but also never speak *of* her again.

I texted, "How about coffee?"

Her response, "Do you want to talk about what happened after the party?"

Fuck! Please, no. I mean certainly, Linda was the most glamorous of the suspects but she was Hamish's girlfriend. Even if I wasn't petrified of the little Bristolian ball of fury, you don't sleep with your mate's partner — it's simple ethics.

As I walked to the café, I felt my heart pounding in my chest. I approached corners with trepidation, expecting Hamish to leap out with his flaming mane blowing in the wind and a mad look in his wonky green eyes.

"Please let there have been some sort of misunderstanding!" I prayed. A misunderstanding seemed unlikely. She'd followed her first text with, "Thank you for coming to me about this and not Hamish." She was either afraid of him, or deeply in love. I pictured Hamish's ruddy face, and decided it was probably the fear.

This was bad. This was very, very bad.

Linda was already in The Boston Tea Party when I got there. She had cut her hair into a severe black bob, which accentuated her perfect features. As usual, her white skin was flawless. She looked sophisticated in long, figure hugging black trousers and a loose, off-the-shoulder white shirt. I imagined her holding a long, slim cigarette, but of course, she wasn't. It was 2011.

The second I sat down, her perfect face collapsed.

Her beautiful almond shaped eyes drooped in the corners, her lip quivered and rippled, and her eyeliner began painting streaks down her face.

"It's okay!" I said, trying to comfort her without touching, as if some restraint now might undo any terrible mistakes.

"I cheated on Hamish. Is it *really* okay?"

"Well, no," I admitted, "it was bloody stupid."

That bit of honesty got me nowhere. She began bawling so loudly that heads turned on the other side of the room.

"It'll blow over. Nobody needs to find out," I said, though I was far from convinced.

"I just feel so foolish," she blubbed.

"Oh come on, you're not the first girl to get drunk and make a mistake."

"He will never forgive me."

"You don't know that."

"But I do! We broke up!"

What? She told him? How was it that I still had use of both of my legs? Was he outside, waiting to pounce? Had she lured me here under false pretences? Was this a honey trap? I looked at her devious black mafia hair and wondered how far I could really trust Linda.

If Hamish knew, then who else knew? How long would it be before somebody told Lizzie? Did Lizzie already know?

Perhaps she was out there with Hamish, hiding in an alleyway with a crow bar ... No, at least I could be certain that Lizzie wouldn't turn to violence. Still, she would dump me, which was as bad. Or was it?

As I found myself weighing up which would be worse, being hit by a steel bar or losing a soulmate, I wondered how I could have let my life become so complicated. *If this is the life of a dickhead, why are there so many of us out there?*

"Why on earth did you tell him?"

"I had to, I can't lie to Hamish."

"Did you tell him who it was with?"

"Yes!"

"Oh Linda! What about Lizzie?"

"What's it got to do with her?" she asked, sounding confused. Suddenly, her tone changed from puzzlement to horror. "She doesn't fancy Sam does she?"

"What's Sam got to do with this?"

"Well, I did sleep with her!"

What? She slept with Sam? But Sam was a woman, and an insane one at that. However, most importantly, Sam was not me! This would mean that Linda and I hadn't gotten squelchy with each other! *Yes!* I began laughing out loud. *I haven't slept with Hamish's girlfriend, halleluiah!*

"Oh that's right! Typical man! Getting off on the idea of two women together. This isn't some sort of lesbian porn! My life is falling apart."

"I am not getting off!"

"Then why were you smiling?"

"Because I thought *we* ... Oh never mind, forget it."

There were already three people in this town who knew that Ross Turpin couldn't remember who he'd taken to bed, and that was more than enough for me.

"Hamish kicked me out," she told me.

Wait, what was this? Was I now Hamish's girlfriend's confidant? That was not a good role to be in, it was practically taking sides. Still, it was better than having slept with her.

Linda had come all the way into town to meet me; the least I could do was listen and be there for her.

"So telling Hamish made things worse?"

"Of course it did."

"Do you wish you hadn't owned up?"

"No, the guilt was killing me."

"Of course it was."

"I couldn't lie to Hamish."

"But if you really love somebody, maybe it's kinder to protect them?"

"If you really love someone, then you respect them with the truth."

"Even if confessing is a merely selfish act, designed to alleviate one's own guilt?"

"Cheating is the selfish act, not confessing."

"But what if you've met the person you want to spend the rest of your life with? Somebody truly wonderful, in every sense of the word. If you really were *truly, truly* sorry and vowed to make them happy every day for the rest of their life ... What if making a mistake made you realise how much you loved a person? What if the mistake was a turning point in your relationship, which actually made you realise how strong your feelings were?"

"I don't think there's any sugar in this coffee. Can I borrow a sugar?"

* * *

Six months earlier ...

"Ross, have you seen my Tim Minchin t-shirt?" Lizzie looked inordinately concerned. Her little eyebrows bowed up in the middle and frown lines wrinkled her forehead.

"Yes, it's in my wardrobe."

"Oh. How did it get there?"

"I found it on the bathroom floor, getting wet."

"Well then why didn't you put it in my rucksack?"

"I don't know, I suppose I thought we've been going out for a while now, and perhaps it would be all right if you kept a couple of t-shirts in my wardrobe."

"Oh!" Her bounce returned.

"Is that okay with you?"

"That's perfect with me!" she sang, grinning. She wrapped her arms around me and gave me a giant hug, while her feet danced up and down on the carpet.

* * *

The thought of making love to Silvia Martin terrified me. Not only was she intimidatingly stunning, almost a foot taller than me, and twice as heavy, but she was the sort of woman who made loud conversation about butt plugs and told of her low scores in purity tests as if they were some sort of medal.

I had previously eliminated her from my enquiries, on the grounds that no matter how hard I tried, I just couldn't visualise us together. Each one of her breasts was larger than my head and her nipples were at my eye-level. She was a Spanish woman of Brazilian decent, and her hips were as wide as two of me. If she got on top of me, I would snap.

Silvia was hardly my type. I appreciated the effect she had on other men and I understood why my fellow males were reduced to jelly when she walked into a room, but I liked my little Anglo-Saxon girlfriend. I liked small but perfectly shaped boobs. I liked a cute little bottom. I loved the long discussions we shared about life.

Silvia had a thick Spanish accent, which I found impossible to follow when drunk.

How does a small, shy man manage to invite a dazzling, curvaceous beauty into bed, without speaking? Words were my strongest suit.

Still, when you have excluded the impossible, whatever remains, however improbable, must be the truth. Unless there was some glaringly probable possibility that I had missed, which seemed unlikely — *I am Ross* — then I had to consider the Silvia prospect.

I decided we had better meet somewhere public. As much as I feared being spotted out with her, Silvia had a reputation for coming on strong, and I didn't want to risk the wrong expression that a discreet venue might give.

The White Hart seemed like a suitable location —

public, but with enough small corners for nobody to see us together.

Good God! What was she wearing? I peered through the window as Silvia Martin strutted down the cobbled path wearing a mini skirt and a red satin blouse with matching stilettos. When a woman is a six-foot walking hourglass, she really doesn't need to spell out her beauty, yet her clothes screamed, like somebody ruining a decent joke by explaining it.

As she came closer, I blushed. Her cleavage was longer than my dick. There was no way that I had slept with this woman.

"Good afternoon Ross!" she said, rolling the "R" in a way that I reluctantly found sexy.

"Silvia," I tried to say firmly, but actually just squeaked.

"I was surprised to get your call," she said, sitting on the sofa next to me. I realised that occupying a double seat was a mistake. I should have found myself a very small stool.

"Linda gave me your number," I responded, defensively.

"And why would you want *my* number?" she asked, tiptoeing two fingers along my forearm.

I winced.

"I think I know why," she added.

"Why?" I asked, nervously.

"You just had to see me again, one on one." She played with the words 'one on one' as if they were the naughtiest she knew, which I somehow doubted.

"No! I mean, I did, but not because ..."

"Do I make you nervous Ross?"

"No!" I squeaked, like a mouse facing an elephant.

"Are you worried about your little girlfriend? Because I can be very discreet ..."

"She's not a little girlfriend!"

"I noticed."

"I meant, she's not *insignificant*. I love her."

"Oh," she said, turning away from me. However, seconds later she'd thought of a new tack. "Perhaps you have a big heart. Lots and lots of love to give?" She actually put an arm around me — *an arm!*

"I don't!"

"A big libido then? The little girlfriend isn't satisfying you? I'm not surprised. She looks like the uptight type. No oral?"

"My girlfriend loves oral!" I yelled. Two little old ladies turned and stared. I felt my face flush.

Who was Silvia to dare challenge Lizzie's sexual prowess? Lizzie was the perfect lover — generous, but selfish enough to keep it interesting; adventurous, but timid enough to keep things safe; ravenous, but calm enough to keep friction burns to a minimum.

"I see, so what you're after is even dirtier than oral. Perhaps ..."

"Stop!"

"Alright, if this is the game you choose, I'll play along, *for now*."

"It's not a game!"

"It's always a game."

"Look here ..."

"When I was in Spain, I met a man who was on holiday with his family. He told me for seven days that he loved his wife, but by day eight, he was ready to leave her and four children to run away with me."

"You're really not a very nice person, are you?"

She seemed to view my remark as some sort of compliment, and chuckled happily. "You called me, maybe you do not like nice?"

Okay Ross, put a stop to this. Find out what you came here to find, and then walk away.

"Did we have sex?" I blurted out.

"What?"

"After the party. It had to be you, I've ruled out everybody else."

Silvia rose out of her seat, a big, seething volcano of rage. "You think you could forget making love with *me*?" she roared. "Nobody has sex with Silvia Martin and forgets about it."

"I wouldn't be so sure," I muttered.

Silva sat down again, this time opposite me. The fury was clearly short lived, and she was smiling mischievously once again. "So ..." she sang, twiddling her hair with a painted nail, "you were drunk, you had a little sex dream about me, and now you're here for the real thing."

She uncrossed her legs. How foolish of me to have thought she was somebody who wore knickers.

"Look, give me a straight answer. Did we have sex?"

"Did you tell your girlfriend that you asked me out to lunch?"

"It's coffee actually."

"Same difference."

"It's not! Coffee is a step down from lunch. It's less significant."

"Shall we let your little girlfriend be the judge of that?"

"No!"

"No? You really do feel guilty about this don't you?" Her fingers were on my arm again, and I did not like it. "Coffee that you can tell your girlfriend about is innocent. Coffee that you have to keep a secret ..."

That was it; I'd had enough. I stood up and waggled my finger at the deluded tart. "Look here you psychotic witch, I've spent the week talking to a woman whose most significant relationship is with a poodle, a woman who thinks psychiatric wards should admit cows, and a woman whose boyfriend may well saw off my toes with a rusty blade. I've been verbally abused, henpecked and punched in the face. But you, you really top it all."

"Wow! That is a passionate little speech. The lady

doth protest too much, methinks!"

"Lady?"

"Well who knows? You've already asked all the women whether you diddled them after the party, that only leaves ..."

"I did not sleep with ..." I began yelling. Then, remembering the two little old ladies enjoying their soup, I lowered my voice. "I did not sleep with a man."

"Are you sure?"

"Yes I'm sure!"

"How?"

"Men don't wear green thongs!"

"Some do. Especially at fancy dress parties ..."

"It was a *women's* thong. You're just trying to rattle my cage because I'm rejecting you, you dumb bitch."

"Oh you're not rejecting me."

"Yes I am!"

"*I* am rejecting *you*."

Then, with a toss of her thick, shiny dark hair, she strutted out of the pub, wiggling her hips as she went.

"Another one down," I thought, grimly. It wasn't getting any easier.

* * *

Three months earlier ...

It was my first outdoor pint of the spring. I was sitting in the garden on a wooden crate, amongst the tulips and primroses, enjoying the smell of lager mingling with freshly cut grass.

Suddenly, Lizzie came storming out of the shed. When I saw her hurt face, I knew that there was only one thing that could have happened. I gulped, then choked a little, and then spat beer onto the patio.

"What is this?" she cried, holding something small in her palm.

Fuck. Fuck, fuck, fuckedy-fuck. She was not supposed to see the box.

"Liz ..."

"I'll tell you what it is!" she said, opening the lid angrily. "It's my grandmother's ring!"

"She gave it to me."

"Yes, I gathered that. When?" she demanded. Little pools of water collected in the corner of her eyes, ready for her to cry.

"She wants me to propose," I said, stating the obvious.

Her hands rose angrily, almost dropping the ring. "How long have you had it?"

"A couple of months."

Lizzie's eyebrows narrowed and I saw her try and disguise a sad mouth.

"Lizzie, do you think I'm going to propose? Do you really think I'm going to ask you to commit your whole life to me without being absolutely, one-hundred-and-ten percent, super sure that I can make you happy? I haven't proposed to you yet, because I'm just not that selfish."

"Yet?" she asked softly, the curve of her lips starting to take a more contented orientation.

"Yet," I repeated, sincerely.

She grinned, then gave me a gentle dig in the ribs and disappeared back into the shed, carrying the box.

* * *

You don't get to be a formidable detective writer such as myself, without having a firm grasp of deduction. This meant that the solution to the mystery was now crystal clear. There was only one logical explanation — Nina was lying. Distraught because I stole her virginity, forgot about it, and then chose Lizzie over her, she had sent me on a wild goose chase.

She had to be the one who owned the knickers; there were no other candidates. I bet, if I went through her drawers, I'd find a matching bra in that exact shade of green!

I would be lying if I said I wasn't exceptionally annoyed, but Nina is a complex character. Her romances usually involve watching men in cafes and talking to penpals online. To her, a moment's eye contact is as important as a marathon shag is to the rest of us. That means that a shag was as important as ... Well, it was important enough to derail our friendship, majorly. I had to speak to her again.

We met down on the quay because apparently Piggins needed a walk. I had always had a problem with Nina calling a dog *Piggins* but then it was a ridiculous name for a ridiculous dog. It yapped, chewed people's hands and sat in shit.

The only good thing about Nina's relationship with her miniature poodle, was that she didn't dye him pink. She had however, resorted to ribbons and a designer dog collar that matched a pair of designer shoes that she had never worn.

It was difficult to know whether Nina over-loved Piggins because she had no boyfriend, or had no boyfriend because she over-loved Piggins. It was also impossible to know which came first: the designer collar or the designer shoes. She was a woman caught in many loops.

"Nina, what's the point of taking Piggins for a walk, if you're going to carry him?"

"I'll put him down in a minute."

Six months ago, I had made a personal pact with myself: *if Nina ever puts her dog in a handbag, I'll call off the friendship.*

"Nina, about the party ..."

"Have you found out who it was yet?"

"No, and I've asked *everybody*."

"Well it must have been somebody else then."

"But I've tried everybody else! Somebody is keeping something from me."

"Well it's not me."

"If it was, I'm not upset ..."

"Firstly, it wasn't me. Secondly, it wasn't me. Thirdly, nobody interviews every woman he met at a party unless he's at least a little upset."

"Okay, fine, I'm upset, a little, but I need to know what happened."

"Oh my God!" she exclaimed. Instinctively, I checked that Piggins was all right. He looked fine. Damn, she was shouting about me. She was using her cross eyebrows again. "You really think it was me!"

"No ..." I lied. "Well yes, maybe a little."

"How long have we known each other?"

"Years," I mumbled, sheepishly.

"And you still think I would lie to you about something like this?"

"Not lie *as such*."

"You could come on my podcast!" she shouted, unexpectedly. I was a little confused, but at least her eyebrows had returned to their usual harmless orientation.

"What for?"

"You could put out a request for information."

"Nina, that's the stupidest idea you've ever had. I might as well make up a sign saying 'I cheated on my girlfriend' and leave it outside Lizzie's front door."

"We don't have to use your identity. We can just say 'A man who wishes to remain anonymous ...'"

"Nina, how many men do you actually know?"

"Lots!" she lied, sounding hurt.

"Okay."

"We say that a man would like to return a green thong to its rightful owner. Then we wait for people to email ..."

"People?"

"Yes."

"Why did you say *people* not *women*?"

"Women are people."

"So are men."

"Yes."

"So why didn't you just say *women*?"

"I don't follow."

"Nina, you don't think there's any chance ..."

"What?"

"Any chance I ..."

"What?"

"Stemmed the rose."

"What?"

"Packed some fudge."

"Huh?"

"Took the backdoor into the gents ..."

"What are you talking about?"

"Silvia said perhaps ... Perhaps the person I had sex with was ... a man!"

I was relieved when Nina laughed out loud. In fact, it's fair to say that she did a full body laugh. She doubled over in fits of giggles and even had to put Piggins on the ground so that she could control herself.

"Yeah, I thought that was funny too. As if! Me?"

"Quite. You're the last person on earth, who would ever do anything even remotely gay."

"Because I'm really self-aware?"

"No, because you're ..." Nina trailed off in a way that I found mildly alarming.

"What?" I demanded.

"What's the opposite of experience seeking?"

"Boring," I frowned.

"No, you're not boring, just ..."

"What?"

"What's the opposite of flexible?"

"Narrow-minded!"

"No, you're not narrow-minded."

"Well what then?"

"Well, you're hardly ... experimental."

"I could experiment!"

"Yes, but you don't."

"Nina! I resent the accusation that I'm too boring to have gay sex. I'm a very artistic person."

This was ludicrous. Nina had known me for years. She'd been there when I wrote a short story about Boris the bisexual bison, there when I wrote a poem about Malc the masochistic moose, and there when I painted a half-naked nun carrying a narwhal. She knew how interesting I was!

"Nina! I'm a writer!"

"I know."

"I could have gay sex."

"But you didn't."

"I might have done."

"Do you think you did?"

"No."

"No."

There was a moment's quiet before Nina started laughing again.

"Hang on," she begun, "you interviewed Silvia?"

"Why's that funny?"

"Well, isn't she a bit ... out of your league?"

"No!" I scoffed, remembering her strategic leg uncrossing at The White Hart.

"Oh come on, she's gorgeous."

"She hit on me."

"In your dreams!"

"No, really. She hit on me."

"What, that night?"

"No."

"When?"

"I met up with her to ask about the party and she hit on me."

"And what did you say?"

"No, obviously! Jesus, Nina! I love my girlfriend."

I took a moment to realise how ridiculous that sounded in light of my current predicament.

Nevertheless, not all the unexplained knickers in the world could lead me to imagine doing anything other than turning Silvia down, or anybody else for that matter. Silvia may be *Maxim*'s idea of perfect, but

Lizzie was mine.

"I may have made a mistake in the past. But it was one mistake, once! I love Lizzie. I can't explain to you how much I love Lizzie. It's un ... un ... it's so something I can't even think of a word for it. I have to make this right. I'm going to confess!"

"What? Why?"

"Well she might find out from someone else."

"Who? *You* can't find out from someone else, and you've been trying pretty hard."

"What if I picked up a disease?"

"That's unlikely."

"Is it? I don't know if we used anything."

"Telling Liz will be relationship suicide."

"Not necessarily."

"Oh come on!"

"You're right. She's going to dump me."

Nina embarked upon a monologue that allowed her to showcase a variety of different voices, none of which sounded anything like the people that they were supposed to be. "You'll be all 'I'm sorry Lizbird, I didn't mean for it to happen, but I was drunk' and then she'll be like 'I can never trust you again' then you'll be like 'Come on Liz' and then she'll go 'Who was she? What was she like?' and you'll be all like 'I dunno' and then she'll go 'How do you know it was only *one*?' Then you'll ..."

"Enough! Do you not think that I've had the conversation over and over again in my head? And I have *never* called my girlfriend Lizbird."

Nina's fondness for making up fictional scenarios was bordering on pathological. What-if conversations were her favourite. I, on the other hand, was not in the mood for imagining my catastrophic plight — if there's ever a mood for that.

"You don't even know for sure that you had sex," she reminded me.

"Yes I do."

"How?"

"The thong, the lipstick and ..."

"And...? Oh yes, male pride."

"No, not male pride."

"Well what else?"

"The other bit's a bit too icky to say out loud."

"You didn't tell me there was ... icky evidence."

"What difference does it make?"

"A thong and a lippy could just be party souvenirs. But icky evidence ..."

"Why do I drink? I'm never drinking again."

"This is bad Ross. This is very bad indeed."

In fact, it was so bad that Nina stopped walking, and took a seat on a bench by the side of the river. She sat with her head in her knees, as if it was her own life shredding into tatters. Piggins pissed against the leg of the bench that I had planned to sit on, so I stayed vertical.

Suddenly Nina sprung into action. She grabbed my torso and started shaking me aggressively. "Think Ross! Think!" she cried.

"I have ..." I tried to begin, but my brain was shaking too much to think clearly. Could grown men suffer from shaken baby syndrome? I tugged away from Nina's urgent grip.

"Who was at the party?" she demanded.

"Well, there was you, Sam, Linda, Silvia ... But I've asked all of you."

"Kelly!"

"What?"

"Kelly was there!"

"Yes, but she left early to go to Timepiece."

"Yes, but then she came back!"

"She did? Oh God, no ..."

This was more bad than I could have ever imagined. Sleeping with Kelly was even worse than sleeping with the others. There was something about Kelly that reduced my heartbeat to a dismal buzz.

"What's the matter?"

"Kelly works with Lizzie. She's practically her best friend in the office."

"Shit monkeys!"

"Quite," I agreed. "What am I going to do?"

"Well surely, if she was going to say something, she would have done so already?"

"Well, you'd think so, but maybe she's waiting for the right moment. I have to talk to her."

"Don't rock the boat. If she hasn't told her so far, she probably won't, unless you do something to stir things up."

"Like what?"

"Well, you could be like 'Hey, Kels.' Then, she could be like 'You're calling so it's not a one-off, now I need to tell Lizbird.' Or, she could be like 'Oh my God! I'd totally forgotten about the sex until you called!'"

"Nina that's stupid." I felt my blood starting to steam and wrongly lashed out at Nina. "Don't you think it's time that you stopped commentating on my life and started living your own?"

"I'm just trying to stop you making more mistakes."

"Why don't you get out there and make some of your own mistakes, instead of sitting on your high horse telling everybody else what to do."

"Are you going to talk to Kelly?"

"Do you think I should?"

* * *

Four days earlier ...

"My sister's broken up with her husband."

"Again?"

Lizzie's sister was like a tall, overdramatic version of Liz. Both had wonderful qualities, but the line of sanity fell somewhere between them. She had crises on a weekly basis, often marriage related but sometimes physical. Since I'd been dating Lizzie, her sister had been in two car accidents, broken a leg skiing and broken up with the same husband seven times. Her reactions to said incidents were often extreme, involving binge drinking, disturbing the peace and public indecency.

"I'm going to have to go around there," Lizzie said.

"But you'll miss the party!"

"I know, gutted. Still, better than having to pick her up from the police station again."

"Do you want me to come with you?"

"No, it's fine. She'll probably want to watch a RomCom and moan about men."

"I'll miss you at the party."

"No you bloody well won't!" she said, elbowing me. "Have a good time!"

"Well, I'll try, but I doubt much will happen," I said grimly. "These house parties are all much of a muchness."

* * *

Kelly was a good twenty years older than me. Still, I was growing used to surprising myself.

As I sat in Costa Coffee, watching the forty-something-year-old Liverpudlian get herself a latte, I wasn't optimistic that she had any information. Surely if she knew something, she'd have told Lizzie by now and, if Lizzie knew, *I would know.*

Kelly had insisted on meeting near their office. A café near work is not the ideal location for a secret meeting to establish whether or not you are in possession of your girlfriend's colleague's knickers. However, apparently she was so busy that being squeezed into her lunch hour was my only option. I looked around awkwardly.

A small brunette stepped into view. I froze. However, when the girl turned I could see that she had sharp features and a particularly acute nose. I felt disloyal for even thinking that this monstrosity might be Lizzie. Still, these were troubled times for Ross Turpin. Who knew what the stress was doing to my visual system?

When Kelly returned, carrying her drink, I noted that she wasn't bad looking for her age. Even so, it seemed unlikely that a woman of such experience would be interested in some casual sex with a toy boy. Surely she should be with somebody sophisticated who wore pinstripes and drank espresso.

"So," she began, pulling up a chair opposite me. "Lizzie tells me you want to be an author."

"I *am* an author."

"What are you writing?"

"Well, I'm actually between projects at the moment ..."

"What was the last project?"

"Well ... "

"Don't worry. I understand — writer's block! I'm a writer too."

"Are you?" *Oh no, not another one.* The worst thing about being a writer, is that everywhere you go, somebody wants to tell you about his or her idea for a novel featuring a vampire Harry Potter with a dragon tattoo.

"It's not my occupation, obviously," she continued. "The likes of you and me need something realistic to fall back on ..."

Thanks.

"But people tell me I'm a natural with words. Scott gets me to word all the signs in the office."

"Signs?" I'd written a two-hundred-thousand-word epic that included inventing a language, and she was talking to me about signs.

"'Would you please leave the toilet the way you'd wish to find it.' That sort of thing."

"Right."

"People usually react better when you give

instructions with a poetic edge. It makes them feel less ... dictated to."

"Right."

"You probably didn't notice the rhyme in there, it's subtle."

"Right."

"I'd like to write a novel."

"You would?" *Oh no, please not vampire Harry Potter.*

"In fact, I've already done the hardest part."

"You have?"

"Yeah, the first line. I read on the internet that that was half the battle."

"You've written one line?"

"Yep! Do you want to hear it?"

"Go on then." I accepted my fate.

Kelly took a moment to compose herself. She closed her eyes, straightened her spine, took a deep breath and then I watched her eyelids slowly elevate. She straightened her head and began. "He shook."

I waited, politely.

"That's it: 'He shook.'"

"He shook what?"

"Himself."

"Why?"

"I don't know yet."

"Well what's the book about?"

"I don't know yet."

"I see."

"It has potential, right?"

"Well, there are certainly a lot of directions it could take."

"Any tips?"

"Not off the top of my head."

"Go on! From one writer to another ... give me a tip!"

"I don't know ..."

"Come on! Come on!"

"Maybe it could do with some planning?"

"Planning? Where's the fun in that? If I already know what happens, I won't want to finish writing it will I?"

"God forbid."

"I like it though. Practical advice from a practical writer. Liz always says you are very practical."

What? "Practical?"

"Yes."

"My girlfriend said I was very practical?"

Why were all of these women calling me practical? I began having nasty flashbacks to my conversation with Nina. I had thought that she was just trying to rile me, but then why would Lizzie say it too, and behind my back as well?

I mean sure, I can change a light bulb, but there is more to Ross Turpin than a bit of domestic handy work. Lizzie had seen me in a *corset* for Christ's sake!

"What's wrong with *practical*?"

"It means boring."

"Not necessarily."

"I am a writer!" I boomed. "I am a creative! Taken by momentary impulses and passions of the soul just like everybody else! I am not practical. I make mistakes like any other person. I am human!"

Kelly started fiddling with her coffee spoon. "Okay, sure." She emptied three sugars into her coffee. "Why did you want to see me anyway, is this about her birthday?"

Panicking, I asked, "No, why? What happened at her birthday?"

"It's in two weeks."

"Oh, right, no it's not about that."

"Oh. Well then, what?"

"You were at the party on Friday, right?"

"I made an appearance, yes."

"Two, I heard."

"You heard? Yes, I thought you might have

forgotten the second."

"Why?"

"You were somewhat wasted."

"I have ... *heard* that maybe I did something I should apologise for ..."

"Oh don't be daft. It was nothing."

"Don't put yourself down."

"People say and do stupid things when they're drunk. It's no biggy."

"No biggy? Maybe not to you, but actions have consequences! Consequences for other people too! For me, for Liz! Liz is your friend!"

"Yeah, and you're the best thing that ever happened to her. I'm not going to let a few minutes in time ruin that."

"A few *minutes*?"

"Look Ross, if you've just brought me here so that you can apologise, there's no need. I wasn't offended."

"Well, at least let me give you back your thong and lipstick."

I retrieved the wretched items from my pocket, delighted to be able to offload them, finally. As I felt the slinky knicker material between my fingers, I sensed that something wasn't right.

"My what and what what?"

Kelly stared at the thong, with a blank expression on her face.

Fuck! They aren't hers! Quickly, I tried to grab them, but Kelly got there first. I tried to prize them out of her hands, but she held a firm grip.

"Ross, what do you think happened between us?" she demanded.

I grappled for an explanation. "I didn't borrow those things?

"Why would you borrow somebody's thong?"

"Wacky party souvenir?" I suggested, trying to laugh it off but actually looking like a demented hyena.

"Ross, did you think we had sex?"

"No. Of course not! Why would I think that? You're Liz's friend! I love Liz. You're not my type — I don't mean that in a bad way, it's just that you're not Liz! I love Liz. I wouldn't cheat on her! No way!"

I paused.

"So, we definitely didn't then?" I added.

"Why would you think that?" she asked. The accompanying shrivelled look of disgust accentuated her age, making me ask myself the same question. "Have I ever shown any interest in you? I mean sure, I smile at you from time to time, and make polite conversation, but that's for Liz's benefit. Why would you think I'd take advantage of you when you were drunk?"

"Well somebody did."

For some reason, Kelly fell about laughing. I didn't like her laugh; it was deep, mean and grating. "You had sex that night?" she chuckled.

"Why does that surprise you?"

"Well, you didn't seem ..." she trailed off. I prayed that she wouldn't finish her sentence, but then it came, that dreadful word: "capable."

"I had sex!" I cried. Obviously, she hadn't heard about the raw power of Ross Turpin Jr. either. Why did nobody know what an animal I was between the sheets? Surely, knowledge like that can't be caged in.

"I did! I had sex!" I insisted.

"Sure."

"I have the thong to prove it! And the lipstick!"

"That doesn't mean you ... *rose* to the occasion." She made a baby erection with her index finger. I hated that mocking index finger. I hated it with a passion.

"Look you deranged poet freak! I rose to the occasion. I shagged somebody that night! I shagged somebody senseless!"

Suddenly, I heard a fruity voice with a painfully familiar Devonshire twang. "What's going on?"

"Lizzie!" I gasped.

* * *

I grabbed the lipstick and knickers hurriedly and stuffed them into my pocket. Had Lizzie noticed? She didn't look as though she'd noticed, smiling politely at her colleague. Was the whole future of my life going to be decided by which direction the love of my life's eyes happened to be looking at one fateful moment?

"I'll leave you to it," said Kelly, taking one last gulp of her diabetes-inducing potion. "Good luck Liz, you're going to need it."

The Liverpudlian stepped away from the table, returned for one more swig of her caffeine-infused sugar, and then hurried off back into the pot of mysterious women, and less figuratively, the street.

I was just about to open my mouth, ruining Lizzie's life forever, when Kelly scurried back to the table and took another swig of her latte. Without saying anything, she walked away again. I carefully studied her exit, making sure that she had really gone this time.

I looked up and saw Lizzie gazing down at me, with a bemused look. For a moment, I considered bolting. I could see the door; there was a clear runway to the exit. I could sprint into the street and disappear into the summer day, with my relationship more or less intact.

Still, explaining the running away would just add to the lies. No, I had no choice other than to bite the break-up bullet. I had to tell Lizzie what had happened.

I gulped as I imagined it: the tears, the apologies, trying to emphasise the fact that there was a slight possibility that nothing untoward had happened. I would approach the subject gently, so that it didn't seem like the big deal that it blatantly was. I would choose every word with care. If anybody could handle this well it was Ross Turpin — words are my thing.

Ideally, I wanted to know where the lipstick and knickers came from *before* troubling Lizzie with them.

However, would I ever really know the truth? Even my best sleuthing tools had failed me. Perhaps being caught thong-handed was the universe's way of telling me it was time to confess.

Although 'Maybe nothing happened' could be my get out of jail free card, part of me wished that I had a concrete confession. Telling my girlfriend I cheated on her would make me look like a prick, but a regular sort of prick. Telling my girlfriend that I didn't know what happened, was a new and special breed of utter foolishness. Ross Turpin would forever go down in history as having invented a new breed of laughable stupidity.

"Were you discussing my birthday?" she asked, taking a seat.

If only. "Something like that."

"I was thinking Paris? Oh ignore me; I know we can't afford Paris. Maybe just a weekend break in the Lakes ..."

Oh no, this is awkward. "Lizzie ..."

"I've always fancied Rome."

She's making this harder. "Lizzie!"

"Don't worry! Kidding! It's not a biggy is it? Not a twenty or a thirty. Nothing ending in a zero, or a five. Not that you have to take me to Rome on biggies either ..."

"Lizzie!"

"Sorry, I was just getting carried away. One birthday at a time, I know. It's just that I saw this poster of Venice ..."

Please stop talking. "Liz ..."

"Okay, I'll stop. I'm joking anyway, I'd be happy with some chocolates and a good book. Well, maybe a good book and a cottage in the country ..."

This time I yelled. "Lizzie!"

"Sorry, sorry. I'm just fantasising. As long as I can spend the day with you, I don't mind where it is. Well, the day and the night obviously. The night being the most ..."

"I cheated on you!" I yelled, in sheer desperation. The words gnashed out of my mouth like an angry interjection, with none of the regret, sorrow and humbleness I had meant them to contain. I tried again, more softly, "I cheated on you."

I braced myself for tears, yelling, perhaps even getting coffee thrown in my face. This was going to be ugly.

"What?" she asked calmly, gazing at me beneath enquiring brows.

"I slept with somebody else," I explained, slowly and repentantly.

"No you didn't," she laughed, completely unperturbed.

Could she not see my fraught face? Could she not see the eyes of regret? The expression of a broken man.

"I did do it," I said gently.

"This isn't funny," she said with a warning glare.

"Why would I make it up?"

"You tell me."

"Lizzie, I did do it. I spent the night with another girl."

"Is this a role play for your writing or something? An improvised sketch?"

"Lizzie, I did cheat on you." God. This was agonising. Sure, I'd earned the villainous role in a hideous confession, but only *one* confession.

"Look Ross! I'm really not in the mood for this. Whatever game you're playing, knock it off."

"Why don't you believe me?" I pleaded. I admired her unrelenting trust, and cursed the fact that I didn't deserve it.

"Do you really want to go into this?"

"Yes!"

"Well, it's because you're ... *you*."

"What's that supposed to mean?"

"You're caring, you're loving, you're ... practical."

"Practical!"

"Yes, practical."

The repugnant word resonated around my skull. *Practical.* It was one of the consolation prizes for a man, like 'you're very sweet' or 'you're like a brother to me.' It was an entirely undeserving adjective for an artistic dreamer like me. Did the women in my life not know me at all?

"I am not practical!"

"Well, you're hardly a philanderer."

"Why is it so hard for you women to believe that I might just have had one night where I went crazy?" Was this some kind of joke? Were the women punishing me for my drunken mistake by undermining my spontaneous streak? Why were they so stubbornly refusing to accept my wanton act of passion?

"Because you're *you.*"

I snapped. Exasperated I began roaring, "I'm a passionate man! I went to a party. I got drunk. I was horny, I took a girl back to mine, and I shagged her! I shagged her rotten. Because I'm Ross! I'm a creative! Taken in by momentary impulses and passions of the soul! I am a man! It may surprise you lady, but Ross Turpin went wild! I'm telling you I shagged someone else, because I did! I *shagged*!"

I stood still for a few moments, refilling my lungs with air, recovering from my passionate declaration of manhood.

When I looked up, Lizzie was sitting with her arms folded and a look of stunned amusement. Her mouth rose into a smile, wrinkling her nose. "Have you quite finished?"

"I was impractical, and experimental, and reckless!"

"There's clearly been a misunderstanding."

"Don't patronise me! I know what I saw."

"I'm sure there's an innocent explanation."

"No there isn't!"

"If you explain to me ..."

"I can't explain! There is no innocent explanation. I have been unfaithful."

"With who? Who have you been unfaithful with?"

"I don't know! I'm *that* reckless."

Lizzie sighed and put her hands in her pockets. "I've had enough of this. Shall I get you a smoothie?"

"Is that it? Aren't you going to break up with me?"

"No."

"But you should, I've been an idiot."

"I don't disagree with you there."

"Well that's what you do when your boyfriend cheats on you, you leave him."

For the first time, she looked genuinely worried. "Do you want to finish with me? Is that why you're making this stuff up?"

"No."

"Well then what?" Her big brown eyes were beginning to well up. Being taken seriously was not the font of liberation that I had expected it to be.

"I'm trying to be honest with you."

"About *what*?" she pleaded, rolling her hands into frustrated balls.

"The party last weekend, when you were at your sister's."

"What about it?"

"Afterwards, I slept with somebody else."

"On Friday night?"

"Yes! That's what I've been trying to tell you."

"At your flat? You took a girl back to your flat, and you had sex with her?"

"Yes," I said, bowing my traitorous head in shame.

I saw her body relax, as if somebody had flicked a switch. "You *are* a moron," she said.

"That's what I've been trying to tell you!"

"But it's okay ..."

"Oh for crying out loud Liz, how many times? I put my cock into someone else's pussy, and I fucked her with it. Wake up and smell the infidelity!"

The whole basis of our relationship was crumbing and Lizzie was behaving as though I'd forgotten to turn the oven off. Perhaps I wasn't the most promiscuous fork in the drawer, but there was no denying that I had made a mistake, a big mistake and Lizzie needed to face that. Good old reliable, practical Ross had broken the mould — it was a *fact*.

All at once, I saw something that made my heart fleet like a headless chicken. My face flushed and I felt prickles dotted all over my skin. My eyes strained to focus as a wave of wooziness washed over me. Surely, I wasn't seeing what I thought I was seeing. It couldn't be ... Could it?

"What's that?" I asked nervously, pointing a trembling finger at Lizzie's shoulder.

"This?" she asked, pinging her bra strap.

I had been reduced to jelly by a brassiere. I had always known that women's underwear had compelling powers, but this bra spoke to me as no bra had spoken before — it was green.

"Yes! That!" I stammered.

"It's my new bra."

"How long have you had it?"

"About a week."

Wow, so this is what it feels like to be gobsmacked. I tried to speak again but there was no air in my lungs and my teeth had been replaced by blancmange. I tried to collect some oxygen but my breathing was rough and shallow. Eventually, I managed to mumble, "Does it come with ... anything else?"

Lizzie reached for my pocket, and grabbed the thong by its dangling thread of a waistband. "What, like this thong?"

I gasped. My eyes widened to dangerously large

circles. I patted my eyes to check that the sockets were still engaged. The world started to spin and I found myself having to sit back in my seat to steady myself.

Four days, *four days* of agony, going over and over that night in my mind, engaging in fraught conversations with hideous women, imagining what Lizzie would say, visualising her walking out the door forever ...

Was it really as simple as Lizzie buying some new items? Was I actually so set in my ways that I couldn't even cope with my girlfriend making minor alterations to her style?

I went through a myriad of emotions: relief — she wasn't going to leave me; anger — she should have kept me informed about new lingerie developments; fear — she might be upset about where my mind took me; love — even after a year, that woman still found new ways to surprise me.

"I didn't have sex on Friday night!" I breathed.

"Oh we had sex!" she informed me, her pink lips forming a curvy grin.

"Together?"

"Of course. Who else would you have been having sex with?"

"I honestly had no idea," I admitted, shaking my head. "But how? You weren't at the party. You went to see your sister ..."

"I did, but then Kelly called and said you were in a bad way, singing Frank Sinatra at her, so I drove over and picked you up."

I didn't know whether to laugh or cry. I grieved for the four days of my life I would never get back and the hair that those days had turned white, but most importantly, I felt delight — delight that my gorgeous, wonderful girlfriend was still my gorgeous, wonderful girlfriend.

"Are you okay?" she asked, rubbing my back, soothingly.

"I thought I'd lost you!" I stuttered, trying to stifle a sob.

"Nope, you'll have to try harder than that."

I locked my arms around her and held her as tightly as I could. It was like being reunited with a lost toy — my girlfriend had been oblivious to the fact that she had been missing, yet I'd pined for her every day.

Even though I knew I hadn't really cheated on Lizzie, it took a while for the cloud of guilt to clear. I was engulfed by an enormous sense of gratitude — gratitude for her soft fingers ruffling my hair, gratitude for the smell of peach body butter on her skin, gratitude for the sound of her relaxed breath.

Eventually I pulled away and looked at Lizzie with a firm, purposeful stare.

"I am a creative though," I told her.

"I know."

"I could have done it."

"I know Ross. Of course you could."

The Other Mother

How can a French girl, with French parents, grow up thinking in English? And, what's so dangerous about England? I may ski, white-water raft and abseil, but Zoe won't let me go to England. I wonder if it has anything to do with my real mother.

We speak French in our house, I go to a French school and my friends are French, but I am English. I know that I'm English. I've always known. I'm fourteen, and it's time for me to find out who I am.

Zoe is French, and Alain was French. They never commented on my nationality, but they did say that I was their daughter and I know that isn't true.

I've never approached Zoe about my parentage, but I don't need her confirmation to know that she's not my birth mother. We have the same fair colouring, but where have my dimples come from? Why do I have a widow's peak? Zoe is left handed, like Alain, but I am right handed, like somebody else.

She's on anti-anxiety medication, Zoe. She thinks that I don't know, but I do. She hides pills inside an insect encyclopaedia. Presumably, she thought I wouldn't touch it, but I'll read anything.

"Claire, have you done your homework?" she asked me today. She tries to play the strict parent, but she's too gentle to be stern. She even looks gentle with her blonde, cotton wool hair and enormous, clear, blue eyes. She has a cuddly figure, which continues to create an aura of safety and comfort.

"Maybe," I replied, with a smile.

"Have you?" Even her voice is reassuring — soft and breezy, like a pan flute.

"No!" I laughed.

"If you don't do your homework, there'll be no dinner."

I knew she was bluffing. She often threatens me, but she never follows through. She has never been able to bring herself to punish me. Besides which, I'm old enough to cook my own dinner. Some weeks I do the online shop all by myself.

Tonight we had fish fingers and jam tarts with little elephants on the lids. I like that she still uses the elephant cutter that we bought together at a school fete, when I was eight. We ate outside on the patio, feeling the evening begin to chill the scorching summer heat. When we finished dinner, we sat down and watched *Amélie*. It's Zoe's favourite film and my second favourite. I prefer *Delicatessen* but Zoe doesn't know that I've seen it.

My homework is still unfinished and I am still unpunished.

Alain used to punish me a lot, before he died. Even when we played games together, they were not fun, and they hurt. I hated them. I hated him.

Then, when I was seven, Alain slipped on the cellar steps and he died.

I remember the moment that Zoe told me. She was shaking and I thought she would never stop crying, but then she did and she became very quiet. She seemed to be in a daze for many weeks. I think I was sad too, at least for a little while, but it's hard to know whether I was grieving for Alain's life or Zoe's vitality.

A few weeks after the accident, things changed. I was allowed to be upstairs all of the time. We even started leaving the house. I remember the first time I saw the sun; Zoe had to warn me not to look at it. I remember how grass felt the first time I stepped on it with bare feet.

However, although those moments felt like new experiences, I'm not sure that they were. Did the grass feel wonderful because it was novel, or because it was familiar? I had a sense that I'd stepped on soft grass before, but I had no idea where or when.

Zoe enrolled me in the local school, which was an overwhelming experience. At first, meeting other children was terrifying. Even though there were fewer than forty pupils, the village school felt enormous. I came home night after night, to run into my new bedroom and cry. However, when Zoe finished redecorating the house, she began inviting other children over to play. After a few weeks, I couldn't wait to get to school in the mornings.

Zoe, or *Mum,* as I often called her, never really fitted in at the school gates. She used to meet me and then scurry away as fast as she could. She's different from the other mothers. I can't describe how, but she is. I wonder if it's because she wears plain clothes, or because she's shy. She doesn't like talking to people she doesn't know very well. She has little contact with the world outside our house. We only just got a computer, and never get newspapers or magazines.

Zoe told me that she used to be a waitress, but I'm not sure how. I can scarcely imagine it. She finds it hard to make eye contact with strangers and she gets nervous easily. She breaks things a lot, and I hear her cursing when she thinks I'm out of earshot.

I can't remember her ever going out to work, and I wouldn't want her to — I like having her all to myself. She's the only family I know.

We play chess and Connect Four. We bake cakes together and ice them in many colours. She taught me how to grow flowers, tomatoes and runner beans. She showed me how to make my own dresses and t-shirts.

I don't like the girls from the village as much as I used to. They gossip about boys and pop music all of the time. They talk to me as if boy-band appreciation is a phase that I'm just about to enter, which fills me with a sense of impending doom. I don't like boys and I don't want to like boys. Growing older is not going to change that and I don't want it to.

The evenings that I enjoy best are nights like tonight, the ones when Zoe makes popcorn and puts on a film that we've seen before. We cuddle up together and laugh before the jokes, quoting lines before they're spoken.

She has given me so many things — the outdoors, school, love and affection. I don't want to upset her, but I want to know who I am, and why my thoughts are in English.

* * *

I've just been sick in the toilet. I've had my first ever big row with Zoe, and I had no idea how draining arguments could be.

We had been fighting about the English exchange trip.

She's downstairs crying right now and I don't know what to do to make it right.

"I'd be allowed to go if it was a German exchange, wouldn't I?"

"Not necessarily."

"Give me a straight answer, please!"

"You're not going on the English exchange trip. That's a straight answer."

It was spoken with an unusual level of force for Zoe, and I was taken aback, but I had to keep probing. I need to know more.

"Is that because it's where my mother lives?"

Zoe froze. Her cup of tea shook in her hand, and she had to put it down. Then she opened her mouth, as if preparing to respond, but before any sound came out, she stopped and her lower lip quivered. Her blue eyes looked not just sad, but terrified.

"I mean, my *other* mother," I said, trying to ease her pain.

"What do you mean?" she asked.

"Just tell me the truth, please. I'm old enough now. Am I adopted?"

"No," she said, softly.

"But I must be! I'm not yours!"

I expected her to say something in response, but

instead she just burst into tears. She started sobbing loudly, clutching at her hair in desperation.

Having never seen Zoe this distressed before, I ran out of the room. I couldn't stand to see her tears, particularly not tears that I had triggered.

Zoe brought me up. I'm going to put her first, whoever my real parents are. But I *do* need to find out about them. I know that I can investigate my past without loving Zoe any less, so why can't she see that?

* * *

I told Zoe that I was sorry, but she's still sad. She didn't eat her breakfast this morning, despite my making her favourite apple pancakes. I heard her crying in her room last night, and the insect encyclopaedia has gone from the shelves.

If only I could find my birth mother, then I could show Zoe that there's room for them both in my life.

I wonder what my mother is like. One of my parents must be artistic, or musical. Zoe's tone deaf and can barely hold a brush, yet I can play the clarinet and paint colourful landscapes from my imagination.

I try to picture my mother but I can't. Is she tall? Is she short? Does she look like me?

Blonde — I think she's blonde. Perhaps it's because I'm blonde, or because I'm used to Zoe's colouring, but I can't imagine having a dark-haired mother.

I've spoken to my friend Charlotte about my parentage. She thinks I can track my mother once I'm eighteen. I don't know if that's true, but I can't wait for four more years. I'm ready to meet my parents now.

That must be why Zoe doesn't want me to go to England, perhaps she's worried that I'll try to track down my real family. She's had me all to herself since Alain died. It must be difficult for her to imagine sharing me.

* * *

I know where I came from and I'm shocked — disgusted even. The news is almost impossible to believe. However, I've read the article over and over again, and every time I draw the same conclusion.

Claire is not even my real name! I'm certainly not French.

I was wrong; finding out who I am may very well have changed the way I feel about Zoe beyond repair. The truth about my origin changes everything.

Today, in English class, we were given newspapers to translate. Our table got one called the *Daily Mail*. It was full of stories about pop stars and pictures of the royal family.

However, then I saw her — my mother.

On page seven, at the top right of the page, there was a picture of a lady. I noticed her image before I read the shocking text — she cried out to me.

Her face was the image of mine. Age differentiated us, of course, but I could see strong similarities between our features — dimples, a widow's peak, the same shaped eyes ...

In some ways, she was scrawny and malnourished looking, yet her features were kind and warm.

She had brown hair with grey streaks. I was wrong, my mother isn't blonde, yet still, I knew that this was my mother.

I *recognised* her. I thought I had no memories of my parents, but as soon as I saw the photo something buried deep within came to the surface. My mother has been there, in my mind, all along.

Beside her picture was a photo of a toddler. The toddler was less familiar, but still evoked a strong feeling of recognition. Did I have a sister?

After I got over the initial shock, I realised I had to translate the text as quickly as I could. My English is not perfect, but I am the strongest linguist in my class. It helped that the *Daily Mail* text was extremely easy to read.

"Mother of Millie Jones Refuses to Comment on Sick Tory Costume" read the headline.

Who was Millie Jones, and why was she in the paper? I read on.

"The son of a Tory MP, Kenneth Sanderson, was asked to leave a fancy-dress party after he arrived dressed as kidnapped toddler, Millie Jones. Her mother, Rebecca Jones, has refused to comment."

Rebecca. That was it. My mother was called Rebecca. The name sounded perfect, like a musical harmony. It slipped right into place.

I looked at the photo — Rebecca — my mother. She looked tired, and I felt an urge to throw my arms around her. I ran my finger across her picture.

Then, the more sinister matter at hand caught up with me. Millie had been kidnapped.

Was that me? Was I Millie? The name did ring some sort of bell, but it didn't fit perfectly, as the name Rebecca had. Was that because I wasn't Millie Jones, or because I had been known as Claire for so long that nothing else sounded right?

In the photo, Millie was blonde, as I am. It wasn't fluffy hair, like Zoe's, but glossy golden ringlets. I tugged at my hair. It was barely even wavy now; could it have been curly once? It was difficult to remember my early childhood, with so few photographs in the house and so many memories of Alain to avoid.

My face is longer than Millie's, and my nose is stronger. I'm used to seeing my face behind heavy-rimmed glasses. I slipped them off and studied my reflection in the silver coating of my pencil tin. My eyes are the same shape as the toddler's, and our dimples match, and are just like Rebecca's. I really think I could be Millie Jones.

I read on. Millie had been kidnapped eleven years

before. She would be the same age as I am now — fourteen. The facts fit. It had to be me. I must be Millie.

"Are you all right?" asked the teacher.

Suddenly, I was aware that I was *not* 'all right'. I was dizzy and nauseous. The thought of having to continue the English class feeling as I did, was unbearable. I grabbed the newspaper and got up from my chair. Despite my light-headedness, I ran. I ran with no goal in mind other than to get away from my school.

* * *

I haven't left for England yet, but I will. I don't have a passport, or any money to buy a ticket. Had I known I would stumble upon my real mother in a newspaper, I would have saved up my allowance.

It feels weird being back at home, but I have nowhere else to go, not without a passport. I could go to the police station, but it seems so final, and so frightening. I'm furious with Zoe and I feel deceived. However, we've shared our lives with one another for eleven years. I don't want to fracture our relationship permanently, no matter how betrayed I feel.

She tried to 'have a talk' with me today. My school called and told her that I had a funny turn in my English class. However, I cannot bear to look at her.

How could she not tell me who I really am? It is almost inconceivable that she was involved in my abduction, but surely she knew about it. The kidnapping of Millie Jones appears not to be common knowledge in our little corner of southern France, but a French woman bringing up somebody else's English child would have found it impossible to ignore such a relevant news item. The story would have been screaming out to anybody with questions. Zoe must have had questions.

Perhaps she knew all along. Perhaps that's why they kept me underground when I was very little.

Perhaps she and Alain were hiding me from people.

Could she really have been involved in something so sinister? It is not possible for a mother to love a daughter more than Zoe loves me, but is that the same as being a good person? Is being loving the same as being right?

Is it ... Is it possible that *she* kidnapped me? Did Alain do it? Could they have kidnapped me together? Or perhaps it is the more palatable explanation that a stranger abducted me, and I somehow found my way into their lives.

Whatever the circumstances, she should have told me! I have a right to know who I am!

* * *

I miss Zoe. We haven't spoken for a whole day. I need her. I need to tell her what I'm going through. I need her to explain. I need her to hug me and tell me that there's been a big misunderstanding, that the past wasn't terrible and everything's going to be all right.

She is a gentle person. Now that the initial shock's worn off, it's easy to see that she couldn't hurt anybody. Whoever it was that kidnapped me, it could not have been Zoe. She's not capable of causing so much pain.

Yesterday, she made a batch of lemon tarts. She made the lids using our elephant cutter. She called to me, and when I didn't answer she left a plate of tarts outside the door. It killed me not to take any, not even one.

I wasn't ready to face her then, but I am now. However, for some reason I cannot bring myself to go and find her. I want her to come to me. I want her to knock on the door with another plate of pies, or laundry, or anything. I just want to see her.

My heart is breaking. I could not stand to lose Zoe. She's always been mother to me. She *is* my mother. However, I can't give up the dream of a reunion with my real parents. I cannot stand to think of Rebecca, alone in England, not knowing where I am, or even whether I'm dead or alive.

I'm all Zoe has. I have no grandparents, aunts or uncles. Now I know why.

Zoe has shown me nothing but love. I feel terribly guilty for doubting her. How could I have believed, for one moment, that she would steal a toddler from another family? How could I have thought she could put another family through so much pain?

My head is all over the place.

Zoe cannot have been the one who kidnapped me, but she must have raised me, knowing that I'd been abducted. Why?

* * *

They've given up on me! The Joneses have given up! I went to the library today. I looked on the internet for articles about my family and they've stopped trying to find me. Have they forgotten me?

Up until three years ago, Rebecca was in the news frequently. The papers told of her constant turmoil. She told them that every morning she awoke to a fresh sense of terror. She said that her heart did not beat without me, and that my empty chair at the kitchen table pained like a knife lodged in her chest. She vowed that she wouldn't rest until my safe return.

Then, suddenly, she told the press to leave her alone, so that the family could get on with their lives. She means their lives *without* me. She stopped giving interviews, she stopped appearing on television, and disappeared from the public eye almost completely.

How could she do that? Does it mean that she's forgotten me? Does it mean that she's stopped wanting me back? Does she think I'm dead? Would it be too much of a shock for her to find out that I'm not? Are they happy now, without me?

However, it's not just Rebecca that I have to think

about. I have a sister too! She's eleven — only three years younger than I am. Her name is Bethany. Her face and the shape of her features look similar to mine, but she's much paler than I am, with a reddish tint to her fair hair, and hazel eyes. She's very beautiful and she has a friendly smile. I'm very excited, but at the same time crushed. I've always longed for a sister.

Is it too late to have a relationship with Bethany? Would she even want to meet me? Do any of them want to meet me?

It's weird to think that there's a girl living in England, being raised by my parents, having the life I should have had. Who is she and what is she like? Are we similar?

I can't remember my dad at all. There was a man called Daniel in the news. They say he's my dad, but he doesn't look familiar. He has thick black hair but, apart from that, looks older than I thought my father would be. It's difficult to know whether I've seen him before because whenever I try to recall a man, Alain's ruddy face pops into my mind. I feel sick. I don't like to think of Alain.

What would my life be like if I hadn't been kidnapped? I'd have grown up in England and perhaps never learnt French.

I would not have met Zoe.

I feel great sadness when I think of Zoe. The news about my identity has made a gaping chasm between us. I miss her. However, sometimes when I look at her, I no longer see a mother that I trust, but a stranger in my mother's skin.

* * *

I came home from school, armed with printouts from the library and scattered them over the dining table. Perhaps it was cruel to spring them on Zoe like that, but I needed to know. I couldn't stand to be fobbed off one more time.

Zoe came in and she smiled. Presumably, she was happy to see that I was finally downstairs and not hiding in my bedroom.

Then she saw them — the news articles.

She froze.

I saw her whole body tense and her hands contracted into involuntary fists. Her eyes twitched and I thought she might start crying again, but she didn't. I noticed that she had begun to shake. Everything about her appearance told me that *she knew*. There was no doubt about it.

I decided to go for it and took a deep breath before demanding, "Did you know I was abducted?"

"Claire ..." she tried to put her hand on mine, but I pulled it away.

"Did you know?" I cried.

She paused, and then nodded, sadly.

I enquired, in almost a whisper, "Did you do it?"

"No," she said, looking me straight in the eye, pleading with me to believe her. Finally, after I failed to put her mind at rest, she added, "Alain did."

Immediately, I knew it was true. She was a good soul. As I recalled, Alain had neither been good, nor in possession of a soul.

"He brought you back here on his boat."

"When?"

"When you were three."

So, I *was* Millie Jones. There was no doubt about it. I felt a hot rush of blood gush throughout my body. My brain felt swamped.

"Why?" I begged.

She closed her eyes tightly, as if the memory consumed her entire body. She began to tremble. Eventually, she opened her eyes again, looking sick. "He was a very bad man."

I knew that was true. I could hardly remember Alain, but I knew that he was a depraved human being. The sick feeling in my stomach whenever I thought of him reminded me of the harm he had been capable of doing.

"Why didn't you call the police?"

"I was afraid of him."

"They would have protected us."

"He said he'd kill you before he let anybody take you away."

"Well, why didn't you take me to the police station yourself?"

"I couldn't get you out of the house!"

"Why not?"

"I couldn't!"

"Did you even try?"

"Yes! Jesus, Claire! You have no idea what a man he was! It's a mercy that you can't remember. I tried to get you out, but he was always watching — always! At night, he locked you in the cellar. I didn't have a key! I used to beg him not to do it! I took punches for you!"

Big, glassy tears were beginning to form in the corners of her eyes.

I imagined it — Zoe pounding the cellar door, rattling the handle, begging him to let me out. I could see myself on the other side of the door, crying out for Zoe. I could almost hear her wail as he threw her roughly away from the door. I remembered her screams ...

"He kept you locked up," she repeated.

"Until he fell down the stairs."

She nodded, miserably.

"Well, why didn't you take me to the police then?"

She said nothing.

"Zoe! Why?"

"I don't know."

"Yes you do! You wouldn't have kept me away from a desperate family without a good reason. I know you, Zoe. Tell me why, please!"

She was quiet for many moments. She closed her eyes again. Finally, when she reopened them, she tried to speak, but no sound came out.

"Zoe! You left my family in the dark. They were desperate. Why did you do that?"

"He didn't fall down the stairs."

I stared at her, wide-eyed. She stared back, willing me to understand. Her eyes were bottomless pools of desperation.

I tried to process what I'd just heard. I knew what she was trying to tell me, but I could hardly find the words.

"You pushed him?" I peeped, scarcely believing it possible, even as the suggestion left my lips.

She nodded. Large tears ran down her cheeks.

I stared. The Zoe I knew was not capable of killing a person, at least not in cold blood. It just wasn't in her character.

"He was a very bad man, Claire." Lost for explanation, she could only repeat what she told me before. "I pray that you can't remember how bad."

For several minutes neither of us spoke. We sat in silence, Zoe letting the news sink in. I'm sure it will be a long time before it truly sinks in, but even then, after just a few minutes, I had a moment of clarity.

I was surprised to realise that I was not cross, or disgusted, by Zoe's revelation. I knew in that moment, that I *could* remember Alain and the utter terror I faced every morning when the light shone down from the cellar door.

Quickly, I tried to think of Disney, to wipe my mind of previous thoughts, but Alain's face reappeared — big, sweaty and grinning sadistically.

"That's why I couldn't turn you in to the police — there would have been an investigation," Zoe explained. "They'd have locked me up and taken you away from me. By that time, I'd been looking after you for *four* years. I was your mother!"

"You didn't report him missing, did you?"

She shook her head.

"But ... Where is he?"

She said nothing.

"Zoe. Where is he?"

She glanced at the floor.

"He's still down there?" I shuddered. Had we been living above a tomb for seven years? Was he really down there right now, rotting?

Zoe looked tired. The effort of making these revelations had exhausted her. "Please don't judge me, Claire. You have no idea what he was like."

I looked at my mum's sorry, terrified eyes. "But I do!" I cried, and threw my arms around her. She wasn't the villain in this story, and she never had been. Rather, she was something of a hero.

* * *

Now that I know the truth, the bitter crack between Zoe and me has mended. I feel even closer to her than I had before. It's comforting to know that whatever may have happened in the past, the relationship I have with Zoe is solid.

Alain's death was a turning point in my life — or, should I say, it was the *beginning* of my life. At least, the beginning of the life I've had in France. I have Zoe to thank for so much.

Today we planted sunflower seeds. We've converted a small area of the lawn into a flowerbed. I love it when we build flowerbeds, turning a little patch of plain into a jungle of colours.

We had a fantastic afternoon. Yet even as we laughed together, and splashed one another with the watering can, I could not get Rebecca Jones out of my mind.

What must she have gone through? What must the Jones family have gone through? It must be terrible to have a daughter by your side one moment, and not the next. It must be agonising not knowing where your daughter is and whether she's come to harm. Rebecca must have been in great pain. Was she still hurting?

And what of my sister? Does she even know that I exist? She must have been a baby when I was kidnapped. She won't have a single memory of me; just years of watching our parents suffer. Perhaps she hates me for being the source of that pain.

Do I remember a sister at all? Is there a Moses basket buried in my memory, or a crib, or a pram?

I suppose they must all think that I'm dead. Eleven years is a very long time. Do they still have *any* hope?

Do they miss me still? Or have they grown used to life without me? Have they moved on?

Did I ever miss them? I yearn for them now, but is it too late? Why did I leave it so long to look for them? And why *do* I yearn for that family? I don't know them. Zoe is my mother and she's incredible. She protected me in the way that a real parent would. She even killed for me. That should be enough for any child, so why isn't it enough for me?

Perhaps if I'd never found out about the Joneses, then I'd be happy to stay here with Zoe and never meet them. However, I *have* found out about the Joneses, and I need to see them face to face. I need to meet them.

* * *

Zoe said we can do it! She said we can go to England! At last, I'm going to meet my family. I'm going to meet my other mother!

It hurts Zoe, I can tell. She's worried that I'll prefer Rebecca. She's worried that I'll want to live with the Joneses instead. However, why would I? Why would I give up my lovely life with a great mother in order to live with three strangers? Of course I won't. I just want to meet them. I just want to find out who they are.

She's worried that she'll go to jail. She thinks

they'll ask questions and find out that she knew who I was and never told. But she's wrong. I won't let anybody take her away! I love her — I love my mum! If it weren't for her, I'd have been raised in a cellar at the mercy of a monster.

I need her, and our elephant-shaped cookie cutter, reruns of *Amélie*, and gardening afternoons. Those things make me happy, and they make me happy because we do them together.

We're going to have to call in a few favours to get me a passport — as Claire, I do not have a birth certificate — but Zoe says we'll work something out.

How on earth will I introduce myself to the Joneses? Can I just ring the doorbell and say, "Good afternoon, I'm your daughter"?

Will they even want me? It sounds as though they're getting on with their lives. I'm worried that they won't welcome the interruption. Perhaps they're happy as things are. Mind you, I'm happy with my life, and *I* still want to meet *them*. Difficult or not, this is something I must do.

* * *

"Bethany, where did you get that from?" My daughter was rinsing a purple trowel in the kitchen sink. It was patterned with painted berries, unlike any of ours.

"The French girl gave it to me."

"What French girl?"

"The one who talks to me at the bottom of the garden."

I felt my blood freeze. "Don't tell lies."

"I'm not. There *is* a French girl. She comes to talk to me in the evenings."

"What have I told you about talking to strangers? You know how dangerous they can be." Of all the families in the world, we had the most reason to be mindful of stranger danger. It was hard to believe that Bethany, who was generally so mature for her age, could be so stupid.

"She's just a girl mum. And, she's never tried to hurt me. She helped me plant the tulip bulbs."

"Are you making this up?"

"No, of course not."

"Well, next time a visitor comes into our garden, you must come and get me, understood?"

"Sure."

"Right away."

"Okay Mum!"

I looked at Bethany as she went back outside. Her auburn hair caught the sun. She was wearing her very first pair of low-slung jeans. Once, her t-shirts had been tattered from years of playing outdoors, but now she ripped them strategically to follow fashion.

She was growing up fast, and was far too old for an imaginary friend. Sometimes I worried about her. She rarely brought friends home from school, and it's especially important to have good friends when you're an only child.

Millie sprang into my mind and the memory stung. I had desperately wanted Bethany to grow up with a sister. Alas, it was not meant to be.

After losing Millie we were too devastated to try for another child, and, eleven years on, it was clear that Bethany was going to grow up an only child. As painful as it was to admit it, my first-born daughter was not coming home. It had been too long.

"Evening, gorgeous!" said a warming voice. My spirits lifted instantly.

"Daniel!" I smiled and turned to meet my husband's open arms. He was wearing a loose-fitting cotton shirt with jeans. I could see the very top of his chest hair peering through the collar, and I loved the way it teased me. Our marriage seemed to be going through a golden age. We were getting on better than we had done for over a decade.

I would never stop longing to have Millie back,

but in the past few years I had begun finding fulfilment in other places. I was starting to live life once again.

It helped that Daniel was more or less the perfect husband. He was a good person, but on top of that, he was somebody who found interesting things to say and new ways to amuse me, even after many years of marriage.

He was often impish in his ways, which could be annoying during my blacker moods. He had also become rather boyish in his hobbies. However, after everything we'd been through, I enjoyed seeing him loosen up, even if it meant a slight regression toward his youth. Millie's disappearance had robbed us both of many years, and we had some catching up to do.

For years, I'd hated the lines on Daniel's face and the pitiful story that they told, but recently he'd grown to look more relaxed and I began to enjoy the tiny wrinkles around his eyes when he smiled. He'd put on a little weight in the last two or three years, and it rather suited him.

Some evenings, when he'd been out all day, I even swooned, like a teenager, when he came through the door. Today, I was wearing a pretty, yellow, summer dress and I'd tied a ribbon into my brown hair. I knew he'd notice.

"How was band practice?"

"Not bad actually, Fuzzy has written another song."

"What's this one about? Another 'I hate women' anthem?"

"No, no. It's a love song."

"A love song from Fuzzy? Bloody hell."

"He's met somebody."

"Fuzzy? No!"

"Yep, he left early so that he could go and see her."

"That's a bit rude! After everything he's had to say about you guys having family commitments!"

"I was quite relieved actually."

"Really?"

"Yes, because now I can come home and do this!"

All of a sudden, he scooped me off my feet. My husband wobbled at first, but then steadied himself. He carried me toward the kitchen door, but my toes collided with the doorframe.

We realised that we'd get to bed faster if we were both on foot. Daniel carefully lowered me back onto the floor, and we scurried up the stairs.

"Where's Bethany?" he asked.

"In the garden!"

"Great!" he said, with a grin, and we hurried into the bedroom and dived into bed.

We were wrapped up in the delight of summer evening sex, when we suddenly heard footsteps on the stairs. Rapidly, we scavenged for the covers.

"Mum! Mum!" cried Bethany, bursting in.

"What is it honey?" I asked, peering out from beneath the duvet.

"What's the matter?"

"It's the French girl! She's back!"

My husband turned to me, "What's she talking about?"

"Oh, hi Dad," added Bethany.

"Oh, don't worry," I told him. "I'll check it out." Then I turned to Bethany and said, "Honey, wait on the landing, I'll be there in a second."

Once Bethany had left, I explained to Daniel, "I think one of the neighbours' children has been coming into our garden. I'd better take a look."

He looked frustrated, but nodded. He pulled me towards him for one last kiss. I wished I could stay there in his arms, but instead I climbed out of bed and went to investigate. I could not leave anything to chance when it came to Bethany's safety.

The garden smelt of summer. The fragrance of freshly-cut grass wafted from next door, and I felt my nose twitch from the pollen.

At first, I couldn't see anybody besides Bethany. I returned to my earlier theory that she had an imaginary friend. I read somewhere that eleven is a common age for children to start making things up — something about the transition to adolescence.

Then somebody stepped out from behind the azaleas. A shadow glided over the path. Bethany had been telling the truth; there was a child in our garden. As my eyes focused, I could see that she was barely a child at all, but a young teenager.

Immediately, something caught my attention — the girl's eyes. Overwhelmed with emotion, I staggered backwards. The girl's eyes were virtually identical to Millie's.

I tried to calm myself. I should not trust what I was seeing. This had happened too many times before — in shopping centres, petrol stations, theme parks ...

However, this girl was not like the others. She didn't just have Millie's eyes. She had dimples too, just where Millie's dimples would be.

I kept staring, incapable of doing anything else. I squinted — did she have the scar on her nose that Millie would have? Could time have erased it?

There was something odd about the way the girl looked back at me. Her gaze was intense. She looked me up and down, as if drinking in every part of me.

I felt a tingle begin at the back of my neck and scurry down my spine. Did Bethany have an imaginary friend, or did I?

The friend looked a lot like I had when I was younger, except with lighter hair. Her face shape was the same, and her hair radiated from a point in the centre of her forehead, just like mine did.

I stopped evaluating a stranger — I was absolutely certain that I was looking into the eyes of my daughter, Millie. Nothing in the world could convince me otherwise.

Immediately, I wanted to reach out to her. Just a simple touch would do, anything to verify that she wasn't an illusion.

Moreover, I wanted to feel my daughter's skin against mine once again. I wanted to wrap my arms around her and bring her close to me. Did she still smell of Johnson's shampoo?

What was I doing, standing there staring? I should have been reaching out to her. I should have been holding her. However, I feared that one touch would turn her to dust, and she'd vanish right before my eyes, as she had done in so many dreams before now.

"Mum," called Bethany's voice, snapping me back to reality. "This is Claire."

The words stung like vodka on a wound. Of course this wasn't Millie, she was French for a start. Besides which, why would Millie play at the bottom of the garden and not come into the house? Had I let myself get lost inside my fantasies once again? I felt giddy.

"Claire?" I said softly, not taking my eyes off her.

She nodded.

I wanted to scream and kick things, but I remained rooted to the spot. For many years after the kidnapping, I'd seen Millie everywhere I went. However, the last few years had been different. I'd allowed myself to start moving on. I could now walk down the street without checking the face of every child. Yet, here I was, seeing Millie's face in a stranger once again. I'd forgotten how horrible the resulting disappointment felt.

"And you're French?" I asked.

To my surprise, and confused delight, she shook her head.

"Then what?" I asked in a hurry.

"Mum! Don't be rude!" said Bethany.

"I think," began the girl, talking with a strong

French accent, "that I am English."

"Millie?" I blurted, before my mind had had time to think.

"Millie?" echoed Bethany.

The girl stared back at me. Her eyes twinkled, and then a little smile began to light up her lips. It was a smile I hadn't seen for eleven years. "Rebecca," she replied, with a grin.

"What?" asked Bethany.

"Bethany, come here," I beckoned. I put an arm around her and pulled her close to my side. We studied the girl together. I desperately wanted to touch her, but I was still paralysed by the fear that she was simply an illusion. I felt as though I was watching a film, not living through a moment in time.

"Are you my sister?" asked Bethany.

"I think so," she smiled, with a nod.

It was extraordinary. How could Millie have turned up after all these years? How could she have just materialised at the bottom of the garden? And how could she have such a strong French accent?

"Parles-tu francais?" I asked.

"Oui," she replied.

"I can't understand!" cried Bethany, and I realised how important it was that she knew what was being said, that she was involved in every step of the process.

"Bethany, it looks as though you might have found your sister," I explained, hardly able to believe the words.

It was difficult to know what to expect. Past outbursts had suggested that Bethany felt threatened by the prospect of her older sister turning up.

I was overjoyed when she turned to Millie and said, "I like you." She wasn't threatened, or jealous, she seemed elated. Then she turned back to me and added, "I like her, Mum! Can she come in for some lemonade?"

I nodded. It was all too surreal. I could say it was like a dream, but it was more than that — it felt as if we were in heaven.

"I like lemonade," said Millie.

"What other things do you like?" I asked, nervously. It felt odd to be a mother who did not know these things.

"Music. I love music."

"I have to get your dad!" I exclaimed.

Imagining telling Daniel brought a tear to my eye. Once the floodgates were open, tear after tear gushed out. This was going to be the happiest moment of Daniel's life. It was the happiest moment of mine. He was going to be overwhelmed with joy.

Abruptly, Millie cried out "Non!" She ran to the fence just as a blue Ford pulled away. "Où vas-tu? Arrête!" shouted Millie. She began trying to climb the fence, but it was too late, the car was gone. "Zoe!" she cried.

I rushed after her, having to use force to stop her from running into the road. She hadn't been returned to me so that she could get hit by a car just moments later. It was the first time we'd made physical contact, and restraining her was far from the loving embrace that I'd imagined.

"Get off me!" she cried. Then she fell down onto the pavement and began crying hysterically. She kept repeating one name over and over again: "Zoe".

"Millie, honey ..." I began, but she didn't seem to hear me. She began hammering on the pavement with her fists. I thought she was going to hurt herself and tried to hold her arms, but she shoved me away.

"What's going on?" Daniel asked. I hadn't heard him coming.

I had so much to explain. I had been so excited about telling him that Millie was alive and well, but not here, not like this.

"It's Bethany's friend from the garden. She's

upset."

He tried to soothe her, offering distraction, putting a calming hand on her back. "How about some homemade lemonade?"

"Get off me!" she shrieked, smacking him away.

After he backed off, she rolled over onto her back and lay there, gazing at the sky and screaming at the top of her lungs.

"Where's your mum?" Daniel asked, an unfortunate question in the circumstances.

"Just come inside," I offered, softly, but she ignored me.

Finally, Bethany sat down on the pavement beside her. It touched me to see my little girl behave so tenderly.

"Would you like me to show you my tree house?" suggested Bethany.

Millie didn't respond.

"Perhaps Zoe will come back," Bethany suggested. "Maybe she just went to get an ice cream."

The girl stopped screaming, and the next time she made a noise, it was more of a gentle sob.

"Let's go up to my tree house, and you can tell me all about Zoe."

I saw their eyes connect. There was already a bond between them.

"Just you and me; no adults," offered Bethany.

Millie eventually nodded and Bethany helped her to her feet. It was astonishing. I watched Bethany guide her sister by the hand, and take her up to the tree house.

"Daniel, look!" I said, deeply affected by what I'd seen. I felt sure I would cry once more.

"What's happening?" asked Daniel.

I grabbed his hand and looked into his eyes intensely. "It's Millie."

"What?" he said coolly, dropping my hand.

"It's Millie."

"Rebecca, I thought we'd moved past this."

"It's not a delusion, or a hope, or a dream Daniel. It really is Millie."

"And she told you that, did she?"

"Yes!"

"Oh, Rebecca!" he cried, burying his head in his hands. "Not again."

"This isn't like before! This isn't a false alarm. We've really found her! Well, she found us."

"Rebecca!"

"You didn't see her! Not properly"

Daniel was livid. In addition to multiple false sightings, a stranger had once executed a sick plot, pretending to be our daughter. Even the police had been duped. He couldn't go through it again. He didn't know that this time really was different.

Before I could stop him, Daniel strode across the lawn towards the tree house. "Hey!" he called. "Excuse me! You, girl! Come down here at once!"

"Daniel ..." I warned, gently.

"I'm not going to put up with this, Rebecca. She has no right to do this to us! No right!"

"Stop shouting!" yelled Millie, peering out of the tree house.

"Bethany, I need ..." began Daniel, but then he realised that the girl before him was not Bethany. In the grey dusk, Millie looked very similar to her sister. His mistake clearly moved him. He stopped advancing and stood rooted to the spot, studying her just as I had done, a mere ten minutes before. "Millie?" he whispered.

"What do you want?" she asked, with hostility.

"Please come down here. Let me see your nose!"

"No."

"She has the scar, Daddy!" Bethany cried. "She is Millie. She is my sister."

Daniel swayed on the spot, and he grabbed a post to steady himself. Then he let his body drop gently onto the grass, which was beginning to soften with evening dew. He sat there, staring up at the tree house.

I sat down next to him and held his hand. "Is this really happening?" I asked him.

"I think so," he nodded, squeezing mine back.

We let ourselves sit there, listening to the sound of our daughters chattering in the tree house, and catching occasional glimpses of them. I would have many questions, and there were many arrangements to make, but right then, everything else could wait. We could just enjoy this moment, knowing it was the pinnacle of our lives.

Of course, I was desperate to talk to Millie, I wanted to hold her and spend time with her, but watching her engage with her sister was so incredible that I could not bear to interrupt.

It was a perfect moment, and we barely noticed the navy summer night creeping in on us.

Some while after it got dark, we realised that the practicalities could no longer be ignored. Millie could not have come from nowhere, and the girls could not stay in the tree house forever, no matter how much they might want to, or how much we might want to allow it.

"Has she come home for good?" I whispered to Daniel.

"I don't know," he said.

"Millie?" I called. She didn't reply. "Claire?"

Eventually I saw Bethany descend the ladder.

"What is it?" she asked. I couldn't believe how grown up she was, looking after her big sister as if it were her life's purpose.

"Can you ask Millie if she wants to stay the night?"

"I want Zoe!" cried a voice from the tree house.

"Why don't you come down here and tell us about Zoe?" suggested Daniel.

"I don't know you!" she shouted.

"Well, why don't you come down here and get to know us?" I offered.

"I'll talk to you," she said, "but not him."

Daniel and I exchanged glances. He looked hurt, but nodded. "All right," he said. "I'm going to go inside to pour some lemonade. You girls come in when you're ready.

I saw that it hurt him to leave, but he knew that what he was doing was for the best.

"Has he gone?" called Millie.

"Yes."

Finally, I saw her shape climbing down the ladder. She was a slim girl with the faintest hint of hips and breasts. She was clearly developing into a young woman. Thank goodness I was here to witness, at the very least, the autumn of her childhood.

"Come and sit down," I said, patting the ground either side of me.

Bethany sat to my left and Millie to my right. For a moment it felt as though the contentment had actually stopped my breath and I might die from happiness. However, reality soon brought me back to life with a painful jolt.

When I put an arm on Millie's shoulder, she flinched. We couldn't simply take up where we had left off. I felt as though I knew her, but she was clearly more uncertain. Eventually, I felt her relax into my embrace. I pulled her closer and she leant her weight against my body.

Despite Millie's reserved manner, it was extraordinary to be able to reach out and touch her. I savoured the moment. During the last eleven years of my life, I'd been to hell and back, but it was all worth it to be able to hold her once again. Did she feel anywhere near as moved as I did? Could she remember me at all?

"Millie, do you mind me calling you Millie?"

"I prefer Claire."

It hurt. In all the years that she'd been gone, in all

my fantasies about her survival, I'd always imagined her known as Millie. It was bizarre to think of her by any other name. However, I realised that I had to respect her wishes. "All right, Claire. Where have you come from?"

"France."

"And how did you get here?"

"Zoe brought me."

"And who is Zoe?"

"She's my real mum," she said.

It was one of the most painful moments in my life. Realising that my daughter had been kidnapped was undeniably the worst, but hearing that she considered another woman her mother was a close second. I felt my chest tighten, and I wanted to cry, but I had to stay strong. I had to be the mother she needed.

I couldn't speak at first, but then I forced myself to go through the necessary motions. "Where have you been staying?"

"In a Travelodge." Her mood seemed to brighten as she realised, "If we go to the lodge then we'll find Zoe! We have to go to the lodge!"

"Perhaps we could phone Zoe?"

"I don't know her number off by heart! It's very long!"

"Why don't you stay here tonight, then we'll go to the Travelodge tomorrow?"

"No!" she cried, shaking my arm off her. "I want to go to the Travelodge now! I want Zoe! I want my mum!"

This was something I needed to discuss with Daniel. I had no idea who Zoe was and whether or not she was safe to visit. I couldn't even be sure that I'd ever see Millie again if I took her back to that woman. For all I knew, she could have been Millie's kidnapper.

"Why don't you both come inside, and get a drink, while I have a quick chat with your father?"

"Why do you have to ask *him*?" she asked,

sneering on the word 'him'.

"Because he's smart. He'll know what to do."

Millie was unconvinced, but she was clearly getting cold, and finally agreed. The two girls walked inside, hand in hand — another moment that touched my heart.

Surely no universe would give me all this, just to take it away again. Surely Millie was here to stay. She had to be.

I recalled, with anguish, past occasions when we'd thought Millie was coming home, only to be disappointed. I wouldn't survive another heartbreak, nor would my marriage.

We slipped into the living room, leaving Bethany telling Millie all about Nana — something that seemed to return her sparkle.

"We should call the police," said Daniel, gravely.

"I agree. But what if they take her away from us?"

"Why would they do that?"

"I don't know. I'm scared."

"This Zoe, whoever she is, might take her away from us if we don't call the police."

"She brought her here today, didn't she?"

"Yes, but we don't know anything about her."

"Millie seems very fond of her."

"I know, but she's fourteen and who knows what she's been through. We still need to call the police."

Suddenly, I heard the door crash and Millie burst into the room, her eyes wide and frightened. "Nobody is calling the police!" she screamed.

"We're just worried about you, honey," I told her.

"I love Zoe. I don't want her arrested. I love her! Did you hear that? I love her. She's my mum and I love her. If they take her away from me, I'll never be happy again. I'll run away. Don't call the police!" she shouted.

Then she turned to me and held my shoulders. "Please Rebecca! Please don't let them take her away," she pleaded.

"Why would the police arrest Zoe?" asked Daniel, but I felt sure that I already knew the answer.

Either she kidnapped Millie herself, or she knew who did. France wasn't far away, and it would have been impossible to bring up Millie Jones without knowing who she was. The press coverage had been immense in the UK, at least some of it must have crossed the channel.

The last eleven years had been a living hell. We almost ruined Bethany's childhood. My marriage hit the rocks. Even during the last few years, after things began to improve, we were still in great pain. I never stopped missing Millie and I never stopped wanting her home. Anybody who could let our family go through *that* deserved locking up.

* * *

Zoe couldn't believe it was over. Nevertheless she had always known this day would come. A pain in her chest told her that Claire was gone for good.

The Joneses would report her to the police, if they hadn't already, and why shouldn't they? She'd robbed them of many years with their daughter. Now, faced with losing Claire herself, she understood how much the Joneses had suffered. How could she have let them go through that?

She hated the thought of prison — the bullying, the boredom, the lack of freedom, but that was nothing compared with the prospect of being separated from her little girl, from Claire.

Would things have been different if she'd gone to the police herself? Would she be in a better position had she turned herself in all those years before? Perhaps, if she'd been honest about Alain, the courts would have deemed her actions 'self-defence'. After all, he had been a violent and terrifying man. Perhaps if she'd done things differently, perhaps if she'd been honest, she might have been allowed some small role in

Claire's life.

Having to watch from the sidelines while another mother brought Claire up would have been agonising, but easier than this — after so many years cherishing Claire with growing love, to face the prospect of losing her.

Zoe had nothing in her life besides Claire. She had no friends, no job and not even any hobbies of her own. She lived off Alain's savings and kept outsiders away, always afraid that, sooner or later, somebody would recognise Claire and take her away.

Without Claire, Zoe had nothing and was nothing; hers would be a pointless, miserable existence.

Claire would miss her, at least for a while, but soon, with the excitement of a new family, she'd move on. The Joneses had things that Zoe could never offer Claire — extended family, money, complete freedom ...

Zoe knew that she had to act before she was arrested. It might not be possible to do it in prison. She must end her life, and she needed to do it tonight.

* * *

As much as I wanted to see justice delivered for the horrendous suffering our family had been through, it was not that simple. Our fragile little girl had been returned to us, and we had to protect her, no matter what.

She seemed to love Zoe. Perhaps she had Stockholm syndrome, but even so, it was clear that she would be devastated if Zoe were locked up.

Besides which, Millie was back now. Over a decade without her had been torturous, but those years were gone. I had to do whatever would make my family happy right now and in the future.

We could always go to the Travelodge, meet Zoe, and then decide for ourselves whether we should get the police involved. It was unlikely that she was dangerous, otherwise why would she have taken care of

Millie for all those years, and then brought her to England, to our street?

"Let's just go and see her," I said to Daniel.

"Rebecca, we can't."

"Yes, we can."

"Why won't you do what she says?" begged Millie. "If dads did what mums told them, the world would be a nicer place!"

The remark frightened me. This was the first time that she'd alluded to a father. The concept of a man bringing her up frightened me much more than thoughts of Zoe.

Millie had bonded with Bethany already, and she was beginning to warm to me, but she was hostile towards Daniel. Had something happened to her? Had a man done something even worse than kidnapping her? It didn't bear thinking about.

I needed to know more. I needed to know what our daughter had been through. How could we prepare for the future if we didn't know more about her past? Still, it might be distressing for Millie to talk about that. We needed to speak to somebody who could give us more information.

"Let's just meet her," I said to Daniel. "If we let the police handle this, it could be weeks, months even, before we find out what Millie's been through. We might never get answers. Please."

"Please!" cried Millie. She was in tears again. "Zoe is a good person, I promise. Please don't let them lock her up."

Daniel frowned. He was an honest man, a man who liked to do everything by the book. However, he was also a man who loved his family and prioritised our wellbeing above everything else.

Reluctantly, he nodded. "Fine, but I'm going in. You stay in the car with the girls, at least to begin with."

"All right," I agreed, reluctantly.

"And if anything, anything at all, alarms us, we're

going straight to the police," he added.

"Thank you, Rebecca!" beamed Millie, and threw her arms around me. "Thank you, thank you, thank you!"

Daniel watched, looking awkward.

* * *

It was an eerie setting for a Travelodge. The building itself was surrounded by fir trees and outdoor lighting was spare. The waxing moon cast spooky shadows. It was almost midnight and the atmosphere was unsettling. Our car was parked by the side of the road, a discreet distance from the lodge. I waited with bated breath for Daniel to return.

Millie clambered around on the backseat, straining to see out of the windows. "There's her car!" she cried, pointing to the car park. "She's here!" Millie unfastened her seatbelt.

"Wait, honey," I told her. "Wait for your dad to get back."

Millie opened her mouth to object.

"Listen to Mum," said Bethany, in a very grown up manner.

I wasn't sure whether the presence of Zoe's car pleased or concerned me. Daniel had gone in there alone. This woman, this Zoe, had spent years with a kidnapped child before bringing her home. She obviously wasn't right in the head. She could be dangerous. Perhaps it would be better if she weren't here.

Suddenly, I saw Daniel come running out of the building. He was holding something that looked like a piece of paper.

"Where is she? Where's Zoe?" cried Millie.

Daniel beckoned me to get out of the car.

"Where is she?" howled Millie.

"We'll find out," I assured her. "I promise. Please stay in the car."

I climbed out of the passenger seat and met my husband by the side of the road. He looked small and badly shaken.

"What is it?" I asked.

He tugged me further from the car. "It's a note." Then he added, under his breath, "A suicide note."

"What? Oh God! Is she in there?"

"No."

"Well where is she?"

"I don't know."

"Well, we've got to call the police!" I cried, grabbing my mobile.

I was surprised when Daniel took the phone from my hands. He had been the one who wanted to call the police in the first place. Why was he trying to stop me now?

"Daniel! We can't let her die! That's if there's still time ..."

"Of course I'm not suggesting we let her die! We need to find her."

"Well then, call the police."

He was silent.

"What? What is it?"

"If we call the police, they'll arrest her and she'll go to jail. That much is clear from the letter."

I tried to grab the note, but Daniel held it tight and I was afraid of ripping it. "She was the kidnapper, wasn't she?"

"No, I don't think she was."

"But she did know?"

"Yes."

"Daniel! We've suffered every day for eleven years. We thought our daughter was dead. We've missed eleven years of her life! Think about Millie!"

"I am thinking about Millie. How could I think about anything else? How do you think she is going to feel if the woman who brought her up gets locked away? Because that's what will happen if we call the police."

"We'll look after our daughter!"

"It's going to take time, Rebecca. We can't just step into the role of parents right away, no matter how much we might want to. She can barely even look at me."

"What's in the letter? Can I read it?"

"It just shows that Zoe is somebody who we should embrace, not somebody we should push away."

I grabbed the letter. At first, he tried to snatch it back, but then he resigned himself to the fact that I would read it and wrapped a protective arm around my shoulder.

The letter was in English.

Dear Daniel and Rebecca,

I am sorry for all the heartache that I caused, particularly for not returning Millie sooner. It was selfish and I'm sorry.

I want you to know that I never hurt her, but somebody did. His name was Alain ...

"No," I whispered.

I could read no further. It was too painful. Daniel pulled me closer to him, but no amount of comfort could take away the expanding sense of dread radiating from the pit of my stomach.

"That did not happen to our daughter. Zoe is just making things up to get herself off the hook. I bet she's the one who snatched our daughter. Maybe she can't have her own kids. Nobody has abused our daughter."

"Whatever may have happened to her, the important thing is that it's over now," Daniel said, softly. "That man has gone."

"It's probably not even true!"

"I really hope you're right. But listen, we need to know what happened and we need to know tonight."

"Why? Like you say, it's over now."

"The truth changes everything. Trust me Rebecca, we need to know," he said, looking at Millie.

"I can't do it. I can't ask her."

"We have to. We have to choose a path tonight. And what we do depends entirely on whether or not the words in that letter are true."

"I don't understand."

"Read on," he encouraged, holding me tighter than ever. How could it get any worse?

... seven years ago. I pushed him down the stairs, and he died. I should have gone to the police right away but ...

Daniel cut in, "If what she's written is true, then Zoe saved our daughter from years of abuse."

"Daniel! She killed a man!"

"She killed a beast. Is that really somebody we can let the police lock up? Can we really take her away from Millie, when Millie is so attached to her?"

She kept Millie from us! Yes, we can! I took a moment to collect my thoughts. Over the years, I'd wanted anybody involved in the kidnapping and subsequent imprisonment to be locked up and punished — I'd even fantasised about the death penalty — but Millie's return changed everything.

The focus could no longer be on retribution. Nothing mattered more than protecting Millie from further suffering. I longed for our little girl to come home and live with us, but would she be able to love us if we were the ones who turned Zoe in to the police? No matter how ludicrous it sounded, she considered Zoe to be a parent, of sorts. Handing her in to the police, would not change how Millie felt about her.

Any involvement of the police would threaten Zoe's freedom. Should we try to find her without including them?

Daniel was right, it depended whether the words

in the letter were true. If Zoe really was a hero, we should do everything we could to protect her. If not, we needed to call the police, and we needed to call them fast.

"All right, I'll ask her." I finally conceded. "Take Bethany, okay?"

It was one of the most dreaded moments of my life, rivalled only by the time we were asked to identify the body of a little girl. Those hours, leading up to the identification, had been horrendous. This moment felt just as lonely and sickening.

I slid into the back of the car, next to Millie. Even thinking the question broke my heart.

"Where's Zoe?" she asked.

"I need to ask you a question."

"Where's Zoe?"

"We'll find Zoe, but I need to speak with you first."

"Is she missing?"

"Millie ... Claire, please, let me talk. I want to help Zoe."

She nodded. Her whole body was shaking. Whoever Zoe was, whatever she had done, she clearly meant a great deal to Millie.

"Claire, do you know that you were kidnapped?"

She nodded.

"And do you know who by?"

She twitched.

"Was it Zoe?"

She shook her head.

"Was it a man?"

"Yes," she whispered.

"And what was his name."

"Alain," she said, with a troubled quiver.

"And who's Zoe?"

"She's the woman who saved me from him."

The words set off a chain reaction. First I felt a cold chill, then I felt dizzy, then I felt my dinner rise in my throat. I tasted fetid lemonade at the back of my mouth.

As painful as it was to admit, it sounded as though Daniel was right. It sounded as though Millie had been abused, or at least had been at serious risk of abuse. I desperately hoped it was the latter.

That would mean that Zoe was on our side. I might hate her for being loved in my place, but without her, Millie's life could have been vile. It sounded as though Zoe really had rescued our daughter from a monster.

"Why does Zoe think that the police might want to arrest her?" I asked.

Millie was silent.

"Claire, I need to be certain. Did she ... Did she hurt Alain?"

Suddenly, the whole car shook. Millie roared, "Well, he hurt me!"

I grabbed her, and wrapped her tightly in my arms. I felt her soft, innocent cheek against mine. I ached from the knowledge that somebody had hurt her, but drew comfort from the fact that I could finally hold her, and help to make it better.

It was difficult to let go of her, but time was of the essence. "I need to talk to Daniel," I told her. "Will you stay in the car? We'll get Bethany back inside. She really likes chatting with you. She'll tell you more about Nana." My voice was dry and broken.

Millie nodded. She was shaking, and it took great strength to tear myself away.

Daniel's eyes were on me, as I climbed out of the car. I looked at him with tears running down my cheeks, and nodded.

He raised his hand to his face and closed his eyes, trying to block out the pain that the confirmation brought him.

"We need to find Zoe," I told him.

"Where do we even start?"

"That's her car," I said, pointing at a blue Ford in the car park.

"She can't have gone far."

"The woods?" I asked.

"There are acres of woodland around here, and we don't know how long she's been gone."

"We should put a time limit on it, Daniel, for Zoe's sake. If we can find her quickly then that's great, but if not, we'll have no choice but to involve the police. It's all very well trying to protect her, but it won't be much good if she's dead."

"I agree."

"What's going on? Where's Zoe?" asked Millie, who had opened the car window.

"We don't know, darling. We're trying to find her."

"How can she be missing? Her car is there!" said Millie.

"She's not in her room."

"Well, maybe she's gone for a walk."

I said nothing, which seemed to alarm Millie even more.

"What aren't you telling me?"

I opened the car door and climbed into the seat beside my two girls. I stroked Millie's hair. "Honey, where does Zoe go when she's upset?"

"She doesn't get upset. She takes pills."

"Well, she's upset today."

Millie's big, blue eyes filled with tears, "I did this!"

"No," I said, holding her close to me. "You didn't do this."

"I made her come to England! I made her sad."

"No honey. We're going to find her, and everything's going to be all right."

Suddenly, an ear-splitting siren broke the still night. I watched as a police car sped past. Where could it be going in an isolated area such as this?

"What is up there?" I asked Daniel.

"Nothing, just a disused quarry."

"Get in!" I cried.

He didn't need telling twice. He rushed into the driver's seat. I fastened my seat belt in the back.

"Get strapped in, girls!" I ordered. *Girls* — it was a wonderful word, and one I'd wanted to use for years. It was a great shame that it wasn't under nicer circumstances.

I realised that I was desperate to find Zoe, and was surprised myself by my growing affection towards her.

Searching for a missing person was familiar territory for our family, but it's not something you ever get used to. I felt cheated; as soon as one painful search had ended, another had begun.

Daniel followed the road. It didn't take long to find the police car. It was parked in a layby with its florescent markings reflecting our headlights and shattering the darkness. We pulled in behind it.

"Girls," he ordered, "stay in the car."

"What's happening?" asked Bethany.

"Where's Zoe?" demanded Millie.

"Your father's right," I told them. "Stay in the car."

"He's not my father!" cried Millie. "You're not my mother. I don't have to do what you tell me."

"Millie," I began, grabbing her hand with both of mine. "We're trying to help Zoe. Now, you want Zoe to be all right, don't you?"

"Why are the police here?" she wept.

"We don't know, but please try not to worry. Please, just stay in the car. Promise?"

There was no time to argue. However, I had similar questions myself. Why were the police here? Had somebody found a body?

I turned to Bethany. "I'm going to put the child locks on. I'm sorry."

A few seconds later I hurried after Daniel, who was already sprinting into the woods. After no more than a few metres, he stopped.

A vast, black chasm stretched before us. I noticed the police officers first, then my eyes detected a figure perched on the edge of the steep cliff.

"Zoe!" I cried.

The officers turned and looked at me. I recognised one of them. He had worked for the local police department for years, although his name evaded me.

Then I noticed another man standing just behind the officers. He was quite elderly, and held a cocker spaniel on a lead. Presumably, he was the person who'd raised the alarm.

"Do you know this lady?" asked the officer I didn't recognise.

"Yes!" I panted. "I know her."

The figure turned her head. It looked like a middle-aged woman, but it was difficult to make out her features in the dark. I could see that she had fluffy blonde hair, but beyond that the night disguised her appearance.

Could this be Zoe? Why hadn't I thought to ask Millie what Zoe looked like?

"Zoe?"

She studied me for a moment and then looked away.

"Rebecca Jones isn't it?" asked the younger officer.

"Yes."

"You know this lady?"

"Yes."

"Could you tell us her full name, please?"

"She's ..."

"She's my sister," interrupted Daniel. I saw the officer take in his jet-black hair and look back to Zoe and her fair colouring. He looked unconvinced. Daniel continued, "She lives in France normally, but she's come over for a holiday."

I saw the lady look back at us with interest. Had she realised we were on her side?

My voice was shaky and hoarse, but I tried to sound as casual as I could. "What are you doing all the way out here Auntie Zoe?" I asked, walking towards her.

"Stand back!" instructed the older officer.

"She's my sister-in-law," I said, ignoring him.

I perched myself as close to the cliff edge as I dared. I felt giddy. All I could think about was Millie, and how devastated she would be if anything happened to this woman.

"Claire wants to see you," I ventured.

"Rebecca," observed Zoe. I wondered if she recognised me from the news, or perhaps from watching me in my garden, or was she just repeating what the officer had said?

"That's right," I said under my breath. Then, for the benefit of the officers I added loudly, "Come back to our house. We've made your bed up."

"Yes, of course you have," she said. Even with her thick French accent, I could identify the sarcasm in her voice.

"Well, we will do," I explained, "if you'll let us."

"I'm not stupid."

"I never said you were. Please come with us."

"The police have put you up to this."

"The police don't know who you are, and we'd like to keep it that way."

She looked away. Clearly, she did not believe me.

"It's true! We haven't told the police anything. We just arrived, looking for you."

"Why would you do that?"

"Millie," I whispered.

"This is a trap."

"No," I tried to assure her, but she was already

gazing back towards the quarry, with an empty look in her eye. "We're on your side. I *know*." I whispered.

"What?"

"I know what you did for my ... for *our* little girl."

She looked back at me, studying my face with a mixture of suspicion and guarded appreciation.

I'd be lying if I said that there wasn't a part of me that wanted to turn her into the police there and then, but I had to be strong. I swallowed and then told Zoe, "She's already had to live for most of her life without one mother. Don't make her live out the rest of it without you."

Zoe seemed to think about this for a moment, and I got the sense that she was starting to trust me. However, then she said, "She doesn't need me anymore."

"You can't really believe that."

The woman was silent.

"She was hysterical when you left. She begged us to find you."

"She did?"

"She loves you."

"She'll get over me."

"No, she won't! Do you think a fourteen year-old could ever get over losing a mother? And like this? Do you think *anybody* gets over suicide? She already thinks this is all her fault. Zoe, she needs you."

After a few moments the moonlight illuminated a tear on her cheek. It had a somewhat morbid beauty as it caught the light, telling me that Zoe understood the suffering her suicide would cause.

She gently rested her hand on mine. "Are you serious? You want to help me?"

"I want to help Millie."

"What would we do? How could we make this work?" she asked.

"I don't know yet, but let's do it together, all right?"

She nodded and her shoulders began to relax. It was weird to look at the woman who had kept me apart from my child for so long and feel warmth towards her, yet I found myself regarding her the way that I might regard a sister. I felt a confusing mixture of emotions and had to make a conscious effort to think clearly.

Suddenly she jolted forward. She was going to jump after all!

I wondered if I could overpower her but didn't fancy my chances. She was plumper than I was, and certainly no shorter.

However, just as I thought she was about to leap, she shuffled backwards, away from the edge of the cliff. I relaxed when I realised that she was not preparing to jump, but simply getting up.

My great relief told me that, no matter how difficult having Zoe in our lives might be, it was the right choice.

The unfamiliar officer rushed forward and wrapped both arms around her, pulling her back from the edge. Millie's best friend was safe. Our new life with our daughter was not going to be tainted by another tragedy.

I didn't know how we would explain Millie's reappearance to the police. I had no idea how our family would function with Zoe in it. I did not know to what extent she would create a barrier to my future with my daughter. However, I did know that I was overjoyed that she was safe. We could work out the rest later.

* * *

I woke up in a strange place this morning. At first, I had no idea where I was. There were Peter Rabbit books on the shelves — actually Peter Rabbit, not Pierre Lapin or Jemima Cane-De-Flaque. Then I remembered that I was in England. This must have been my bedroom when I was a little girl.

It had changed, of course. Some parts of the room showed that my family had begun to move on. There was an amplifier in one corner and craft supplies in another. That upset me for a moment, but then I asked myself whether I would have wanted Rebecca to keep my room the same for eleven years, and realised that I didn't — it would have been rather creepy.

Other parts of the room told the tale of my past — books and a collection of Beatrix Potter figurines gave me the warming reassurance that the Joneses had never forgotten me, nor ever wanted to.

Zoe popped into my head and I felt a pang of fear. Was she still here? She hadn't run off again, had she? What good would my new family be without my mum? Hurriedly, I crossed the hall. I prayed that she was still here, and tried to remember which door led to the spare room. Eventually I found it, and threw the door open. I needn't have worried, a mane like candyfloss covered the pillow. I saw her chest rise and fall; she was fast asleep. I relaxed.

I knew that Zoe had been through a dreadful time and needed to get her energy back, so decided to let her sleep. I didn't know what had happened in the wood, but I knew that she was upset. Quietly, I closed the door.

Which was my sister's room? I was overjoyed to have a little sister. She's a bit less mature than I am, of course, because she's only eleven. However, I have more in common with her than with any of the girls in my school. I wondered if I would ever go back to that school — back to France.

Suddenly, I heard a toilet flush and Daniel Jones stepped out onto the landing beside me. I jumped, and he moved backward to show that he didn't mean to alarm me. It doesn't feel as though I'll ever be able to call him Dad, but he helped to find Zoe, so at least I can begin to call him a friend. We nod at each other. I wonder if I will ever be able to cope with having a man in the house.

It's a funny situation, and I don't know what's going to happen next. However, I feel good about the future because now, finally, all of the players are together at once. Having two families feels better than having one.

I ran my fingers along the white, glossed banisters. It was peculiar how things could seem both novel and familiar at the same time.

I hurried down the stairs and into the kitchen. Rebecca greeted me with the biggest smile I've ever seen. She was holding a whisk.

"Are you making pancakes?" I asked.

"Yes, lemon and sugar."

"Lemon and sugar?" I said with a disgusted giggle. "You want to be making apple pancakes! Give me that!"

I grabbed a peeler from the draining board and began searching for the fruit bowl. When I looked back, Rebecca had tears pouring down her cheeks.

"Sorry," I said. "We can make lemon pancakes if you want to."

"I don't mind what flavour pancakes we make, Millie," she laughed through her tears. "Sorry, I mean *Claire*."

"Ah, ça m'est egal," I told her. "Either will do."

Knitting Man at the Door

If only Knitting Man would whisk me off to dinner. I let myself slide down the magnolia wall, and collapse into a lovesick heap on the carpet tiles. Ah, Knitting Man — a man on the train who was knitting. I remembered the blueness of his eyes, like two little pools of tenderness amid a face so handsome it warned 'DANGER!'.

My doorbell rings. I inspect my body for signs of nakedness. Living alone can lead to tardiness in the clothing department. It's all right — I appear to be fully dressed. I pat my nose — no neglected face packs either. Just one more thing — am I wearing my fluffy, pink, penis slippers? No I'm not! Hoorah! I'm OK to face the outside world.

I explore the option of opening the front door, trying to remember if I ordered any new reams of paper, memory sticks or dildos. Nothing springs to mind. It's probably an energy salesman. Still, I'd better open the door, just in case it's somebody without a clipboard.

"Good evening, Evelyn," says a voice.

What the—? *Knitting Man?*

"How the hell did you know where I live?"

"I asked around."

"But you don't even know me. Our eyes met across a grubby train aisle, that's all."

"Yes, but as our eyes met across that grubby train aisle, I detected an unmistakable signal that you wanted me to ask you out to dinner."

"Not by turning up at my house unannounced! And, what do you mean, you asked around? I was alone on that train. How do you even know my name?"

"I have my ways."

"I'm calling the police."

"Wait!"

I try to slam the door, but he puts a polished, black, leather shoe in the way. They look like shoes of danger. Perturbation is rapidly turning into absolute terror. I look up at his seductive face. Damn that thrilling beard. Where was a nice, safe, bald-chinned admirer, when you needed the comfort of not fearing brutal assault?

I catch a glimpse of my ankle — prickled with coarse, angry, black hairs. Why don't I adhere to a more strict grooming routine, so as not to frighten unexpected visitors with the unsightly terrors of badly depilated body parts? I bet the spot on my nose is glowing like a beacon, having worked its way through this morning's thin covering of foundation. Is the waistband of my baggy, granny-pants showing too? I bet I'm the portrait of an unkempt, modern spinster.

Then I remember that this is a man I am deeply disturbed by. This is a man who appears to have stalker tendencies who has issues with taking 'no' for an answer. He deserves to see stubbly shins — in fact, he deserves bulging, sweaty, gorilla legs. He needs to leave, and he needs to leave now.

"Are you going to leave or am I going to have to scream?"

"Dammit Evelyn! Why can't you have idealistic fantasies like everybody else? This preoccupation with realism is drastically inhibiting your personal pleasure."

I thought about it for a moment. Perhaps he had a point. "Maybe you're right," I conceded. "I'll just grab my coat."

THE END

RosenTrevithick.co.uk

Facebook: RosenTrevithick
Twitter: RosenTrevithick
Newsletter: RosenTrevithick.co.uk/subscribe/

Seesaw – Volume II

Will writing erotica save a grandmother from financial ruin? Where is Emma's baby and why hasn't he been returned to her? And will a boy be able to stop his little sister from being made into a gourmet girl burger?

Following Rosen's acclaimed Seesaw collection, Volume II continues alternating between outrageous comedy and more sinister, psychological tales. At the core are two very different novellas – My Granny Writes Erotica and The Ice Marathon – alongside nine brand new short stories.

The preface will continue Rosen's own story, inviting you to share in her rocky but exciting journey from long-term incapacity to professional author.

Pompomberry House

A writer's retreat seemed the perfect chance for Dee Whittaker to take her mind off her marital difficulties.

However, she meets five of the most hideous writers ever to have mastered a qwerty keyboard, and her problems quickly multiply. Things escalate further when the handyman winds up dead.

After fleeing from the island, Dee attempts to get her life back on track but begins to notice that something strange is going on. The stories written on the island are coming true and hers is next - complete with a murder.

Her estranged husband makes an unlikely sidekick as the two of them try to stop the literary copycat killing an innocent woman.

Packed with topical references, *Pompomberry House* provides a satirical look at the emerging world of indie publishing.

Novels
Pompomberry House
Two Shades of the Lilac Sunset
My Granny Writes Erotica - Threesome

Collections
Seesaw Volume II

Short Stories
The Other Daughter
London, the Doggy and Me
Lipstick and Knickers
The Selfish Act
On the Rocks
A Royal Mess
No Shades of Grey

Novellas
The Ice Marathon

Non-Fiction
How Not to Self-Publish

Children's Books
The Troll Trap
Mr Splendiferous and the Troublesome Trolls
Trolls on Ice
Gourmet Girl Burger
The First Trollogy
Monster Avengers (co-written with 300 children)

Printed in Great Britain
by Amazon

78609644R00149